TANGLED THREADS OF FATE

HANGING BY A THREAD
BOOK ONE

GRACE MCGINTY

Cover Art by DAZED Designs.

Editing by Aubergine Editing.

ALSO BY GRACE MCGINTY

<u>Hell's Redemption Series</u>: The Redeemable/The Unrepentant/The Fallen

<u>Damnation MC Duet</u>: Serendipity/Providence

<u>The Azar Nazemi Trilogy</u> : Smoke and Smolder/Burn and Blaze/Rage and Ruin

<u>Dark River Days Series</u>: Newly Undead In Dark River/Happily Undead In Dark River/Pleasantly Undead in Dark River

<u>Black Mountain Mates</u>: Hunting Isla

<u>Eden Academy Series</u>: The Lost and the Hunted (Prequel)/Heart of the Hounded (Prequel)/ Rebels and Runaways (Book 1)/Sweethearts and Savages (Book 2)

<u>Shadow Bred Series</u>: Manix/Frenzy/Feral/Crave

<u>Stand Alone Novels and Novellas</u>: Bright Lights From A Hurricane/The Last Note/ Inside The Maelstrom/Pay-Per-Heart/8 Seconds to Fly/Make My Heart Race/The Daymakers

<u>Penalty Box Players</u>: Sticks and Stone/Break My Bones

<u>Omega Lottery:</u> Tryst In The Dark

TANGLED THREADS
OF FATE

CHAPTER I
WREN

Have you ever been violently attacked by a watermelon? I have. Twice.

Once at Ashley Michael's eighth birthday party, when her mom tried to use a watermelon instead of a piñata. It was filled with grapes and lychees; her mom was one of those almond and yoga parents. I don't think I ever saw Ashley smile, because she didn't want wrinkles.

Long story short, Ashley hit the pinata, making the oversized yet hollowed-out fruit flail wildly. The hemp string snapped, sending the watermelon careening at my face.

I ended up with a bloody nose and a fear of flying fruit. The Fruit Ninja period of my life was rough.

The second time was today, when a watermelon rolled across the sidewalk and right under my feet, sending me hurtling toward the concrete, arms wind-milling uselessly. I hit the ground with a bone-jarring thud. The wail of an elderly woman—who was still clutching the handle of the overturned fruit cart she'd been pushing—was almost lost beneath the sound of early-morning traffic.

Ugh.

I looked at the sky and sighed heavily. I was definitely going to be late. Hopefully my boss would understand, but he was a bit of an asshole. Actually, he was a giant, gaping, hemorrhoid-infected asshole. He was a stickler for rules and time stamps, and he "had a business to run, and if we were spending six minutes in the bathroom, then that was a customer who was inconvenienced for six minutes, which was six dollars worth of revenue, and if every employee lost six dollars of revenue…" *Blah blah blah.* Dude was an asshole, but I'd worked at Java Llama for a long time. It had half-decent benefits and free coffee for employees.

And it was damn fine coffee.

Rolling onto my hands and knees, I scooped up some stray grapefruit—and the offending watermelon —while the little old lady hefted her cart back onto four wheels with the help of a dude in a business suit. The woman said something effusive, but the guy just took one look at me, and the mess on the sidewalk, before hurrying away.

I couldn't even blame him, not really. No need for us to both be late, and I'd already resigned myself to the fact I was going to get an ass-chewing, so may as well go big.

My Java Llama shirt was a little oversized, so I used

it as a basket to scoop up grapefruit, oranges, and lychees, making a bunch of trips back and forth to the elderly woman's cart. All the while, she threw her hands up and gushed at me in a language I didn't understand. I just smiled, hoping it reached my eyes, and tried not to look at my watch.

Finally, I'd gathered most of the fruits off the ground and placed them back into the decorative wooden boxes they'd fallen out of. There were still a few oranges on the road, but they were on their own. They'd be juice by the end of the morning rush, and no one wanted to eat dirty road fruit anyway.

She repeatedly told me to "Eff Harry's Toe," which I imagined was *thank you* in whatever language she was speaking.

"You're welcome. Have a good day," I said quickly, turning to rush away. I was definitely late now, and I'd have to run to not be more than five minutes late. I didn't have to sit through the Boss Man giving me a fifteen-minute lecture about being six minutes late.

"No! No!" She gripped my hand, pulling me back with a strength that belied her frail appearance. She thrust the shiniest red apple at me repeatedly, until I took it.

"Uh, thank you?"

She mimed eating it. Sighing, I took a bite, and she smiled widely as she watched me chew. Man, old people were weird. But still, it was a really good apple. Sweet, crisp, juicy.

Before I knew it, I'd eaten the whole thing. Even the

core. The old lady's smile was infectious, and I grinned back.

"Thank you again. That was really delicious, especially if I don't think about the fact that it was rolling across the filthy ground only moments ago." God, I hoped she had no idea what I was saying. "Now I really, *really* have to go to work. Be safe."

I hightailed it out of there before she could stop me again, clutching my purse to my side and sprinting to work. My knees hurt, and I felt like I'd jarred something in my shoulder, but I didn't have time to do anything more than dry swallow down a couple of Advil before I slammed through the doors of the coffee shop seven minutes late.

Bob was already waiting for me. *Fuck.*

"I'm sorry, Bob. An old lady tipped her cart on my way to work, and I tripped over a watermelon, and I couldn't just walk away and not help her, right? Especially when I'm wearing my business-branded shirt. What if someone saw and reported me to Headquarters for inhumanity?"

Always use the underlying threat of HQ to get your way. Surviving Micro-managers 101.

I gave him a soothing smile. "But I'll make up the time in my lunch break." I rushed past him, praying he'd just let it go, hopefully appeased by the fact that he only had to give me thirteen minutes of my government-mandated twenty-minute break.

Apparently, luck was on my side because he just heaved a heavy sigh and returned to his office, where he'd probably stare at an empty spreadsheet and play solitaire until one of us fucked up enough that he could come out and give us a teamwide "pep talk."

One of the baristas, Tammy, was on the drive-thru window, and I tapped her out. She gave me a thankful smile.

"Sorry I'm late," I puffed, throwing my apron around my waist and liberating her from the headset. "Got caught up on the walk here."

Although my boss Bob was a festering butt nugget, my coworkers were really nice. I guess we'd all banded against a common enemy in Bob the Boss, so there wasn't much of the workplace bickering I'd had in other hospitality jobs.

"No worries, Wren. Honestly, I don't know how you do it, talking to people all the time. Car number four thought I should know her order just by the sound of her voice. Can you believe that?"

I looked out at car number four and indeed knew her order, because she was a regular, but I didn't tell Tammy that. Instead, I just rolled my eyes—the universal sign of *people are so annoying, especially in customer service.*

Sucking in a deep breath, I got on with the day. "Welcome to Java Llama! Can I take your order?"

Then I got to work, trying to clear the backlog of cars in the drive-thru, now that there were two baristas behind the machines. Fortunately, we were purely a drive-thru coffee place, so no one had to serve on the front counter, a small mercy that I knew both Tammy and the other barista Camila appreciated.

I worked through my lunch break, even though Bob didn't deserve it, and before I knew it, the end-of-day routine had begun. Java Llama closed its drive-thru lane at two p.m., thank goodness. The six a.m. starts weren't so bad in summer, but in winter, they were hell.

But if I had to get up at six *and* not leave until six? I'd probably throw myself off the overpass on the way home.

I helped scrub everything down and did the food prep for the following morning, before leaving behind Tammy as she locked up. Bob usually went home at midday every day, because he opened the store. I mean, he didn't do anything except unlock the door, but I guess he had to wake up early and drag his skinny ass here.

I was starving, and I'd reached the point of nausea. All I'd eaten all day was that apple, and it was sitting badly in my stomach. Or maybe it was the two double espressos I'd had during my shift, just to keep me going.

Waving at Camila and Tammy, I headed back to the street. "See you guys tomorrow." Fortunately, tomorrow was Saturday. We were only open Monday to Friday, really preying on that early-morning commute crowd, so at least my weekends were my own. It wasn't a bad gig, which was why I'd never told Bob to shove it.

Walking home on autopilot, my brain flicked through random, distracting topics. The kind where you thought about them so hard, you arrived at the front of your house and realized you'd been contemplating the mating habits of jellyfish for fifteen whole minutes, with no recollection of crossing any roads or making any turns the entire trip home.

Tonight was the premiere season of *Lust In The Sun*, a reality show filled with B-list celebs from all over the world, living on a small island near Aruba, trying to find love with lucky commonfolk. It was supremely cringe, but man, was it compelling. Which meant I needed at least one pint of ice cream to kick the season off in style.

Luckily, I already had to stop at Rossi's on the way home to pick up a grocery delivery for my landlady, Mrs. Byrne, who was ninety, with the wit and humor of someone much younger. In a tragedy that happened far too often, her body was failing her long before her mind. When I'd first moved in five years ago, she'd seemed a lot more spry, but she was aging fast.

So we had an arrangement: I'd pick up her groceries, and she'd make me a plate for dinner. It made her feel like she was doing me a favor, and not like she needed to be cared for in some way. She wasn't wrong; she was caring for me far more than I was caring for her.

Five years ago, back when I was a grieving eighteen-year-old kid fresh out of high school, Mrs. Byrne's meals had been the only thing that stopped me starving to death. I hadn't wanted to do anything, let alone cook.

My parents had been devout Catholics, though apart from getting me christened and then confirmed, they'd never pushed me into it. But when they'd gotten back from a tropical holiday and had both succumbed to some weird virus that enlarged their heart and inflamed their lungs, the last thing my mom had done was reach out to some of her church friends, finding somewhere that I'd be safe and cared for, in case the worst happened.

And it did.

Their loss was still like a stab through my heart. I didn't think I'd ever recover from losing them both.

Mrs. Byrne had been friends with my maternal grandmother, and a member of my parents' church. She'd been a widow longer than I'd been alive, living in a three-story walk-up where she rented out two of the three floors. She'd agreed to rent me the top floor for as long as I needed it, no matter what happened. She'd held my mom's hand as she was dying and had sworn she'd make sure I was okay, easing a worry in my mother's mind enough that she could let go, and stop suffering through days of pain.

Getting Mrs. Byrne's groceries was the very least I could do. I owed her so much more than I could ever repay.

Swallowing down the emotion, I turned onto a familiar street. Rossi's would just be winding down from the lunch rush, and I was hoping I could snag a hoagie as well.

"Wren! Are you here for Mrs. Byrne's groceries?"

Valerie Rossi was my age, and we'd attended the same school, but we'd never been friends. Still, I enjoyed stopping for a chat, especially when I knew that I wouldn't talk to anyone else again for the next… oh, sixteen hours or so.

I smiled politely at the elderly Mr. Lunetta trying to get a tin of tuna from the bottom shelf. Squatting down, I grabbed one of each variety and held them up for his inspection as I responded. "Yes please, Val. And do you think Uncle Antonio could make me a Rossi's Special, extra provolone?"

"Can do, Wren!" someone yelled from the back of the store. I could only assume it was Uncle Antonio.

Old Mr. Lunetta tapped the tin of tuna in lemon, and I stood, putting it in the cart for him. "Thank you, dear," he said. I patted him softly on the arm and wove around him, heading back toward the old-fashioned register. Handing Val the big reusable bags Mrs. Byrne gave me to haul her groceries to and fro, I helped her load the food carefully inside.

"And how is your sexy neighbor?" Val asked, waggling her eyebrows at me like she always did every time I came in.

The apartment between my top-floor place and Mrs. Byrne's ground-floor apartment belonged to Nate, who I thought might have been her nephew. I hadn't really had a single conversation with him in the last five years, just passing pleasantries. Sometimes, he'd help me carry my groceries to the top floor. He did all the handyman stuff and yard work for Mrs. Byrne, and I didn't know if that was in exchange for food too.

There was one small reason I'd never really spoken full sentences to Nate.

Simply put, he was smoking fucking hot. Like, holy shit, my ovaries had started a fan club and named it the *Let Nate Impregnate Us Club*. Total members: two.

I mean, the rest of me kinda wanted to join the fan club too. He was universally handsome, in a rugged kind of way. Messy dirty-blond hair, sparkling blue eyes, sun-browned skin, and so many damn tattoos that I daydreamed about tracing every single one with my tongue.

Every time he was in my presence, I turned into a bumbling simpleton. So eventually, I'd decided to be cool and mysterious myself, and usually ran away anytime he came close.

Rolling my eyes, I shrugged. "I have no idea. I don't see him any more than you see your neighbors."

Val snorted, stuffing a baguette into the bag. "That's what you think. My neighbors are my cousin Antonio Jr. and his six hundred kids, and my aunt Valencia with her on-again, off-again boyfriend, Vinnie." She huffed, casting her eyes to the heavens. "I pray every day that I don't see them on my way home, but inevitably, there's a relative knocking on my door within ten minutes of me stepping across the threshold."

Shaking my head at her exasperation, I pushed down the sad feeling that welled in my chest whenever I thought about how truly alone I was. I'd give anything for Val's big, messy, loud family.

"Well, I'm going home to watch *Lust In The Sun* with

my hoagie and a pint of ice cream, so I'm kind of hoping I don't see anyone tonight either."

Uncle Antonio appeared with my sandwich, all wrapped up tight, and put it on top of the groceries. "You tell Mrs. Byrne she should come down and see me one day soon. Maria misses their chats, though I think they just gossip about everyone at church. But they both used to enjoy it. And my Maria, she gets lonely, even with all the family." He gave Val a stern look, and she gave him an unimpressed expression in return. With a sigh, he turned back to me. "I can only imagine how lonely Mrs. Byrne must get."

She always seemed happy enough to me, but I knew she was getting on. The meals she slipped me now were more often just meat and potatoes, and even the meat was questionable. How she hadn't given herself food poisoning was beyond me, though she'd been brought up in a harder time, that was for sure. Cast-iron stomach.

I'd offered to cook for her once, and I'd never forget the outraged expression on her face.

I grabbed the bags up in my arms. "I'll tell her, Uncle Antonio. Give my love to Zia Maria." I hustled it out of Rossi's before I got trapped there for another thirty minutes. Rossi's was an institution, and if you'd lived in the neighborhood a while, everyone knew everyone.

The bags were heavy today, and I shifted them up my body to get a better grip. It wasn't a long trip home, but I'd swear some days, Mrs. Byrne ordered bricks. I was red-cheeked and out of breath by the time I made it to the front door, which whipped open before I could put the bags down and get my key out.

Nate stood there, his face stormy as always, though I was fairly sure that was just his natural resting dick face. He was wearing a tight black shirt and jeans that were actually well-worn, rather than bought pre-distressed. His tattoos were on full display, swirling patterns that ran up his muscular forearms and always transfixed me like a moth to a flame.

The tattoos, not the forearms.

Well, maybe the forearms, just a little. Especially when he flexed.

I pasted a smile on my face and hoisted the bags higher. "Hi, Nate. How are you?"

He grunted, but reached out and took the bags from me, ignoring my protests.

"Seriously, you don't have to. They're only going over to Mrs. B, and I'm sure you're going out somewhere…"

"It's fine," he grumbled, already turning toward Mrs. Byrne's door. He shifted both bags to one arm, making his bicep bulge, like someone had over-inflated an inner tube, then knocked with his free hand.

I stood behind him, like an idiot. I didn't want Mrs. Byrne to think I was slacking off on my job, though I doubted she would anyway. So I'd just loiter here, looking like a weirdo. It always took her ages to get to the door—had I mentioned she was, like, ninety?

I stood there in awkward silence with Nate. I didn't

do awkward silence. Well, the silence part. I did awkward just fine.

"So, how's work?"

Fuck, I didn't even know if he had a job. What if he didn't and that was a sore spot for him and I'd just put my foot in it?

"Actually, that's presumptuous of me. I didn't mean to insinuate that you only have worth if you have a job. I'm sure whatever you do is amazing. So I guess, uh, how's life? The yard looks good, and the handrail at the front is looking amazing since you repainted it. The stairs in this place are so old, I'm surprised that it's only the outdoor ones that need fixing. Actually, the third step from my apartment landing is squeaky, so if that wakes you up, I'm sorry!"

Just murder me now and throw my body in the bay.

"Don't hear it," Nate grunted as the door swung open.

"Oh, Nate, my boy. How have you been?" Mrs. Byrne gushed, waving him into her apartment. It was a proper old lady apartment, filled to the brim with ruffles and knick-knacks of a life well lived. As Nate got his big shoulders through the doorway, she finally spotted me. "Sweet Wren, there you are! I was beginning to worry, I was. Come in. I have some supper for you, girl."

"Thanks, Mrs. B. How did you go with the doctors?"

Mrs. Byrne had no family close by, except Nate, so I tried to keep tabs on her medical issues, in case she passed out one day and the paramedics asked me hard questions. Someone needed to know the answers, right?

Mrs. Byrne's face fell, and my heart thundered in my chest. *Oh no.*

"Oh, my darling Wren. It was awful news today, me'girl." She reached out and held my hand. "They diagnosed me with this terrible condition… Old age." She threw her head back and cackled. I frowned at her, but already, my lips were turning into a smile.

"Not funny, Mrs. B! You had me worried."

She passed me a plate of food from her fridge, covered with plastic wrap. "Oh, let an old lady get her kicks somewhere. I have one foot in the grave, and no matter what they tell me at the doctor's office, my time isn't coming any sooner than it was supposed to."

I really didn't like to think about Mrs. Byrne dying.

Nate finished putting away her groceries, then folded the bags and handed them back to me. He leaned down and kissed Mrs. Byrne's cheek, before giving me a respectful nod as he left.

She watched him go with a frown, then turned back to me. "Wren, I know I tease, but when I go, ya must know that this house goes to Nate, and he'll ne'er kick you out as long as you want to live here." There was always something comforting about Mrs. Byrne's soft Irish accent.

"I know, Mrs. B. But you're going to live another sixty years, because you've been pickled from all that whiskey you keep in your kitchen cabinet."

She chuckled. "Aw, away with you. It's time for Judge Trudie."

Kissing her on the cheek, much in the same way as Nate had, I closed her door, making sure it was locked first. She was vulnerable down here on the first floor, but she liked her independence, and she couldn't manage the stairs.

A wave of exhaustion swamped me, and suddenly, Judge Trudie and suspicious-smelling pickled pork sounded like a great idea. The step outside Nate's door squeaked, but I didn't have to worry too much about disturbing him. I was pretty sure he'd left after putting away Mrs. Byrne's groceries.

As I dragged myself up to my apartment, my stomach cramped, and I sighed. Great, I was getting PMS on top of being tired. My ovaries hated me, for sure. Still, I made it to the couch and flopped down, grabbing the remote and flipping on the television. I'd just have a little nap, and then I'd get up for dinner.

CHAPTER 2
WREN

THIRTEEN WEEKS LATER

I had brain cancer. Or cancer of the eyeball. Or maybe my ex had given me syphilis, and that was affecting my vision? Considering I'd broken up with him twelve months ago, when I caught him being spanked in his apartment by the building's Armenian maintenance man, syphilis *could* be an option. I probably should've gotten checked way back then, but I'd been heartbroken, and honestly, poor as hell.

I regretted it now, because obviously whatever venereal disease that fuck had given me had migrated to my brain. For weeks, my eyes had been blurry. No, blurry wasn't quite the right word. I'd gone to an optometrist in the mall, who'd told me I had perfect 20/20 vision. But that couldn't be right, because there were strange disturbances in my sight. Little streaks of light danced through my vision, as if my eyes were on a slower shutter speed, creating stars.

It had been the optometrist who'd told me I should go and see my family doctor. He'd suggested what I was describing was maybe some kind of synesthesia, though it didn't present with colors like it normally would.

My doctor had transferred me to a specialist, and at this point, I was pretty sure that if I didn't die of some kind of brain-melting disease, I'd die of starvation, because the medical bills were killing me. Not even Java Llama's decent benefits covered MRI scans, which was what the specialist had suggested during the previous appointment.

Luckily, I didn't have to take the day off work, instead setting my appointment for after two, but I still had to get a rideshare to the doctor's office, and it was all eating into my meager savings.

I thanked the driver and stepped out in front of the shiny neurosurgeon's office. It was a sleek building made of walls of glass. It was obviously architecturally designed, all sharp angles and economy of space, and held all sorts of specialist offices, from brain surgeons to podiatrists.

A couple walked out in front of me, smiling sweetly at each other. He squeezed her hand, and the light flared around them, the streaks of light wrapping around both of them like a ribbon, and their faces transforming into someone else. Some*thing* else, with longer faces and bigger teeth. They looked like monsters.

"Argh!" I screeched, scrabbling away, shaking my head. When I opened my eyes again, they were staring at me like *I* was the monster, these two perfectly human-looking people.

Fuck. This was bad.

Tears welled in my eyes, and I felt my lips form into an apology, but the couple were hurrying away, the man's arm wrapped protectively around the woman's back, like he was ready to throw himself between us if I attacked.

I was going crazy.

I couldn't breathe as I slid into the elevator, relieved when no one hopped in after me so I could rest my head against the glass of the mirrored wall and breathe.

I'm going to be okay.

I'm going to be okay.

I hit the button for the floor I needed, and deep-breathed the entire trip up.

When I stepped into the reception area, the receptionist frowned. "Name?"

"Wren Mahone."

She looked at her screen, then nodded. "Take a seat."

I sat beside the water cooler, grabbing a paper cup and filling it. Gulping down the ice-cold water, I filled it once more. And then again. And again, until I was feeling more alive.

I suddenly realized I was sweating, my skin cold and clammy, but my insides felt like they were on fire. I stared down at the water as if it might hold the answers to why I felt like this, but all I saw was my reflection and the long fluorescent lights.

"Wren?"

I dragged my eyes from the water up to the concerned face of Dr. Kash. He was around sixty-five, but he had barely any lines on his face, which told me he either had really good genes or a great hand at Botox.

I stood, dragging my backpack up with me. There were coffee stains on my shirt, and my hair was probably a wild mess, but I didn't care. I walked through to his office, with its beige furniture and great view of the river. He waved at the same hard leather seat I'd sat in last time.

"Take a seat. How are you feeling, Wren?"

I tried not to cry. I really did. I'd even forced a smile onto my face, but someone hadn't given my tear ducts the memo, because tears started pouring down my cheeks.

Dr. Kash handed me a box of tissues. "So, not well?"

I shook my head. "It's getting worse. I feel like I'm losing my mind." I didn't tell him about the fact I thought I'd seen monsters exiting his building earlier. I didn't want to get thrown in a padded cell.

He looked at the screen of his fancy laptop, a frown on his face. He winced, and my stomach fell out of my butt. It must be cancer. A brain tumor. Something bad.

"Well, the blood test determined a significant possibility for what's causing your visual disturbances."

"Is it a tumor?" I breathed, and when he shook his

head, I couldn't help the relieved whoosh that blasted from my overfilled lungs.

But he was checking for parasites too, right? Sometimes, they could lodge in your eyeballs or in your brain… *Ew. Ew, ew, ew!* "It's not parasites?"

Dr. Kash looked almost amused. "Well, yes, some would say so, by definition." He chuckled, though I failed to see what was amusing about a hookworm in my eyeball.

Though surely the optometrist would've seen a worm in my eyeball, right?

"You're pregnant."

Obviously, that meant the parasite had to be in my brain. That sounded bad. Did they do surg—

Dr. Kash's words suddenly permeated my panicked fog. "Excuse me, *what?*"

"Pregnant. We won't know exactly how far along until you have a scan, but your blood work suggests you are definitely pregnant."

I shook my head. "Um, no."

"I know this might be a surprise—"

I shook my head more vigorously, making the lights dance and sway like a disco. "Not a surprise, Doc. An *impossibility.* I haven't had sex in… a long time. Like, twelve months."

Dr. Kash was frowning again. "You haven't had any late nights out in the last few months, where you may have imbibed a little too much alcohol? Any time you might have been sexually active?"

The only time I'd even partied in the last three

months had been Camila's farewell. Her boyfriend had gotten an acting gig in LA, so they were moving to the West Coast. We'd gotten rowdy, but definitely not black-out drunk. I remembered most of the night... didn't I?

Even as I thought it, doubt crept into my brain. Maybe there were a few blank spots, but I'd remember fucking someone, I was sure of it. I wasn't that type of person. I was more an *I'll take your number and call you* kinda girl, and sometimes I called and sometimes I didn't. Sure, more often than not I didn't these days—after my ex and the Armenian—but that still didn't mean I'd hook up with a person and not remember it. Right?

Fuck, maybe I had. Well, *obviously* I had, because the doctor was looking at me expectantly. I realized my head was still shaking from side to side. "I don't know. I don't think so?"

Jesus fucking Christ on a Christmas cracker.

"I'm not trying to be insensitive, Miss Mahone, but regardless of how, the fact still stands that you're pregnant, and I believe this may be causing your visual hallucinations. It isn't unheard of, though exceedingly rare. I'm going to rule out any conditions that may have this effect with an MRI, and then I'll transfer your case to the perinatal mental health department of Brighams. Sometimes, it can be a sign of pre-eclampsia, or even gestational diabetes, so I've referred you to an obstetrician in this building. I've also had my receptionist book you an appointment with the ultrasound techs the next floor down, just to confirm." He smiled softly at me. "In case the tests were wrong."

"Is there a chance of that?" I couldn't keep the hope from my voice.

He shook his head. "No." He stood, coming to stand around the other side of his desk. I felt shaky; my whole world had been not just turned upside down, but pile-driven into the ground. "I know this seems like the end of the world, but I have to tell you, Miss Mahone, that the rest of the tests are perfect. You're a healthy, pregnant young woman. There are no signs of anything else to worry about, and I hope that eases something in your mind."

I snorted. *Eases something in my mind?* Fuck, he'd just dropped a baby on me, and he hoped that not having a brain tumor made me feel better? I still managed to mutter, "Thank you," through my incredulity.

I stood, and he ushered me gently toward the door. "You're welcome. See the receptionist; she'll give you the bill and also direct you to your next appointment." With that, he stepped back into his office, closing the door in my face, like he hadn't just fucked me right over.

Fuck.

FUCK.

The receptionist handed me a bill that made me want to cry again, then pointed over at the elevator. "Level two. Your appointment is in forty-five minutes."

And that was how I found myself sitting in a waiting room, surrounded by six pregnant women, one guy with bronchitis, and a lady who was jigging around like she was about to pee herself. Each one was encased in imaginary streaks of lights that hurt my eyes.

I looked down at the bill in my hand and opened my bank account app on my phone.

Then I cried yet again.

CHAPTER 3
WREN

The ultrasound tech was running behind, so it was actually more like an hour and a half before I was in the tiny room, climbing onto a bed covered in glorified paper towels, while a tech in a mask fiddled with the ultrasound machine.

"When was the date of your last period?"

I shrugged. "I don't know. A year ago? I've consistently used an implant since I turned sixteen, and I stopped getting regular periods, like, the first year?"

The tech nodded. "Okay. Well, this wouldn't be the first contraception-fail baby I've seen, and I can tell you, it won't be the last." She gave me a look that was probably meant to be reassuring, but was ruined by her next words. "We'll see what we can with this wand, but if it's too early, we might have to try a trans-vaginal ultrasound."

"Is that a train that goes across Virginia?" I joked, because I tended to make jokes when uncomfortable, and the idea of this woman poking any kind of instrument up my hoo-haa *definitely* made me uncomfortable.

She raised an eyebrow and talked me through the next steps like I was a child. "I'm moving up your shirt… I'm squirting a lubricant on your stomach… The wand will be cold… I'm searching for your uterus…"

It was all going fine until her eyebrows rose two inches toward her hairline, and she let out a soft little, "Oh," that echoed around the room like a gong.

It was a single syllable. Two letters. It shouldn't have been as terrifying as it was. But that "Oh" had my heart hammering in my chest. "What?"

She gave me a tight smile, or at least, that's what I thought she was doing behind her mask. Unfortunately, a smile that didn't reach your eyes may as well not exist if your mouth was hidden. "I just want to get my colleague to check an anomaly. One moment."

Then she disappeared, and I stared at the grainy screen grab of the Rorschach painting she'd been reading. I tried to see what she was worried about, but it made no sense to me at all.

When she returned, she brought along an older technician, whose smile was far more reassuring. This tech had curling gray hair and a quietly confident demeanor that bled through the room.

"How are you doing, sweets?" When she smiled, she meant it, and a part of me relaxed a little.

Flicking her glasses down her small, stubby nose, she picked up the magic wand thing and dug it into my stomach. Her fingers flew across the machine, taking screen grabs every now and then, before her eyebrows rose too.

"Ah, I see." She didn't seem as worried as the other tech, which told me that my baby probably didn't have two heads or an extra leg, or something growing where it shouldn't. She moved the wand again into another position, humming to herself. Another screen grab. And another.

Looking at my notes, she hummed again. "I'll send these through to your doctor, but everything looks fine. I'd say you're about thirteen weeks along." She gave me a look I couldn't quite decipher. "No need to panic at all." She moved the wand until a familiar shape came into view. The profile of a face. "This is Baby A."

"Baby A?" I breathed, but I was transfixed. This little gray blob had a profile. Sure, it looked more like a shadow puppet of a baby than something living and breathing, but still, there it was, its little heart fluttering on the ultrasound.

She moved the wand, but then the profile was back again. "And Baby B."

"*Baby B?*" I squeaked, and as she moved the wand again, my hands started to shake.

"This one is a little harder to see, but there's definitely a Baby C back here too."

I was going to pass out. I was going to puke. Probably both. "No, no, no, no…"

The kind nurse rested a hand on my shoulder. "It's okay; it'll be fine. They are fraternal, which means they all have their own amniotic sacs, and that definitely lessens the risks for both you and the babies. Your OB-GYN will be able to give you more information, and I suggest you find one immediately, if you don't already have one."

I was shaking. I could hear her talking, but it felt like bees were buzzing around my head. She wiped the jello stuff off my stomach and printed me out pictures, before leading me from the room, telling me firmly to book an appointment with an OB-GYN as soon as possible.

I collected another bill from the reception desk, and they sent me on my way, like my life wasn't in fucking shambles.

I looked down at my stomach, poking it gently. I felt like an idiot. How could I have not known? It was harder than it should be, but I mean, I'd been binge eating Rossi's beef rolls like a lunatic because I'd been craving them so much.

Guess I knew why now.

Stuffing the bills into my backpack, I walked to the bus stop. I definitely couldn't afford cabs anymore. Or Rossi's beef rolls. Or anything. I grabbed the next bus and sat by myself, staring out the window as it wound its way across town.

How was I supposed to take care of three babies by myself? *There's no way…*

I swallowed down the emotions that seemed to still be riding way too close to the surface. The world was alight with golden slashes of light, and right now, possible brain damage was the least of my worries.

I kept my head down until I made it back home, so close to being able to break down properly. I walked up my steps, sneaking through the door so I didn't run into Mrs. Byrne.

Fuck. I'd have to move. I couldn't have three babies in a three-story walk-up. What if I tripped and dropped one down the stairs?

I was on the second-story landing when I ran into Nate. "Sorry," I mumbled at the ground, dodging around him.

His hand shot out and wrapped around my wrist. I looked down at his long fingers on my skin. This was the first time in five years he'd ever touched me. He usually went out of his way to not even brush shoulders with me.

"Are you okay?"

I looked up into his gruff face, his short beard messy, and his wild, burnished red-brown hair piled on top of his head in a messy top-knot. He should've looked like a hipster, but I'd dare anyone to call him that to his face.

"Wren?" he prompted.

Don't you do it, Wren. Don't you fucking do it.

My body was now possessed, because despite the fact I was warning myself repeatedly, when I looked up into those sky-blue eyes, I burst into tears. I sobbed like my world was ending, slumping down onto that squeaky damn step.

I wouldn't have to worry about the step waking him up soon—it would be the screaming babies. Babies who'd quickly realize fate had handed them the worst beginning ever by giving them an inexperienced single mother who couldn't even tell them who their father was, because she didn't remember.

Nate took two steps into my space, his face furious. "Are you injured? Who hurt you?" His hands gripped my shoulders gently, and it felt nice. I really was losing my mind.

I just shook my head, and he bundled me up into his arms and marched me into his apartment. I'd never been in here before, and while the layout was the same as mine, the place couldn't have been more different. Firstly, there were a lot of plants. They made the whole place appear green, with soft tapestries lining the walls, giving it a cozy feel.

Well, except for the display of medieval weapons that hung on his wall, including a double-sided ax and a sword so long, it would take a giant to wield it.

He sat me on the couch and moved across to his small kitchen, pouring me a dram of whiskey. Coming back to squat in front of me, he pushed it beneath my nose. The smell made my stomach curl.

"I can't."

"It'll calm your nerves," he cajoled softly. It was the softest voice I'd ever heard him use.

Shaking my head, I didn't even attempt to stop the fall of tears anymore. "No, I can't, because I'm pregnant."

Nate looked like I'd slapped him as he rocked back on his heels, his face contorted into a mask of surprise. "Pregnant?"

"*With triplets,*" I shrieked, hysteria setting in. "That means fucking *three*, Nate."

Nate lifted the dram of whiskey to his own lips and threw it back, before walking back over and pouring himself another one. He cleared his throat, moving to sit down on the intricate stone coffee table across from me. He was so huge that it groaned ominously, and I was a little worried it might fall right through the floor and onto Mrs. Byrne's head.

"Who's the father?" he asked, looking as confused as I felt.

"That's just it. I don't *know*. I swear, I haven't had…" I snapped my mouth shut. Was I really about to tell the hottest guy I knew that I hadn't gotten laid in twelve months? At this point, if I died of mortification, it would probably be a blessing. I cleared my throat and continued. "I haven't had sex for a really long time. But I don't remember being unsafe. And I have a damn contraceptive implant."

"No boyfriend since that jacked-up douche from across town?" he asked.

My ex. Nate had never liked him. Thomas hadn't liked Nate much either.

"I went out to a club a couple of months ago for Camila's going-away party, but I didn't drink that much!" I wasn't sure who I was trying to convince, Nate or myself. "It's a little hazy, but I wasn't black-out drunk, I swear. But *something* must have happened…" There was nothing else. No other explanation. I just buried my head in my hands and cried some more.

Nate moved to sit beside me, hesitantly wrapping an arm around my shoulders. "Don't cry. It'll be okay."

"Everyone keeps saying that, but I can't see how!" I shook as I curled my legs up against my chest. Well, I tried to, but couldn't, because my stomach was in the way. "I thought I was just getting fat!"

"Yeah, me too."

I looked up at him, horrified.

"In a *good* way, Wren. I thought you were getting curvy. It suits you." His cheeks flushed, which was kind of adorable. He looked down at my stomach. "Three, you say?"

Yeah, nice save, buddy.

I nodded, and he patted my back. "A real blessing."

This time, I snorted rudely at his words. I didn't feel blessed. I felt cursed. My whole life had been cursed.

"I need to get drunk, but I can't," I muttered, flopping back and sinking into Nate's warmth, even though I'd regret it later when I relived this horrifying encounter over and over. "I'm going to have to move, because how will I take babies up and down the stairs? Plus, Mrs. B. doesn't want to spend her remaining years listening to babies screaming their lungs out. But I can't afford anywhere else.

"My boss will fire me, because I probably won't be able to work for the last trimester, since triplet pregnancies are dangerous. I wouldn't be able to lean out the drive-thru window to hand people coffee anyway. I won't be able to afford the doctor's bills. Or the hospital bills. I'll be paying the babies off until they're thirty. Not that they'll be speaking to me by thirty, because I'll have had to raise them all under a bridge in our three-room cardboard box, since I won't be able to afford to keep a roof over their heads—"

Nate placed his hand over my mouth to stop the absolute vomit of words from tumbling out. Was it weird his hand kind of tasted nice? Like vanilla or something.

"Wren, no one is kicking you out of here. Mrs. Byrne is going to be over the moon. She couldn't have children herself." I hadn't known that. "You can move into this apartment, and I'll move to the top level. There'll still be stairs, but not as many."

I was going to cry again, but I swallowed the tears down. "That's really nice of you, but you're what, six hundred feet tall? You aren't going to fit in the top-level apartment." The third-floor apartment had lower ceilings to account for the eaves. It didn't bother me, but I was short as hell. Nate was not. He'd be insanely uncomfortable up there; I couldn't do that to him.

A low grumble in his chest made me look up at him, suddenly acutely aware that I was snot-balling all over a guy I barely knew. He shook his head at me. "Take the help, woman. If I didn't want to help, I wouldn't offer. You're going to need it, and you aren't in the position to turn it down out of stubborn pride."

I swallowed hard. He was right. So fucking right. "Okay," I agreed meekly.

We sat in silence, and I stared at the painting on the wall opposite his couch. He didn't even have a TV. Just that massive painting. It had a whole herd of horses running over green grass, their manes spread out behind them in the breeze. Below them was what appeared to be a farmhouse made of stone. It was a beautiful painting. I could see why he liked it.

"What am I going to do?" I whispered the words, but Nate heard anyway.

His huge hand stroked circles over my shoulders. "Doctor's appointments, I imagine. A lot of them."

I gave a mirthless laugh. "I hope they let me pay the bill with sexual favors, because I have no money." I sighed heavily, closing my eyes against reality for just a second. "I'm so fucked."

He may have replied, but exhaustion dragged me down into oblivion.

CHAPTER 4
WREN

The next day, I stared at myself for way too long in the mirror, trying to work out how I'd been so delusional to think the little round podge of my belly had been gas. Or like, a big burrito. Or just extra chub. It was hard and round, and the more I stared, the more it couldn't be anything but a pregnant stomach.

I'd always been a little soft around the middle. Wide hips, a little pooch. I was never one of those flat-belly babes out in their bikinis every summer, getting a golden tan. So I'd kinda just assumed I was putting on weight because I was basically eating potatoes and Rossi's subs every day.

Sighing, I buttoned up my stretchiest pair of work pants and a sweater that was pretty but also baggy. I had to hide my pregnancy from Bob for just a little longer; he didn't need an excuse to fire me. It wasn't like he didn't have a filing cabinet full of people who wanted to replace me.

I walked to work, my brain running a million miles an hour. I needed to find a doctor closer to my house, because there was no way I could keep traveling to the other side of town for my appointments. Luckily, Mrs. Byrne's house was in a nice neighborhood of Boston, and there were some good OB-GYN around. None I could actually afford, but I'd done some Googling last night and had scared myself into forking over the money.

The risks for me, and for the babies—they were huge. Multiple births were an anomaly, but triplets were even more so. With each extra baby came a higher risk factor. At least I could be thankful I wasn't having quintuplets.

I strolled into work five minutes early, just so I didn't have to look at Bob. My stomach was roiling, but luckily for me, my morning sickness had decided that it wanted to strike every day at six p.m. At least by then I was home from work, and I was no longer deluding myself that I had bad food, or a gastro bug, or whatever the hell else my brain had come up with to justify the fact I'd been puking for two weeks straight.

Nope, it was straight up morning sickness.

I smiled tightly at Tammy as she bustled around, doing the opening checklist. Picking up my apron, I got to work too. I needed the distraction. Too soon, the store was open, and the steady stream of coffee drinkers didn't stop until one. We all rotated out to have our lunch breaks, but I couldn't bring myself to eat anyway.

I was hanging out back at the machines as Tammy

made coffee, and the new girl Priya was working the window. "Tammy, did I give my number to anyone while we were at Camila's farewell? The night is a little fuzzy."

Tammy frowned, pouring a hazelnut shot for a mocha. "I don't know about your number, but you were dancing with a cute guy there for a while. Tall and built."

Yeah, I remembered that guy. I also remembered when he'd wandered to the next girl. "Hmm, I see."

Tammy stopped what she was doing, giving me a frown. "Is someone harassing you?"

I wanted to laugh at the ridiculousness of it all. "No, nothing like that. Trying to piece some things together, is all. I didn't disappear or anything at the end of the night?"

She shrugged. "You went to pee, but that's about it. You were gone for ages, but when you came back, you just grinned and said the lines were long."

I didn't remember that, but taking a pee wasn't exactly something that stuck in your brain. It must have been then, not that it mattered. That horse had bolted. The ship had sailed. The tadpole had turned into a frog. Three frogs.

I didn't get time to talk much more as lunch finished, and I was relieving Priya again. "Someone just ordered a pup cup for their tarantula." She visibly shuddered, and I tilted my head.

"Wouldn't a spider be lactose intolerant?" We got

some weird customers, and a tarantula wasn't even the strangest thing I'd seen in the window.

Priya rolled her eyes. "He ordered it with almond milk." She hightailed it back to the breakroom, and I didn't blame her.

It was a day for weird customers. I had a guy whose husky tried to jump through the window to kiss me. Followed by a woman who wanted me to measure exactly how much milk was in her latte—eight and a half ounces, not a single drop more—and gave it back to me twice, until I made Tammy come over with a measuring jug so she could watch the pour.

That backed us up, meaning we had to hustle to clear the line. When someone ordered an extra-large caramel macchiato with cherry syrup and chocolate whip, I was about ready to reach through the window and shake them if they were another prank order.

The car that pulled up was hot pink. It seemed to have chia seeds growing in heart-shaped chunks on the doors. I decided that the disgusting order probably wasn't a prank. This lady looked like she'd love an unholy combination of flavors.

"Caramel macchiato with cherry syrup and chocolate whip?"

The woman just stared at me. Her hair was in a beehive on the top of her head. Her eyelashes were fake, and her red lipstick was a touch too orange for her skin tone and bleeding up through the wrinkles around her mouth.

I cleared my throat. "Uh, that's $6.90, thanks. Cash or card?"

"You should go to Crete."

I stared blankly at her. It was too late in the day for this shit. "Pardon?"

"You should go to Crete if you want to survive. Amourgeles. They'll come for you soon."

Her voice was monotone, and her eyes… They were freaking me out. It was like storm clouds were moving across her irises. The lights coming off her were intense, and I squinted as they hurt my head. "What do you mean?" I breathed.

"If you want the children to survive, go to Amourgeles. If you stay, you'll die."

I swallowed hard. "Ma'am, I don't have any children."

Her eyes snapped to my face then, and they were an eerie pearlescent. "Crete. Only they can help you." Then she blinked slowly, and when she opened her eyes again, they were a deep brown. "Did you say $6.90? Have the prices gone up?" She handed me a handful of money, and I took it on instinct.

My eye twitched, my heart now thundering in my chest. "Uh, yeah. Sorry. Management, you know?" I fell into the natural excuse I gave anytime someone whined about the prices. I gave her back her change as Tammy appeared with the drink.

When I turned back to the lady, she was regarding me silently, her eyes the normal color but the golden lights jumping around her still extra strong. Man, I was losing it. I thrust the drink at her, hoping she'd disappear and I could just write the whole exchange off as another crackpot weirdo.

And I'd met a few. You couldn't live in a city this long without meeting a few kooks. There was a guy who walked through the drive-thru once a month, even though it was against the law, because he insisted he was on his flying horse.

In the end, we just served him, because who was I to argue with invisible winged horses?

I finished out my shift, pushing the weird lady deep down into the box of shit I wasn't examining too closely.

My baby daddy.

My finances.

Three babies.

Crazy lady in the drive-thru.

All of that was going straight into the "worry about later" box as I just focused on how I'd survive the day. And then how I'd survive the week. And then the month. For like, eighteen more years.

I walked home slowly, the tiredness that I'd attributed to some kind of illness still plaguing my bones. I had to stop and get Mrs. Byrne's groceries, but soon I'd probably have to ask Nate if he could do it. Maybe Valerie would deliver them for me, even though it wasn't part of their service. Mrs. Byrne had been going to Rossi's since there first was a Rossi's; surely that had garnered a little loyalty, though I was pretty sure they were still selling her canned vegetables for a quarter.

I walked in to find Mr. Lunetta—who was always there—looking at canned tuna on the bottom shelf again. Walking over, I plucked the can he'd chosen last time from the row and handed it to him. "Thank ya, girlie," he said in his gruff old man voice.

I weaved my way through to Val at the register. She grabbed the sacks that I'd dropped off earlier and handed them over to me.

"No sub today?" Uncle Antonio yelled from the other side of the store.

I shook my head, giving Val a tight smile. "Not today, Uncle Antonio," I called back, grabbing the bags.

Val stared at me, a small crease between her brows. "Everything okay, Wren? You're looking sick."

Ha. If only she knew. "Nah, I'm fine. Just tired. Crazy day at work today."

Val didn't seem convinced, but I hightailed it out of there before she asked any more questions. The bags seemed extra heavy, and I was puffing by the time I got home. Plus, my stomach was happy to swirl with nausea early today.

Dammit.

Knocking on Mrs. Byrne's door, I heard the squeak of her recliner, then the clip-clop of her uneven gait as she shuffled across the room. Finally, she opened the door and smiled brightly. "My sweet Wren, come in." She ushered me inside, but I didn't miss that she was a little stiffer today. She was also a little grayer.

"Afternoon, Mrs. B. Are you using your oxygen while you watch your soaps, like you're supposed to?"

She waved me off with a huff, which I was pretty sure meant no. "Have you come to tell me you're pregnant?" she asked haughtily.

I gaped. She smirked. *Touché, Mrs. Byrne.*

"How the hell did you know that? I didn't even know until yesterday!"

She raised a wispy eyebrow at me. "I'm old as dirt. I've seen a fair few pregnant women in my time. I just know. I was waiting for you to tell me. You must be halfway along, judging by the size."

I huffed a disgruntled laugh. "I wish." I slumped down at her small table. "It's triplets." Mrs. Byrne clutched her chest, her eyeballs rolling heavenward, and I bolted to my feet. "Mrs. B, are you okay?"

She flapped her hand at me. "Of course I am, child. I'm probably no closer to a heart attack than you were when you found out. Three!" She shook her head. "I don't know whether I should pray that your parents watch over you, or curse out your grandmother for letting this happen." She shook her head at the ceiling again, like she was actually cursing out the spirits of my dead ancestors. "And the father?"

I flushed red. Fuck, it had been easier to tell Nate that I didn't know the father than Mrs. Byrne. "Uh, he isn't in the picture." See, a way better explanation than *I have no fucking clue who he is and therefore he can't be in the picture.*

Mrs. Byrne clicked her tongue in disapproval, but

moved over to her bags of groceries. I stood and helped her put everything away, and somehow, her not tossing me out on the street as a harlot made me feel better.

Finally, with everything put away, she pulled out a large pot and sat it on the stove. She took out half the vegetables we'd just stacked into the fridge, as well as some meat from the small drawer freezer.

I watched her totter around for a moment, before it became too much. "What are you doing, Mrs. B? You should be resting and sucking in that good oxygen."

"Psh. I'm making you soup. You're eating for four now. You need your strength. A big pot of vegetable soup, that's what you need." She was using too much of her weekly food rations as she tipped vegetables into the pot, muttering to herself the whole time. I was going to have to replenish her stocks, but the thoughtfulness of it made me want to cry.

And throw up.

Fuck.

"Thank you," I murmured quietly. "I appreciate it."

I appreciated her. I always had. She turned at the sound of my quavering voice and held her arms out wide. I stepped into them, and she held me tightly, despite how frail she seemed lately. She was disappearing in front of my eyes, and I didn't know how to keep her here with me.

"You never have to thank me, sweet Wren. Having you here all these years has given me something I thought was gone forever. A purpose. I appreciate you just as much. And I'll adore these little ones too," she said softly, cupping my stomach in her pale, crepey hands. "Now, you look like you want to lose your lunch, and I'd prefer you didn't do that in my apartment. Come back down before seven."

"Yes, ma'am." I rushed out of her place, making it up the stairs and into my bathroom with moments to spare. As I hugged the toilet bowl, I cried. Not in self-pity—okay, a little in self-pity, but more in fear. And thankfulness. Thankful that I had Mrs. Byrne, but fearful that one day I was going to wake up and she'd be gone. The last anchor I had. The last person who cared about me.

Then who would I lean on?

CHAPTER 5
WREN

After two weeks of coming to terms with the fact I was going to be someone's mother soon, life went on bizarrely like normal. As normal as it could be, considering I was knocked up, I was still seeing things that weren't there, and the whole community had figured out I was pregnant.

It had started with Tammy at work, though I made her keep it quiet from Bob. He was pretty oblivious, and I was going to keep him in the dark as long as I could. Then Val at Rossi's. Then my mailman. It was awkward as hell, but I settled on a lie and stuck to it. I'd had a secret boyfriend, and when he found out I was pregnant, he had run off. It garnered mostly sympathy, but a few dirty looks too. No one knew it was triplets, though, of course.

What I hadn't really expected was the huge outpouring of help. Uncle Antonio had his grandson, Christos, start to deliver Mrs. Byrne's groceries. He put extra vegetables on my hoagies. Zia Maria started knitting baby clothes at an alarming rate.

How she'd managed to knit twelve pairs of booties and a cardigan in two weeks was a marvel. I stood at the counter at Rossi's and tried not to cry as Val put the knitted items into a paper bag for me, shaking her head. "Nonna has gone wild too. They're lighting candles for you—because you're pregnant out of wedlock, of course." She rolled her eyes, making the sign of the cross sarcastically. "But the baby is going to have enough blankets and outfits to last until they're five, now that she's got her church group involved. Do you need anything else? A ride to any appointments?"

I shook my head. "Nate, my neighbor, is driving me to my OB-GYN appointment tomorrow."

"Is he now? Does he want to roleplay as daddy?" The way she said it made it very clear she didn't mean to the babies, but something infinitely dirtier.

"No, he's just being a kind neighbor," I grumbled, and Val laughed. Literally laughed in my face.

She dropped her voice conspiratorially low. "Girl, you're so delusional. But hey, pregnant chicks are definitely some people's kink, so I say if you can lock down that hunk, you should do it. Silver lining and all that," she said with a wink.

Incorrigible.

Honestly, though, I hadn't seen much of Nate since my breakdown on his couch. I'd run into him walking up the stairs once, and we'd made polite conversation. Somehow, my appointment had come up, and he'd offered to drive me. I didn't really have the energy to turn him down. My feet hurt, and I was so goddamn *tired* all the time. Breathing made me feel exhausted, let alone working ten-hour shifts and walking home. Climbing the stairs some days seemed like divine torture.

So I'd take the help, just like he said.

I smiled as old Mr. Lunetta came up to pay for his groceries. He patted me gently on the back. I looked into his basket. "No tuna today, Mr. Lunetta?"

"Not today, girlie, but I got you this." It was a wooden rattle that had three moons connecting together at a single point. Each moon was carefully carved with vines and words in… possibly Greek? Or Latin? It was gorgeous.

"Mr. Lunetta, I can't accept this. It's beautiful. You have to let me buy it from you," I gasped. It looked completely hand carved.

He waved a dismissive hand. "Forget it. I make these to keep my fingers nimble. I have dozens lying around my house." He gave me a shaky smile. "You're a good girl. Consider it a thank you for your help reaching things on the bottom shelf."

I felt like I was about to cry, but instead, I hugged him. Did he look a bit brighter today? I was thankful the golden lights were starting to fade slightly. "Thank you, Mr. Lunetta. I appreciate this."

He mumbled something gruffly under his breath and patted my back three times in a clear dismissal of the hug. Swallowing down the emotion, I stepped back so he could grab his grocery bag.

"See you tomorrow," he huffed at Val, lifting his chin at Uncle Antonio as he left.

Val and I watched him go. "What a sweet old man," she sighed, and I nodded my agreement. She turned back to me. "Antonio Jr. says you can have any of the baby stuff you need from his garage. He got the snip, because he said six kids is enough. I say he should have stopped at two, but the man loves chaos. I bet Guilia is ecstatic; the poor woman's been pregnant for like, a solid eight years."

I talked with her for a little longer, resting my aching feet before I headed home, armed with Antonio Jr.'s phone number so I could come and collect his crib. I just needed two more now. The thought made me want to cry, again.

I went a couple of blocks out of my way to a baby store at the strip mall. I really needed to start pricing things so I knew how much to save. Hopefully I'd have enough so that the babies didn't need to sleep in boxes.

Mentally, I began making a list. Cribs. Car seats, though I had no car. Hell, maybe I needed a car? A stroller as long as a bus. Clothes. Diapers. Holy shit, so many diapers. Blankets. Thermometer. Bottles. Formula.

The list kept going on and on and on. I sat down on a bench outside the mall and took out a notebook. Writing a list would make me feel better—there was something about putting things down in black and white that settled me when the world was chaotic.

I could feel people watching me, though maybe it was just my imagination. I was sensitive to the staring of others now. I looked up, but no one was being obvious about it.

Finally, heaving a sigh, I strode into the baby store. It was time to rip off the bandaid and stop being in denial. Pretending it wasn't happening wasn't going to unsplit the egg.

I WAS a sweaty mess by the end of the following day. I'd missed my lunch break, and I desperately wanted to put my feet up for five minutes while I waited for Nate to come and collect me from the staff parking lot.

But when Bob poked his head out of his office, I knew I probably wasn't going to get the rest I so sorely needed.

"Wren, can I speak to you in my office?"

His office was just a retrofitted supply cupboard, so it was cramped and awful. I nodded, doing my best not to clutch my aching spine. I slipped past him and sat down on the edge of the hard plastic chair by his desk.

Bob pulled out some papers, shuffling them loudly. "Wren, I have to let you go."

My whole world screeched to a halt. "*What?*"

"You've been late three times in the last three months, for which you were warned. You're also taking prolonged bathroom breaks, against company policy. We're a small team, and if one of us doesn't pull their weight around here, the job doesn't get done."

I gaped. "I was *two minutes* late this morning. I followed you into the building!"

He scowled at me, clearly not appreciating his hypocrisy being thrown back at him. "It's a pattern of behavior that I can't see changing in the next nine months." He looked pointedly at my stomach, but didn't say anything else.

Fuck.

He knew I was pregnant. I hadn't told him, so he couldn't say it was the reason he'd fired me. *Fucking fuck.* I'd have no legal leg to stand on.

"You're a real piece of shit, Bob," I hissed. "You're a weak weasel of a human being, and I hope your dick gets the rot from masturbating too much and falls off." I stood and pushed past him, trying not to cry.

"Where do you think you're going? We weren't finished," he shouted after me.

I glared at him over my shoulder. "Finish this, asshole." I flipped him the bird, grabbing my stuff from my locker as he came barreling out of his office. I stuffed everything into my backpack and stomped out the door.

Bob really didn't like his subordinates walking away from him. "You are contractually obligated to stay for a week and train your replacement," he yelled as he followed me into the parking lot.

"I don't *have* to do anything, especially if you fired me for being pregnant, you slimy fuck."

He smirked. "Oh, you're pregnant? I didn't know. I thought you were just getting fat."

I let out a noise that could only be a suppressed screech of rage. I wanted to hit him *so fucking bad.* "Screw you." I stomped away again, but he grabbed my arm.

"Listen, you little bitch—" he hissed low, his hand tight around my wrist.

He didn't get any further than that, because Nate was suddenly between us. "I suggest you remove your hand, before I remove it for you." He leaned close, his eyes ominous. "From your fucking arm. Permanently."

Bob was a coward, and he backpedaled so fast, he almost tripped over the curb. He gave Nate a greasy smile. "Just a misunderstanding. I was informing my employee about her schedule next week."

I folded my arms across my chest. "He just fired me because I'm pregnant."

Nate stood to his full height, and I swear, it was like he grew a foot until he was glaring down at Bob. "Is that right?" His Irish accent, which I hardly ever noticed, had gotten thicker.

Bob was shaking his head furiously. "No, of course not. That's against employment law here in Massachusetts. Uh, she was let go due to multiple policy and procedure violations, as per her contract." Clearly, Bob thought he was talking to a well-meaning member of the public.

Nate's jaw flexed. "I find it hard to believe that Wren would break the rules so badly that you'd need to fire her."

A light went on in Bob's brain, as he realized this

wasn't just a passerby. This was someone who had a vested interest in me. He was also huge, tattooed, and broader than the side of a barn.

Still, no one had ever accused my former boss of being smart. "The terms of her employment termination are confidential." He looked at me, but I could see the whites around his eyes. He was playing tough, but was shit-scared. "I'll find someone else to replace you. Don't bother coming in tomorrow."

With that, he escaped back into Java Llama like the very devil was on his heels. Nate grunted, stepping forward to follow him, but I was suddenly too exhausted to care.

"Leave it, Nate. Let the weasel stew in his own self-righteousness. I don't want to be late for my appointment."

An appointment that was going to eat through the last of my money.

Nate continued to stare daggers at the building, but when I turned toward his truck, he followed behind me.

CHAPTER 6
WREN

"It's wonderful to see you, Mrs. Mahone. And you've brought Daddy along to see the babies." The receptionist cooed in Nate's direction, as if just turning up to medical appointments made a man Husband of the Year.

I was irritable. Bob had made me pissed beyond measure, and that made me snarkier than the poor receptionist probably deserved.

"Oh, he's not the father of the babies. He is Daddy, though, if you know what I mean." I gave the woman a lascivious wink, making her flush bright red. I purposefully didn't turn to look at Nate. That might've been a little too ballsy, even for me.

"Well, uh, okay. That's good?" The poor woman was flustered, and now I felt bad. She'd only been trying to make conversation. "The techs are running on time, so if you want to take a seat, someone will call you in soon, then Dr. Cho will see you afterwards to discuss your care."

I gave a tight nod and headed into the waiting room, where I would be surrounded by my brethren. The pregnant and the rotund. I flopped down in a chair gratefully, because damn, I was exhausted. Emotionally and physically drained, and perilously close to crying. Yet again.

Fuck this shit.

"I'll be fine here, if you have something else you want to do," I said, attempting to ignore the last few minutes. I couldn't believe I'd insinuated he was some kind of Dom to a perfect stranger. Damn my mouth. It would be best if he left, because then I could overthink everything without his scrutinizing gaze.

It didn't matter if I was terrified about doing this on my own; I'd have to learn sometime. This was a good first step.

Some of my terror must have shown on my face, though, because Nate shook his head gently. "If you'd like, I could stay with you. It's always good to have another set of ears at appointments." He raised a single golden eyebrow at me. "After all, I am Daddy."

All the blood in my body rushed to my face, and I choked. *Serves me right.* "Sorry. That was awkward, and I had no right to, uh, call you that."

His shoulders shook, and I suddenly realized he was laughing. I could hear the low, muffled rumble of his chuckle. It was like a physical prickle across my skin.

I'd never seen the man laugh. Ever. I wanted to bathe in the sensation.

"Don't be. I've been called worse things."

I was saved from answering by a tech calling my name. Nate rested his hand against my spine as I stood with a little less grace than a couple of months ago. He followed me in, and unlike the receptionist, the ultrasound tech didn't make any assumptions about our relationship.

"Your notes say you're expecting spontaneous triplets?" she asked, giving me a wide smile. "I bet that came as a wild surprise."

I shook my head as I climbed onto the bed. "You have absolutely no idea. It was… a lot." That was an understatement. It had forever altered my life; I doubted anyone could be adequately prepared for that. "I thought I had brain parasites."

Nate barked out a laugh, drawing the gaze of both me and the tech. She stared for an inappropriate amount of time, her lips slightly parted. *Girl, do I get it.* As he laughed, his face pulled into that smile again, and it was dazzling.

As I cleared my throat softly, the tech dragged her eyes back to me. Her cheeks were pink, and she looked slightly horrified. "Uh, well, pregnant is better than brain parasites. That sounds awful." She pulled out a squeeze bottle. "The gel should be warm, but if not, I apologize for the slight chill." She squirted a good dollop of gel on the wand as I wiggled up my shirt.

Once upon a time, I might've been self-conscious of

showing my stomach to someone like Nate, but now? My body felt like it was a timeshare, so I had to get over my insecurities.

The tech ran the wand over my stomach, and immediately, I heard the whoosh of heartbeats. Looking over at the screen, I could see a face. She took a few measurements, marking it as Baby A. Then she moved further down, and for a brief moment, I wondered if maybe the other ultrasound tech had been wrong. Maybe she'd had faulty equipment, and I was really only carrying one baby. A big one. Or hell, maybe just twins. I had two arms, which meant two babies would be workable, right?

"Okay, Baby B is here, and they both look really good. Let's try and find baby C, shall we?" She poked her tongue out through her teeth as she stared at the screen, navigating my womb like it was the world's most convoluted video game.

I held my breath as she searched and searched. "Is there something wrong?" What if there was something wrong with the third baby? Why couldn't she find it? My heart felt like it was pounding in my chest.

Nate reached up and gripped my hand in his. Just completely encapsulated it with his large palm and long fingers. Instantly, I felt calmer.

The tech gave me a reassuring smile. "No, nothing is wrong. Just a lot of business going on in there at the moment, so it's a little hard to navig—aha! There he is."

"He?"

The tech shook her head. "Figure of speech. It's a

little too early to really tell the sex just yet." She did her measurements, moving the wand around. "Baby C is a little smaller, but nothing to be worried about. He's still within the acceptable parameters." She went back to work, and when she was done, she printed me out a long strip of pictures. "Babies' first photo," she joked.

I was mesmerized by the tiny images. This was real. They were real. I looked up at Nate to check if he was seeing what I was seeing, but his gaze was fixed on my face, his blue eyes intense.

I passed him the ultrasound photos. "Babies. All three of them." I was choked up, tears brimming at the edges of my eyes.

"Your babies, Wren," he said softly, like he wasn't sure I knew who they belonged to. "They're beautiful already."

Thankfully, the tech wiped off my stomach for me, distracting me from the heavy emotional blanket of the moment. Nate helped me sit up, holding my arm as I climbed down from the hospital bed. His hand stayed on my back as we returned to the waiting room to wait on the doctor, who wasn't quite as on time as the tech.

An hour later, I was feeling sore and restless, my back was aching, and I felt guilty that I'd stolen so much of Nate's day. "I can get the bus home," I told him for the second time in thirty minutes.

"I've got nowhere to be," he said gruffly, not looking up from the pregnancy magazine he was reading.

Women in here had been throwing him hungry looks for fifty-nine of the last sixty minutes. That was something they'd never told me about pregnancy. We might cry a lot, but man, pregnant women were also horny as hell. I wasn't sure why; it seemed like an odd quirk of biology. I mean, we were already knocked up— why did our libido need to be ratcheted up to eleven?

One woman, who was so round that I was a little worried she'd legit explode, looked like she was ready to ride Nate all the way to the delivery ward of the hospital across the road.

"Wren?"

I realized I'd been giving the woman across the room the stink-eye when the doctor's voice made me start. Dr. Cho was a female doctor in her late sixties, and there was something reassuring about her presence. I moved toward her, doing my best not to waddle just yet.

I was a little surprised when Nate followed me into the office, but not upset. Relieved, maybe. He'd been right; another set of ears didn't hurt, and it felt like I was sharing the weight of this burden with someone else. Not that the babies were a burden.

No, you know what? They *were* a burden. I wasn't going to pretend like being knocked up meant I was suddenly ready to be a mom. There wasn't a switch inside me. I still had to come to terms with it, and then I knew, deep down in my soul, I would love them.

But they'd derailed my life. A life I could barely keep up with myself. I hadn't been to the dentist since I was ten. There were weeks when I only bought crackers and cheese for food. I wasn't the picture of responsibility, just because I was pregnant. There would be a learning curve.

They might be a burden now, but I would love them and care for them to the best of my ability, and if that meant that right now, at this moment, I needed a little extra help, then there was nothing wrong with that.

So I was glad that Nate was here to hear what the doctor said, because my brain had been a permanent tilt-a-whirl for weeks. What if I forgot something and made a mistake and somehow caused them irreparable damage?

"Take a seat, Wren. Can I call you Wren?" Dr. Cho asked, and I nodded. "So Dr. Kash has sent me the notes he had on your condition. Are you still seeing visual hallucinations?"

I cast a quick look at Nate, whose face was pulled down in a frown. Guess I'd left that part of the story out.

"Uh, yeah, but they aren't as, I don't know, bright anymore?" Well, most of the time anyway.

The doctor made a humming noise as she wrote notes. "Sometimes, disturbances in the vision or hearing can be an early onset sign of pre-eclampsia, though your blood pressure and blood work all look quite good. But we'll keep an eye on it anyway. I see Dr. Kash also authorized an MRI, and I can see why he ruled out any organic cause of your disturbances. These things, if related to pregnancy, usually dissipate by the end of the second trimester, so we'll watch it but not panic just yet.

"I've reviewed your ultrasound, and that all looks fine as well. A miraculous event, three fraternal triplets. Safer for the babies, and for you. Baby C is small, but we'll watch and ensure he's growing before we think about any drastic actions. They're all well within the margins we'd expect at this stage."

She talked more, about prenatal vitamins and regular ultrasounds and bed rest, and it all began to blur. But Nate, apparently, was taking extremely good notes.

"Is there any exercise she shouldn't be doing? Or should be doing? Foods she can't eat?" He quizzed, and I melted a little inside for my surly neighbor. I shook myself, because down that road only lay heartache.

As Dr. Cho unloaded an absolute wealth of knowledge onto Nate, I rested my hand on my stomach. Inside, there were three whole humans 3D printing, and it was hard to imagine that my body would ever be the same. It might be vain, but I was going to be like a deflated balloon.

No matter how sweet he was being now, Nate was not the kind of guy who would've been attracted to me normally, let alone once my body was all stretched and marked from carrying three tiny miracles into the world. No, Nate needed to stay well and truly in the friend zone, both for my sanity and my self-esteem.

Finally, we left the doctor's office with a fistful of pamphlets and another appointment in two weeks. As I looked at the amount on the bill, I tried not to wince. Maybe I could push it out to a month's time, because these visits were going to eat into my savings now that I was unemployed. Maybe I needed to look into a free clinic across town.

Nate opened the passenger door of his truck for me. "Come on, Wren. We'll stop at the drugstore on the way home." His voice was gentle but firm, and I found myself nodding.

It was a shame the receptionist had been wrong—he'd have made a good father.

"Seatbelt," he reminded me, and I let my lips curl into a smile.

Actually, he'd have made a good Daddy too.

CHAPTER 7
WREN

I hadn't realized quite how exhausted I was until I stopped going to work. I started sleeping late, and for the first time in so long, I got the amount of rest I needed. My body still ached, but after a couple of days, I felt refreshed. As refreshed as someone could be, while being used as an energy bank for three other human beings.

I hadn't really seen Nate since the appointment, but he'd started delivering food outside my door, the way I had with Mrs. Byrne. It was sweet—too sweet—and I gave myself another stern talking-to about the hazards of getting attached to him. Hell, attached to any man.

I'd sat down and budgeted once more, applied for other jobs, even applied for welfare, because the days of being too proud for government handouts were long gone. I'd researched what I should eat, what I should be doing, and had thrown myself into the role of being an expectant mother.

I was staring at the vegetables in my fridge, wondering what I could make that would stretch the week, when there was a knock at my door. Padding over to it in bare feet—because all my socks were uncomfortably tight on my swollen ankles—I looked out the peephole. I was surprised to see Nate, and my gut did that bubbly little swooping thing.

I opened the door to see him holding a big bag of takeout. The smell of garlic bread hit me, and my mouth watered.

"Hey, Nate." I stepped to the side so he could come in. He had to duck his head to get through the door, and I once again felt residual guilt that he was so willing to give up his apartment for mine. He looked like a giant in a doll's house.

"I brought you dinner." He made it sound almost like an accusation. "Italian. You need the carbs." He placed it on my tiny dining table, then turned back toward the door.

"You aren't staying?" I tried to hide the disappointment in my tone by sifting through the bags, but I doubted that I'd done a great job.

His eyes took in my face, those blue irises burning like flames. I wanted it to be from desire, or need, or something other than pity, but I hadn't reached that level of delusion yet. Still, when he shook his head, my chest felt tight with disappointment.

I walked him back to the door and held it open. "Thank you for this, Nate. Actually, thank you for everything. You've been a lifesaver."

He paused just inside the doorway, his eyes snagging on my lips, and for a crazy second, I thought he might kiss me. These hormones were like being on a bad trip; I second-guessed everything.

He raised his hand and traced my cheek, and my lips parted. Okay, maybe I wasn't imagining it then. But instead of leaning forward and taking my lips with those mesmerizingly plump ones, he stepped out onto the landing. "Goodnight, Wren." He shut the door softly, and I stared at it, my heart pounding like a drum behind my ribs.

What the hell was that?

Shaking my head and extra confused, I walked back over to the food. Complimentary bread sticks weren't confusing—they never gave you mixed messages. Indigestion occasionally, but never mixed messages.

He'd bought me enough pasta to last a week. Spaghetti. Lasagne. Some kind of thick noodles with a pumpkin sauce. There were also two loaves of garlic bread. I tried not to get teary at his thoughtfulness.

Taking out the pasta that I thought wouldn't last quite as well in the fridge, I broke off half a loaf of bread. I was suddenly starving. Loading up my goodies, I went over to the couch to watch *Lust In The Sun*. There was nothing like forgetting about your own problems by watching a bunch of people make out in a hot tub, then fight about it the next day.

I was so full, I was fairly sure that the babies would have to make room for the food baby I'd just ingested, and I wildly hoped it would stay down. I wasn't sure my carbonara would taste quite as good coming back up.

Mentally, I rearranged the apartment to fit in three cribs. Maybe if I got rid of the dining table, and possibly the couch, I could fit three in. It wouldn't leave much space, but it would be doable. Luckily, they wouldn't need a lot while they were young, so I'd have some time to figure out the next step.

I spent the next hour researching how to transport three babies. There was everything from baby-wearing devices, to how to strong-arm three baby capsules at once. Transporting them was definitely going to be the hard part. I really was going to need a car.

By the time I stopped doom-scrolling my way through YouTube videos, it was late. I'd already put the rest of the Italian food in the fridge, and I quickly washed my bowl.

There was a noise on my landing, and I wondered if Nate had come back. Maybe one of the dishes was actually his? I mean, that had been a hell of a lot of Italian food for one person. Or maybe it was the rat that Mrs. Byrne had been trying to get rid of for at least a year, which somehow managed to dodge death, like he was Splinter from Teenage Mutant Ninja Turtles.

Or maybe he wanted to kiss me.

Nate, I mean. Not Splinter the Rat.

I smiled at the thought as I watched the shadow stop in front of the door. Lifting my hands to my mouth, I tried not to worry that my breath now smelled like garlic and I had indigestion from the rich cream sauce.

The shadow outside my apartment didn't move. Was he summoning the bravery to knock? Nate didn't seem like the type to hesitate, but he also didn't seem like the type who wanted any kind of romantic connection either, so what did I know?

I watched the shadow for a little longer, and when it disappeared, I tried not to feel too disappointed. *Platonic friends. Platonic friends.* That was my new mantra.

The door crashed open, making me scream, scrambling backwards until my ass landed back on the couch. The shadow in the doorway definitely wasn't Nate. I didn't even know *what* the fuck it was. It was huge and black, like a creature from a nightmare. It didn't move so much as ooze its way into my living room.

This wasn't real. It was a nightmare caused by too much garlic and carbs before bed. That's all it was.

I tried to wake myself, pinching my skin until it turned red, but nothing happened. The nightmare was still right there, moving toward me in a way that made my hindbrain scream to *run.* But run where? There was only one way out of my apartment, and the shadow monster was standing in front of it.

I screamed again, hoping Nate would hear me. The thing moved around, hissing, and I scrambled to my feet, dodging behind the breakfast bar.

It had a wide-open maw, baring teeth so razor sharp, they looked like knives. Its black flesh was dripping from its skeleton as it moved forward again, and my heart thundered so hard I was worried I'd have a heart attack.

"Get the fuck away from me!" I screamed.

It lunged, its long, skeletal claws reaching for me, and I held my breath. It smelled of damp earth and trash, but that wasn't why I'd stopped breathing. Terror had clogged my throat. I was about to die at the hands of a monster, my babies right along with me.

Before those claws could so much as scratch me, an ax swung down and removed its hand. At least, I thought it was an ax. It shone so bright, it was like a spear of light through my retinas.

When I peeled my eyes open against the piercing brightness, Nate stood in front of me. Well, kind of Nate. He was also luminescent, and I had to squint against the light bursting from his skin.

The monster spun on him with a pained screech, flying at him like it had no bones. It wrapped itself around him, smothering his light with the oily, dripping darkness of its body. The glow where Nate had been flickered under the terrifying blackness. It was like an abyss had sucked Nate down deep.

"Nate!"

The shadow gave an inhuman shriek, and pinpricks of light burst through the membrane of its flesh. With a roar that made all the hairs on my body stand on end, Nate's glowing ax burst through what I assumed was the middle of the beast, making shadowy ooze splat against the walls, like gore in a Tarantino film.

Then the creature disappeared, just like that. Even

the oozing flesh that had hit the wall was like invisible ink, fading away like it had never been there in the first place. Staring at my clean white wall, it all could have been a bad dream.

Except Nate was still glowing and he seemed… bigger. I couldn't explain how, but he'd grown at least a foot, as if a normal-sized Nate couldn't contain the enormity of his aura. I could feel his presence like a suffocating weight on my chest.

Fuck. "Maybe there really is a brain tumor," I whispered. None of this shit was making sense.

"You don't have a brain tumor, Wren," he grumped, wiping his glowing blade against the rough fabric of his pants. "I think you might be seeing the supernatural."

My eye twitched, and a hysterical laugh bubbled up from my chest where the hard block of fear still sat heavily. "The supernatural," I repeated.

"Yes. That creature was a Verserpent. A creature of the night." He frowned. "At least, I think it was." As I watched, he cracked his neck, and it was like the opposite of a glowstick; his light shrunk in on itself, like a roaring fire smoldering down to a glowing ember. Now that I'd seen it, I couldn't unsee the light that shone from his chest, banked for now, but not gone.

"Verserpent," I repeated dumbly as my brain tried to cling to… anything.

He nodded, dropping his ax so it leaned against the back of the couch. "Yes." He walked over to the window, looking out into the small backyard. "There were two. I dispatched one on the stairs before I heard you scream." He gave me what would be considered a lopsided smile. "It was lucky we didn't fix that squeaking step after all."

I slumped down onto the couch. "How? Why?" *Why did it break into my apartment and try to eat me? How did it get up...* "Mrs. B!"

Panic flashed across Nate's face, and he was out of the room before I could even get up from the couch. I ran to the stairs, forcing myself to grab the handrail and go slowly down so I didn't trip.

"Mrs. Byrne!" I yelled, panic edging my tone. "Mrs. Byrne, answer me!"

I reached the bottom of the stairs, and Nate was there, blocking the door to her apartment, the look on his face laying bare my worst fear.

"No. No, Nate. Let me past," I screeched, shoving at his chest.

"Wren, you don't want to—"

"Let me *past!*" I screamed at his chest, and he slowly stepped back, letting me through.

At first, I convinced myself she was just sleeping. She was lying in her recliner, the late-night shows playing on her TV. The remote was still in her hand. But as I got closer, there was an unnatural stillness about her. An unnatural angle to her body that screamed death, not sleep.

Her face was contorted in horror. Her other hand was clutching her chest. She'd died in fear, and that broke something inside me.

"No, no, no," I breathed, clutching at her hand. I

sank to my knees beside her recliner, shaking. She couldn't be dead. She was the last person left in the world that I had. She couldn't die and leave me alone.

I sobbed into the couch, clinging to her hand. At some point, I felt the warm chest of Nate wrap around me, giving me someone to lean against as I cried.

"I've called 911. They'll be here any minute." He gripped my chin and lifted my face so I was forced to meet his eyes. "You have to hold it together, Wren. You can't say anything about monsters or shadows, because they'll throw you in a psychiatric ward. We came down here and found Mrs. B. That's all that happened, okay?" His voice was softer than I'd ever heard it, the Irish lilt comforting, like it was wrapping around my bruised heart. The same soft Irish lilt that Mrs. B used to have. "You've been such a brave girl. Just be strong a little longer. For Mrs. B. For the babes." He rested his forehead against mine.

When the police arrived, shortly followed by the EMTs, I let Nate do most of the talking. When the paramedic wanted to check me out, asking me a few questions, I answered them robotically. I was having triplets. No, I didn't feel any pain. Yes, they could take my blood pressure.

They declared Mrs. B deceased, loaded her onto a gurney, and wheeled her out the door. Probably a heart attack, the EMT told us—after all, she was very old.

When the cop asked Nate why we had come down to check on her in the middle of the night, he shrugged. Shit, we hadn't gone over that.

I looked up at the cop, my eyes brimming with tears. "Pregnancy instinct, maybe? Something felt wrong." I'd heard about that kind of thing. Sounded like something a mom would develop. Mrs. Byrne had certainly had those instincts.

The cop gave me a soft smile, and Nate tucked me under his arm. "Oh yeah. That mom gut feeling. Once, my wife woke up in the middle of the night with a bad feeling. Caught our three-year-old on a chair, trying to escape out the front door of the house. That mother's instinct is some wild stuff." He reached out and rubbed my arm. "I'm sorry for your loss. We'll get out of your hair and let you grieve."

Nate kept me pressed tightly to his chest as he bid the officers and EMTs goodnight. Then he led me up the stairs into his apartment, and I slid beneath the covers of his bed like I'd done it a hundred times before.

"Sleep, little one. I'll guard you tonight," he whispered, going to sit in the chair across the room.

But he couldn't guard my dreams, and when I drifted off to sleep, it was filled with shadows and monsters, and Mrs. B's fear-filled face, which would be forever etched in my mind.

CHAPTER 8
WREN

Grief sat heavily on my chest, weighing me down so it felt nearly impossible to climb from Nate's bed. As soon as I set foot outside the apartment, it would mean that it was all real. Shadow monsters and Mrs. Byrne's death would be more than a nightmare. The supernatural would be real.

So I stayed in bed. Even as Nate left to go and make arrangements for the funeral, I stayed in bed. He brought me food that I ignored, and water, which he watched me drink, standing over me and muttering about staying hydrated.

He was gone now, and I had to pee. Grabbing my stomach, I shuffle-rolled from beneath the blankets. I grumbled at the babies for sitting right on my bladder even as I stroked my belly soothingly. It was odd how quickly I'd no longer felt alone.

I was still scared. Petrified, actually. Dusk was starting to settle, and I hoped that Nate returned soon, even though it made me feel like a complete chicken shit. Apparently, I was going to develop a phobia of the dark at the grand old age of twenty-two. Every shadow now seemed more ominous, and I only felt slightly guilty as I flicked on every single light switch between the bedroom and the bathroom.

Much like my apartment, there was only an open-plan living room and kitchen, then a bathroom and bedroom side by side. I stepped out into the living room, and my eyes snagged immediately on the giant ax hanging on the wall, looking like a normal ax that you might use at a renaissance festival, or LARPing. It wasn't a beacon of glowing light, though if I concentrated, I could almost imagine a hum of power emitting from the etched blade.

Averting my eyes, I hurried to the bathroom. After relieving myself, I stared in the mirror. I looked like crap. My eyes were red-rimmed and sunken. My hair was lank around my face, a rat's nest forming on the back of my head from tossing and turning.

I looked like absolute shit, but I didn't care, because Mrs. B was dead, and it was kind of my fault. I quickly splashed water on my face before I started crying again.

Hearing the front door open, I froze. I didn't breathe, my hands hovering over the sink as I waited, my heart pounding in my chest. What if it was back?

"Wren?" Nate called, and I didn't miss the panic in his voice. Apparently, last night's attack had shaken us both.

"In here." I moved back toward the living room in time to catch the relief on Nate's face.

"Are you doing okay?" he asked softly, moving toward me as his eyes ran over my body repeatedly, looking for injuries or illness, or something that only he could see.

Shrugging, I sat down on his couch. "Okay is relative."

He gave a tight nod and walked into the kitchen, pulling out a plate of sandwiches from the fridge, covered by plastic wrap. "You need to eat now."

It wasn't a request anymore. Apparently, now that I was out of the fetal position, he was going to shuck at least one of the kid gloves.

He dropped the plate in front of me on the coffee table, and I felt my stomach rumble. I was hungry, even if the thought of eating made my stomach turn. But I sucked it up, taking a nibble of the first perfect triangle. It was chicken salad, and tasted like ash.

Swallowing hard, I gave him a grateful smile. "Thank you." I chewed another mouthful, and then another, until that triangle was gone. *Okay. I can do this.* "How did… arrangements go?"

I couldn't say the word funeral. Because that would mean she was gone and never coming back.

I watched his jaw flex. "Fine. It's set for Friday."

The ball of grief grew in my chest. "So soon."

He nodded, sitting down beside me. "She was old, and it was clearly a heart attack." A heart attack caused by coming face to maw with a monster. "I went and saw the lawyer. I was the only beneficiary of her will, but I told him to sign half the house over to you too."

"What?" My eyes went wide as my brain tried to grapple with what he was saying.

"Zelda and I had been talking about it anyway before she died. It's what she wanted. What we both wanted. She wanted you and the babies to always have a roof over your head. If you decide you want to leave Boston, I'll buy out your half so you have something to start with. A nest egg."

"Nate…" I didn't know what to say. He didn't have to do this, even if it was Mrs. B's last wish. No one would have ever known. "I…" Fuck, I didn't know what to say, but tears threatened to run down over my cheeks, no matter how vigorously I blinked them back. "Thank you." I threw my arms around his waist and felt him stiffen slightly, before relaxing into the hug.

"It's what she wanted," he said dismissively, like he just hadn't given me more security than I'd had since my parents died. But he didn't let me go, just stroked my back as I cried silently against his chest.

It FELT like Mother Nature was taunting us on the day of Mrs. Byrne's funeral. It was the most perfect, beautiful sunny day we'd had all month. It felt *wrong*. It should've been as gray and miserable as I felt. As the whole crowd behind me felt.

Dressed in black, I sat in the front row of the graveside service. Beside me, looking stoic, was Nate, the black button-up shirt he wore clinging tightly to his shoulders and setting off the tattoos that peeked above his collar. His beard was trimmed close to his jaw, and his eyes were covered with dark sunglasses.

It felt like everyone I knew in our tight-knit community had turned out for the funeral. The ladies from the church were all there. Rossi's was closed for the day so the entire Rossi family could attend. Even Mr. Lunetta had come. There were former students from when Mrs. Byrne had been a teacher, her knitting circle, even the President of the Eire Society of Boston. It felt like everyone who'd ever crossed paths with her had come out to pay their respects.

The Catholic priest at the front of the crowd droned on about piousness and goodness, and the amount of people whose lives had been bettered by a true stalwart of the faith. He went on and on, and I could feel myself starting to burn under the heat of the midday sun.

Nate lifted one of his huge hands and held it above my head, sheltering me from a little of the heat. I looked over and smiled at him gratefully, even if it was a little soggy around the edges.

People stood up and spoke about their experiences with Mrs. Byrne, and I couldn't help but smile through the tears. She'd helped Hal Wallers when he broke his hip falling down icy steps out the front of his house; she'd taken him food every single day for weeks. He described how she'd sat with him and watched *Jeopardy!* for hours, just to keep him company while he was bedbound.

Zia Maria talked about how Zelda—Mrs. Byrne, it really was weird for me to think of her as Zelda—had come over to drink wine with her when her youngest son enlisted and was sent off on his first tour of duty, then lit a candle for him every day until he returned.

Finally, it was my turn, and I waddled to the podium set up in front of all the folding chairs. There was a murmur in the crowd as they took in my pregnant belly, and I steeled my spine. I guess those people who hadn't known about my pregnancy did now.

Clearing my throat, I looked out over the crowd. "Mrs. Byrne saved my life. A few times, actually. I remembered her from my childhood, a friendly face I'd sometimes see at my grandmother's house when I went to visit, who'd always sneak me candy with a grin and a wink." There was a low chuckle through the crowd.

"When my grandmother died, and my parents soon after, I was adrift and alone in the world, yet she didn't hesitate to step up and throw me a lifeline. She stepped in to be my surrogate grandmother, without caring that taking on a teenager might be hard work. She gave me a space in her home, three meals a day when the idea of cooking for myself—of going on at all—seemed too hard. She was my lighthouse for so long, and I'm adrift once more without her."

My voice broke, and I watched Nate shift in his chair, like he wanted to come and rescue me from this too. I held a hand up in his direction, keeping him in his seat.

"But even in death, she made sure I had a safe

harbor, and that was just the kind of woman Zelda Byrne was. She was good down to her very core. She was giving, even to the detriment of herself. She was tough—so fucking *tough*—but she never let it make her bitter. She is a woman I admire, and still someone I'd like to make proud." I looked down at the grave, her shiny wooden coffin glinting under the sun. "I'll miss you, Mrs. B. I love you."

I'm sorry.

With that, sobs shook my body, even as I tried to swallow them back. Nate stood, coming over to usher me back to my chair. The rest of the funeral slowly wrapped up, and as the priest committed her body to the earth, I began to build myself back up again, brick by brick.

The wake was going to be held at the church hall, catered by Mrs. Byrne's bible group, but I had to wait until they lowered her into the ground and started covering her over before I could move. I was almost waiting for her to pop up from her casket and say, "Sweet Wren, you spoke beautifully, child." Nate stayed by my side the whole time.

Finally, swallowing hard, I stood. I needed to move. To leave and go and pay my respects at the wake. People would expect me to be there.

"I'm okay," I murmured as Nate gripped my elbow, though my shaky knees flew directly in the face of that statement. Merely grunting his disagreement, he wrapped an arm around my ever-expanding waist and ushered me up the small aisle between the chairs. The funeral directors stood at the end like gargoyles.

This day had dragged on, and all I wanted to do was go home and curl up in bed—well, Nate's bed, because I was still too chicken to go back to my own—but I needed to show the proper respect first. Mrs. B deserved that from me. I'd drink a cup of tea or two, have a finger sandwich, then use pregnancy exhaustion as an excuse to leave early. Hell, it wouldn't even be an excuse; I was exhausted.

But as we headed into the shade of the trees bordering the cemetery, I audibly groaned. Because there, standing beneath the trees, was my panicked ex-boyfriend.

"*Fuck*," I swore beneath my breath, and Nate went tense beside me, his eyes darting around, looking for threats. However, there were no shadow monsters or anything else that oozed. There was just Thomas, who was a douche canoe, but not a monster.

"Is it mine?" he gasped out.

Had I mentioned he was really stupid too?

"Thomas, we broke up twelve months ago. Unless you're the Messiah and can impregnate me with a thought, it seems unlikely, don't you think?" I had the patience of a saint, really. How I'd managed to stay with this guy for three years was actually a real miracle. Call me Saint Wren, Patron Saint of Dumbasses.

Nate actually growled in Thomas's direction, and Thomas gave him the side-eye. Obviously, he had no self-preservation skills either.

"Nate."

"Thom-ass," he replied. I was pretty sure he'd done it on purpose, though you couldn't really tell with the slight lilt of his accent. I had a suspicion he played it up at times.

I let out a heavy sigh. "Why are you here, Thomas?"

He shrugged. "My mom told me about Mrs. B, and I wanted to pay my respects."

Mrs. Byrne had never thought Thomas was right for me, mostly because she believed he was as stupid as a box of rocks and not half as useful. *"Simple men want simple things, and you, my sweet Wren, deserve more than simple. You deserve someone who'll give you the whole world."* That was what she'd told me when we broke up, and I had to admit, it had lessened the burn of the fact I'd caught him cheating on me.

Still, I reached out and squeezed his arm, ignoring the fact that Nate pressed me tighter to his side. "She would have appreciated that." I dropped my voice. "How's Ivan?"

I knew cheating was cheating, but there was something reassuring about the fact that he'd cheated on me with someone who could give him something I couldn't. A hairy chest. And an equally hairy back.

Thomas looked around as if his mother might appear, like the vengeful old hag she was. He was still firmly in the closet. "He's good. He sends his condolences."

The silence stretched between the three of us. "We

should go," Nate muttered, and Thomas narrowed his eyes.

"Yeah, sure. Is it"—his eyes dropped to my stomach, then flicked back up to Nate disapprovingly—"yours?"

"No."

"Yes."

My denial and Nate's affirmation melded together, and I whipped my head up to stare at him. *The fuck?*

My cheeks flushed pink as my eyes darted back to Thomas. "They aren't yours, and I think that's all that should matter to you, right?" I asked lightly. "I'll be seeing you, Thomas."

I strode off, forcing Nate to follow along, ignoring Thomas's shouted, "They?!" as I made it to Nate's truck. He held the door as I climbed in like an ungainly beluga whale, shutting the door softly behind me. Then he climbed in the driver's side, buckled me in, and put the keys in the ignition, all the while not looking in my direction, which was kind of impressive.

And because he wasn't stupid, he didn't start the truck.

I turned to stare at him, my eyes trying to bore holes in his face. "And what the hell was *that?*"

He grunted and started the truck. Okay, maybe he *was* stupid. "You need a father for the babies so people will stop looking at you like a jezebel."

I slow-blinked. Like, I could feel my eyelids flutter at the patriarchal bullshit of that statement. "Let them look, Nate. I don't care."

"I care. Makes me want to wring all their necks. Do it for their health, if not for your own reputation."

I shook my head, like that would improve the crap spilling from his mouth. "You are *unbelievable*, you know that?"

I thought I might've seen his lips curl before he schooled his features back into his normal grumpy mask. "Thanks."

"It wasn't a compliment," I huffed, crossing my arms over my chest. As we drove, I stared out the window, trying to squash the tiny bit of my heart that fluttered at the thought that Nate cared enough about me—about us—to claim my babies in public.

CHAPTER 9
WREN

Three days after Mrs. Byrne's funeral, I knew it was time to go back to my own apartment. Nothing else had happened. There'd been no more shadow monsters or supernatural things, and I was beginning to wonder if it had ever happened at all. Nate didn't glow any more than normal, and his ax was on the wall where it had always been. The longer nothing happened, the longer I wondered if the streaky lights in my vision had just expanded into full-blown delusions.

If it hadn't been for the fact that Mrs. B was still dead, and that Nate hadn't ever contradicted that the events of that night were real, I'd really begin to wonder.

In fact, Nate was still pretty against me going back to my own apartment, even though he'd been sleeping his six-four ass on the couch, which had to be uncomfortable. But I'd imposed enough, and I hated sitting around his apartment all day while he went off to work.

I'd discovered he was an employee for an equestrian center outside of the city, where he worked as a stable manager, teaching children how to ride. My brain had almost exploded at the idea that the gruff, tattooed man who lived in the apartment below me had been out there teaching preschoolers how to ride ponies all these years. He also donated his time to helping people overcome their fear of horses, and ran a program for teens and adults with disabilities who wanted to ride and do animal husbandry.

Who freaking knew?

I slowly walked up to my apartment, wearing one of Nate's oversized hoodies. I needed to get around to buying maternity clothes, because nothing I owned fit anymore. I was hooking my jean shorts together with hair elastics now. Even my comfiest sleep shirts just fit as regular shirts these days.

If I thought the nightmare creature had just been a delusion, one look at my apartment fixed that assumption. My furniture had been flipped, and the long scratch marks on the walls were straight out of a horror film. My heart thudded loudly in my ears, and I backed away.

I couldn't stay here. I couldn't.

Turning toward my room, I rushed in and grabbed some of my things. Clothes. Shoes. My laptop. The picture of my parents. Things that I needed until I was feeling stronger. Until Nate was with me and we could come and scrub the evil feeling from this apartment.

I needed an entire army of wiccans with a barrel of sage to smudge the fuck out of this apartment.

Stuffing everything in my bag, I slung it over my shoulder and got the hell out of dodge. I locked the door, like a lock had kept out the last thing that went bump in the night. Gripping the handrail, I waddled down the stairs, trying to think of ways to explain to Nate that I had to stay with him permanently, because my apartment had bad vibes, and Mrs. B's apartment was too painful to live in. He was going to be stuck with me for a little longer.

"Excuse me?"

I spun around and gasped. I hadn't even heard the woman on the stairs. She had a package in her hands and a tan outfit. *Crap.* I'd forgotten I started buying baby shit online.

She winced. "Sorry, I didn't mean to scare you. The front door was open, and I thought that maybe this was an apartment complex. You didn't have a package drop at your front door."

I waved her away. "It's fine. Just let me get the door."

As I turned to open Nate's door, the hairs on my neck stood up. I looked over my shoulder at the delivery woman, scanning her from head to toe. She was pretty, with honey-blonde hair and a wide smile. But there was something wrong; I knew it in my gut.

Stepping inside the doorway, I white-knuckled the

heavy wooden front door. "Just leave it there, and I'll get my husband to bring it in."

Her smile never faltered. The uniform she was wearing looked too big, almost like it wasn't made for her. "I can bring it in. It's absolutely no problem," she crooned at me, and her voice made goosebumps rise on my skin.

I was already shaking my head. Every instinct I had was screaming to get away. "It's fine. Have a nice day." I tried to shut the door, but the box was jammed inside.

"Let me in, Vessel," the woman growled, her voice no longer sweet. I raced across the room and grabbed Nate's ax.

And then promptly dropped it. That fucker was *heavy*. How did he swing it like it weighed nothing?

The woman was still on the other side of the doorway, and the pretty visage of a delivery driver peeled away, leaving something from my nightmares. She had huge, sunken eyes, and lips that were raw and red, like they'd been burned into her face. A long snake tail whipped behind her in agitation.

She screeched as she lunged at the doorway, but was propelled back by some unseen force.

"We're coming for you, Vessel! You have to leave these wards eventually, and we'll be waiting. You won't always have the Celtic traitor with you." She licked her lips. "And when you die, I'm going to eat the young from your stomach."

I clutched my rounded belly protectively. "Fuck you!" I screamed at her. I ran into Nate's room and hid in the closet, like that could stop her. I seemed to be protected here, but I couldn't stand there and listen to her vitriol, and my heart was beating a million miles an hour.

Grabbing my phone from the front pocket of the hoodie, I dialed Nate's number. He answered in two rings. "What's wrong?" I could hear him puffing, like he was already running.

"There's some kind of monster here. A snake woman. She—" I choked on the words. "She can't get in, but she said she's going to eat the babies. I'm so fucking *scared,* Nate." I was trembling so hard, I dropped the phone. I could hear the snake monster taunting me from the doorway as I picked it back up.

"The fucking Lamia. Where are you right now?"

"In the closet in your room."

I heard the door of his truck slam shut and the engine roar to life. "The apartment's warded against the supernatural. Don't move from there. I don't care what she says."

"Okay," I whispered.

I could still hear the Lamia alternating between shouted obscenities to cajoling promises. "I'm going to burn you out of your hole like a boar hunt of old, Vessel. It does not matter to me if your flesh is cooked," she sing-songed from the doorway.

I was breathing so heavily that my lungs were burning. "Did you hear that?" I whispered, hoping Nate was still on the other end of the line.

He growled. "It's going to be okay. I'm almost

home." I could hear horns blaring in the background. "Three more minutes. You'll be okay. She can't get in there, and it would take longer than that for a fire to spread through my apartment. Get up and shut my bedroom door, then get back in the closet and shut that one too. Put clothes along the bottom, in case it gets smoky."

Doing as he asked, I slid along the floor, blocking out the demon's ranting vibrato voice. I repeated his instructions back to myself.

Shut the bedroom door. It would keep the fire from spreading into here.

Shut the closet door. That would keep the smoke out.

I climbed to the very back of the closet and buried myself beneath a pile of Nate's clothes, like the scent of him could protect me from monsters and fire. I wrapped myself protectively around my stomach, the phone beside my head.

I could hear Nate's hissed swear words as he drove through traffic. "Two minutes, Wren. Don't move. It'll be okay."

Don't move, he said. Where the hell would I even go? I rubbed my stomach soothingly, hoping the babies couldn't feel my fear. "It's okay. It's okay." I wasn't sure if I was reassuring them—even though they were no bigger than a baby squirrel right now—or myself. Probably both.

"One minute," Nate growled, and the banging outside the door stopped. I could smell smoke now, though it was faint. That crazy bitch had actually set Nate's apartment on fire.

I wanted to be my own damn hero. I wanted to be the old Wren who would've gone out there fearlessly and fought off the crazy bitch. But it wasn't just me in harm's way now.

I could hear Nate's roar of rage, and a quick scuffle, then silence. I heard the hiss of a fire extinguisher, then the door was pulled open.

"Wren!" Nate dug me out of my cocoon, pulling me easily to my feet and patting me down. "She fled as soon as I showed up. Are you okay?"

I was numb. My eyes were burning, but no tears came out, so maybe it was the smoke. "I think I need to go to Crete."

Pulling back, he stared at me like I'd lost my mind. "What?"

"Amourgeles. I need to go to Crete." I sighed and sunk into his chest, soaking in his strength like a vampire. "I'll explain."

And that's how I found myself lying on Nate's bed, my head on his chest, explaining about a crazy lady in the drive-thru and my upcoming trip to fucking Greece.

My life was a mess.

CHAPTER 10
NÉIT

By Dagda's fucking hairy testicles, what had Wren gotten herself into? Fucking Crete? I didn't know much about Greece, but I did know that all the creatures that had been trying to kill her were from the Greek Pantheon.

There'd been a long-standing rule—a division of territory, even. When humans settled in an area, the gods that were worshiped there all divided up the area. Sometimes, it was fine, and we lived in harmony. Sometimes, it was a bloodbath that spilled over to the human world.

But Boston, up until now, had been pretty uncontentious. There were enough Boston-Irish mammies rolling around who sat in the Cathedral of the Holy Cross on Sundays, but still celebrated Imbolc and Samhain to warrant a Celtic presence. Mammies like Zelda Byrne, who'd learned the practices and traditions from her mother, who'd learned from her own mother before that.

And that was how the disgraced and supposedly dead Irish God ended up in the new country, living in the house of a God-fearing Catholic, while holding a very pregnant, unwed woman in his arms.

Personally, I stayed the fuck out of the politics. I might be Néit, ancient God of War, but there was a big difference between war and petty political struggles. I left that to the new Celts and the Tuatha. I was happy working with the horses, watching the pretty, broken Wren from afar.

At first, when she had come to live in the house, I'd followed her with my eyes, mostly out of curiosity. She'd just been this sad, pathetic little creature who, for a long time, looked like she just wanted to sink into the earth and never emerge. That Wren didn't interest me so much. I came from a time when only the strong survived, and if she couldn't pull herself out, then I had no interest.

Even now, the world was no place for the weak. But still, I felt protective of her, maybe in the way I'd felt protective of Zelda Byrne. She was part of my domain.

But eventually, after grief had stopped marring Wren's face, and she'd picked herself up, something about her caught me and took hold. The fire returned to her eyes, though there were still shadows of grief that I didn't think would ever leave. She'd dusted herself off and gone on with her life, spreading her wings after the deaths of her parents, and *that* woman? She was something special.

When she came home with that gobshite Thomas, I'd had to stop myself from chopping his head off every time he talked to her dismissively. She deserved better, but I couldn't tell her that. I barely spoke to her. I grunted hello on the stairs occasionally. I was an eternal God, and I had no business becoming obsessed with a mortal whose life would be over in what was essentially seconds in the course of my existence.

Still, I watched. Like a fucking creeper, as the people of this age would say. I got invested in Wren's life, even as Zelda gave me the side-eye. Celebrated when she broke up with that *hoor.* Worried when she worked so hard.

But when I'd found her crying on the steps about the babies, my ability to keep my world separate from hers shattered in the wind. I'd had to acknowledge that I was invested in her happiness as more than a bystander. She was strong and so beautiful.

Zelda had noticed my preoccupation, and actually had the audacity to slap me, the God of fucking War, upside the head with her rolled-up TV guide. "She is not for you, Néit," she'd said sternly. "With you lies only heartache, and Lord knows, that child has had more than enough heartache in her life." I'd known she was serious when she called me by my real name.

I'd rolled my eyes in her direction. "I'm just helping her out, Zelda. Just like I'd help you. And she's not a child. She's about to be someone's mother."

She'd just huffed and dismissed me. Even the memory made me smile.

I was going to miss Zelda, who'd been my companion for more years than I could count. I would feel her loss for a long time.

I stroked Wren's back softly, soothing her. I didn't understand why she was being targeted, and I wasn't inclined to ask. I was more inclined to get my ax and thin the number of Mythics in Boston until they got the point that Wren Mahone was off-limits.

I listened to her explain about the woman in her drive-thru, how her eyes had gone white and her voice monotone, and it sounded like an Oracle of some kind. A lot of the Pantheons had Oracles, though, so it was hard to judge if this one was working on behalf of whoever was trying to hurt her, or if she was a separate entity entirely.

I'd never heard of Oracles being able to lie during a prophecy, but was I willing to stake Wren's life on it?

"What should I do, Nate?"

She should stay here, where I could protect her. But three supernaturals had already breached the outer wards, and even if I extended them to the front door, she would be trapped like a caged animal. That couldn't happen. She had appointments and had to give birth and shit.

That preemptive bloodbath was back on the table.

My grumble of frustration was almost soundless. I didn't know what to do, and I could tell she was relying on me to help her decide. I couldn't take out a whole

Mythic faction by myself, and to say I hadn't made many friends with my own people over the last millennia was an understatement. She couldn't stay trapped here either.

"What does your gut say?"

She looked up at me, her big eyes shiny. "It says that going to Crete is the right idea, but that's crazy, right?"

Hell yeah, it's crazy. "Then I guess we're going to Greece."

"We?"

Yeah, fucking we. Because there was no way I was letting a vulnerable Wren walk into an unknown country, into an unknown situation, by herself.

"We."

She stared at me, the fear and trust in her eyes making something in my chest clench. When she stretched and brushed her lips across mine, I was too stunned to move away. Her lips were so soft, and she tasted sweet. But before I could deepen the kiss, taste her more thoroughly, she dropped her cheek back to my shoulder.

"Thank you," she whispered, and I wanted to shout at her that she shouldn't thank me. I hadn't kept her safe, just fixed problems as they arose.

Instead, I kissed the top of her head gently and held her tighter. We'd make this work, and I would try and keep the hard-on I had for my sweet neighbor to myself, even if it was getting more difficult every time I touched her.

I needed help. That much was clear. And I fucking

hated asking for help. There was only one other from our Pantheon that I even associated with, and I knew she was going to give me so much shit about this.

THE FOLLOWING DAY, I brought Wren along, partly because I needed Cliona to meet her and partly because I was worried about leaving her behind. The other supernaturals seemed a little more hesitant to attack Wren when she was in my presence, and I was banking on that fact.

Driving further out of the city and into Revere, I kept casting Wren small looks. She was pale, her eyes smudged by dark circles. I'd watched her toss and turn last night, leaning against the doorjamb like a voyeur.

"So, who are we meeting again?"

I turned off the freeway. "An old friend. Cliona, but she prefers Clio now."

"And she's... like you?"

"Irish?"

Wren frowned at me. "You know what I mean."

I held back a smile. "She's immortal, yes. She is a *bean-sidhe*."

"A banshee! You're taking me to see a banshee?"

Technically, Clio was the queen of the *bean-sidhe*, but I didn't think that would make Wren feel better. "Yes. I want to know what the hell is going on, and Clio keeps better tabs on the politics of the supernatural world than I do."

Wren nodded. "And by the supernatural world, does that include, you know, things like werewolves and vampires and stuff?" She was putting on a brave face, but I could hear the subtle shake of uncertainty in her voice. It was probably a lot to take in for a human; I mean, they lived their lives as if they were the apex predators. It'd come as a shock that most supernaturals, especially the Mythics, considered them only marginally more interesting than sheep.

Definitely less interesting than cats.

"Those are human labels, and I wouldn't say that there are *exact* matches in the world, but humans didn't come up with these things themselves. At some point, they probably ran across some supernatural being that looked like a wolf—maybe one of the indigenous deities?—and then called it a werewolf."

Dumb name, but whatever.

Wren shook her head, chewing her lip until it was puffy. I wanted to reach over and kiss her until she stopped. Instead, I consoled myself by patting her knee. "There's so much history and mythology, even theology, that some humans dedicate their whole lives to a small portion of it, and they still don't know everything there is to know. You can't expect to understand it all in a month."

She looked out the window, and we completed the rest of the drive in silence. Clio lived down a random street in suburbia, which would make you think she was hiding out. But you'd be so wrong, which you'd soon discover as you pulled up to her little colonial house.

Because the whole thing was blacker than a widow's veil. The cladding, the trim, the door, even the letterbox were all pitch black. The windows were tinted the darkest shade money could buy. There was a spindly fence around the whole place, sharp spikes on the top. It was a foreboding kind of house, the kind the neighborhood kids would dare each other to knock on the front door as a rite of passage.

Clio loved that shit.

"Woah," Wren breathed, trepidation written all over her face.

Shaking my head, I climbed from the car and walked around to her door. I helped her out, my hands wrapped around her waist. "Don't let it fool you. Clio enjoys theatrics." I opened the squeaky gate and strode down the path. There was no Mythic on this planet that scared me, least of all Clio and the *bean-sidhe*.

Using the knocker shaped like a woman screaming, I slammed it down three times. I held my breath as Clio opened the door, taking in me and then Wren. I waited for her to scream. The wail of the *bean-sidhe* that would tell me that I was working against the very hands of fate. She opened her mouth, and I tensed.

Instead of the wail that you would feel in your very soul, she laughed in my face. "How'd you manage to knock up a mortal, Néit?"

Wren flushed, and I growled. "Are you going to invite us in?"

"Sure. Welcome, Wren Mahone."

I didn't know if it was reassuring that Clio knew her name or not. And I didn't know how to interpret the shit-eating grin Clio threw my way as we stepped into her house.

CHAPTER 11
WREN

I didn't know what I'd expected of a banshee, but it wasn't the woman in a Nirvana shirt and leather pants. I'd expected the inside of her house to be as dark and gloomy as the outside, but instead, it was like a cottagecore wet dream. Everything was shiny, dark wood and flowers. Prints on the wall, vases on every flat surface. Comfy leather furniture and coarse wooden benchtops. It was… quaint.

Unlike Nate, I looked at Clio and something inside me immediately knew she was different. Not wrong, just not… right. Perhaps that didn't make sense, but you know when you meet a person and there's something about them you find immediately unsettling?

It didn't hurt that she was ethereally gorgeous. All fine-boned and willowy. Her hair was fire-red, and her blue eyes sparkled wildly.

Nate huffed. "Wren, this is Clio. Clio is the representative for the Celtic Pantheon here in Boston. I obviously don't have to introduce you to her, because she seems to know your name already?" There was a question, and maybe a little threat, in his tone.

Clio waved a hand, ushering us over to her kitchen table. "My fluffy little retired Godling, it is quite *literally* my job to know every person." She sighed. "However, I can't really claim credit for this, because our girl here is being whispered about in all the dark corners."

I sucked in a breath. "But why?"

She shook her head. "I don't know, girlypop, but the boons they've put on your head for proof of death are wild. Only for the Greeks, though. They're a pompous bunch of fucks, but at least that means none of the other Pantheons give a flying fuck about you, right? Silver linings and all that."

Nate stood up and paced around the kitchen. "She's a fucking human," he grumbled, though his accent seemed to be thicker in the room with Clio, so his *fucking* sounded a little more like *fooking*. It was kinda cute, not that I'd ever tell him that. I swallowed down my grin as he continued. "What the hell could she have done to piss off the damn Greeks so much that they'd send the Lamia?"

Clio's brows rose high. "The Lamia?" She whistled. "Girl, you really did shit in someone's Wheaties." She eyed me with an expression that said she'd like to dissect me for parts.

Jesus fucking Christ.

Nate came over and rested a hand on my shoulder; a

gesture that wasn't lost on Clio. "Have you heard anything else?"

She shook her head. "Just the usual squabbles and shit. West Africans want East Boston, and I say let them have it, because it's just the damn airport, right? But no one can agree on how much, and obviously, no one wants to cede a damn inch. Very tedious." She stroked her chin. "There have been rumors that we've reached the tail once more."

"The tail?" I asked, because honestly, it was like she was talking in riddles.

It was Nate who answered. "If there's one thing we all agree on, it's the circle of time. The passing of ages. When the Ouroboros—or Jörmungandr, Leviathan, whatever other name they've given the Great Serpent—reaches the point where his tail is consumed by his mouth, it is a time of destruction and recreation. Civilizations and religions fall, and something new is built in its place. It has happened many times throughout the long history of the world, and will happen again.

"When I was, uh, deposed during the battle for the Emerald Isle, it was one such recreation. Both when the Roman Empire rose, and fell again. Sometimes the cycles are long, and sometimes they are short, but inevitably, the world changes." He was gazing into the distance thoughtfully. "The real question is, what does that have to do with a mortal girl?"

Clio shrugged, pouring me tea and putting cookies in front of me, like it was the most natural thing in the world. "Rooibos. No caffeine," she said offhandedly, still looking at Nate. "Tell me again what they said to her?"

Between the two of us, we recounted both attacks. The unhinged taunts of the Lamia, and the vague threats of the Verserpent. We also told her what the drive-thru Oracle had said. Nate even told her about my surprise pregnancy and the fact I didn't know who the father was, which made me wince and feel all sorts of guilt that I didn't need to be feeling.

That had made Clio pause the most. "No idea at all?" I shook my head, and she hummed. "You live in a house with a God, so I doubt anyone snuck in through the window. We can probably rule out the incubi."

I blinked at the two of them. "An incubus was an option?" *Fucking hell.*

"You're having triplets. Three is the magic number in the world of mythos. It stands to reason that it was the babies that put you on the radar, but why?" She looked me dead in the eye, and any trace of mirth left her face. "I'll make some inquiries, but I know one thing. You shouldn't ignore the prophecy of an Oracle. I think you need to go to Crete."

Nate groaned. "I was worried you were going to say that."

This was all insane. Completely insane.

PACKING to travel was surprisingly easy when you only had three sets of clothes that actually fit. In fact, it was all really easy. Nate had insisted on buying the plane tickets, getting first class because he was too tall and I was too pregnant to be stuck back in economy.

When I'd told him I'd pay him back, he'd just rolled his eyes. "I've had a thousand lifetimes to accrue money, Wren. I can pay for a couple of flights," was all he said, shutting down my arguments.

He also didn't like talking about the fact he was some kind of God. Enough to allude to the fact he was really old, but not enough that I could do any decent research.

Luckily, I still had a passport from the time I took my senior year trip to Cabo, just before my parents died, so I didn't have to worry about any bureaucratic hurdles.

Clio had come around and helped Nate ward our entire building, locking it up tight against intruders and harm. That eased something in my chest. I hated the thought of people rifling through my things while we were away.

The more they worked together, the more I realized that Clio and Nate were friends. Maybe they'd even been lovers once upon a time? I tried to ignore the jealousy that sprouted in my chest at the thought. He'd lived thousands of years. He'd probably had more lovers than I'd had chocolate bars.

The idea that they'd been something more was only compounded by the fact that Clio drove us to the airport in her vintage Mustang. I wasn't a car girl, but even I could appreciate the awesomeness of this machine. They talked up the front in Gaelic, while I sat in the back, trying not to feel nauseous. Motion sickness was not my friend right now.

Finally, we pulled up in front of Logan Airport. Clio double-parked, ignoring the parking attendant and flipping the bird to a cab that honked behind her. Nate climbed from the car and opened my door for me, holding out an arm so I could lever myself out. He grabbed my huge tote and duffle that contained everything I'd packed. We wouldn't be gone too long—at least, that's how I consoled myself. Our return flights were in two weeks, so we could be there and back before we knew it.

Settling me on the sidewalk, Nate went over to the popped trunk and grabbed his own bag, including his big fucking ax. How we were going to get that past the TSA was a mystery.

Clio surprised the shit out of me by coming over and hugging me tight. "Be careful, Wren. Trust no one but Nate. And if either of you need me, call. I haven't been in a good battle in like, a thousand years." She said the last part almost wistfully, and I eyed her like she was insane. She might actually *be* insane.

Still, I nodded and agreed.

She smirked at me. "And take good care of Nate. He looks tough, but he's really a big fucking marshmallow."

I chewed my lip. "Are you and he... you know, together?"

Clio threw back her head and laughed, the noise both melodious and slightly off-putting. "Shite no. That big hairy bastard is not my type. I prefer armor-clad battle maidens soaked in the blood of men's misfortune."

I shuddered at the visual. "Must make it hard to find a Tinder date."

She gave my cheek two hard pats. "Girlie, you have no idea." Someone honked again, and she let out a stream of foul-mouthed Irish cuss words that sounded like English, but made no logical sense. "Oi, fook off, you drippydick cuntwaffle!" With that, she climbed back into the Mustang and roared away.

Nate rolled his eyes, grabbing our bags and loading them onto one of those little carts. I followed behind him as we moved through check-in, noting how people watched him as he strode through the crowded terminal. Most moved out of the way naturally, although sometimes they just stood in his path and gaped, like a deer in headlights. He would stare those people down, until their synapses decided to switch back on and they got the fuck out of the way.

As he stood in the first-class line, women ate him up with their eyes. I could almost see the wheels turning in their brains. Tall. Strong. Rich. Handsome as hell. It didn't really matter that I was standing there beside him, obviously pregnant. If anything, watching him dote on me, his hands gentle as he directed me, only made their gazes hungrier.

I mean, I got it. We loved a good provider. A big boy to make us feel small and treasured. I couldn't even feel territorial, because he wasn't mine. I was just his obligation. A responsibility he'd inherited from Mrs. Byrne, like the house.

In a whirlwind of first-class lounges and polite smiles, we were being ensconced on a plane. The flight attendants bustled around, cooing over me, giving me sparkling apple juice and ignoring Nate's gruff demeanor as they fussed.

I'd never had a nanny as a child, but first class felt a bit like being the toddler of rich parents. They fed me almost immediately, trying to tempt me with gourmet food and drinks, and after we'd been flying for a couple of hours, they gave me pajamas and guided me to the bathroom to change. The bathrooms were bigger than the one in my apartment back home.

When I emerged in my silky PJs, they'd even reclined my seat and made me up a little bed. They might be treating me like an infant, but that didn't mean I wasn't enjoying the absolute heck out of it.

The divider wall between Nate and I was lowered as I snuggled down to sleep. My eyelids were starting to drag down, the subtle movements of the plane lulling me.

Nate sat beside me, his seat still upright. I blinked at him groggily. "Aren't you going to sleep?"

He looked down, pulling my blanket up to my chin. "Later. Sleep, Wren," he rumbled softly, and the sound made me sigh with contentment.

He didn't have to tell me twice.

CHAPTER 12
WREN

Nate rubbed his hand down my side, over my flat stomach and down between my thighs. I sighed happily; that's where I wanted—no, *needed* him to touch me. His fingers dipped further down, brushing over my clit. I sucked in a breath, curling into his hand.

Yes.

He stroked me slowly, and I groaned, trying to move against him faster. I needed more. So much more. I needed him inside me.

"More," I moaned, gripping his wrist as he finger-fucked me in the forest. I'd never been to this forest, but man, Nate looked so wild here. He looked powerful, and as he moved my body, spreading my thighs wider so he could go deeper, I knew that I wouldn't ever be the same after he fucked me. It didn't matter that there was a stick jabbing me in the ribs, or that I couldn't quite press my breasts to his chest for some reason, just as long as he kept touching me.

I ached so much. I was going to die if he didn't get inside me soon.

"Wren," he breathed softly.

"Nate," I moaned back. "Please."

I moved my body faster, getting so close. I needed it harder, faster.

"Wren, wake up."

Oh, I was more than awake. My body had never felt so alive. I felt like every square inch of my skin was electric. I could feel the pleasure shooting through my veins, making my heart beat fast.

"Wake up, *mo stóirín*. You're… dreaming."

I frowned. No, that wasn't right. I looked up at Nate, as his hands ran over my hips and flat stomach.

That wasn't right either. My stomach wasn't flat anymore. The babies were already stretching it to the max. I wanted to ignore it. My body was on fire, and the need to come was almost painful.

But it was too late. I was drifting back to wakefulness, and horror quickly replaced lust as I became aware of my position. At some point, Nate had reclined his seat flat too, essentially turning our two seats into one big bed. I was pressed tight against his denim-clad thigh, one leg flung over his, and I was rubbing my… *Oh god.*

His hand was tight on my hip, and I could feel the hard press of his dick against the rounded curve of my stomach.

I'd been humping his thigh, like some horny toy poodle.

Fuck my life.

I was so fucking wet, and I could feel my silk pajamas were soaked. No matter how horrified I was, I was still so fucking aroused. All it would take was a few more strokes and I could have some relief.

Instead, I was frozen. I'd just violated Nate.

"Wren…" he choked out. "Are you okay?"

"Yep. Yeah. Totally fine," I whispered.

The whole plane was dark, but I could feel the soft puffs of his breath on my face. "Do you need something?" he murmured back, and his thigh moved. The friction sent an electric, but taboo thrill through my body.

I bit back the moan that was bubbling up my throat. I needed something, all right. I needed *him*. But I couldn't tell him that. I didn't want to make things weird with the last person who gave a shit if I lived or died.

He moved a little closer. "Tell me what you want, *mo stóirín*. I will give you whatever it is you need."

Fuck. Was he suggesting what I thought he was suggesting? Or was my horny-ass brain still caught up in the dirty dream?

I considered asking him for a drink of water, sending him away until I could get myself under control, but in this blanket of darkness, thousands of feet in the air, I felt brave. Or stupid. Definitely one of the two.

"I… I need to come."

The groan that rumbled from his chest was a primal

sound that somehow made my clit throb. "Tell me you want me to help you, Wren. Tell me you want me to touch you until your tight little cunt squeezes around my fingers."

Oh my god. If he kept talking like that, he wouldn't need to touch me—I would just come on the spot.

"Please, Nate," I breathed so softly, it was a wonder he could hear me at all.

"Please what, sweet one?"

"Please touch me. I need you inside me." My voice was a breathless whine.

That was all he needed. His hand dove beneath the blankets that covered us, his fingers brushing over my stomach, the skin stretched and sensitive. Then he slid further down, under the waistband of my fancy airline PJ pants and underwear, until he found my slippery, wet folds.

He buried his face in my hair and hissed out a breath. "So wet," he growled. "For me?"

"For you." I was trying to be as silent as possible. I didn't want to give the other people in our cabin a free show, but when his index finger flicked over my clit, I bit down on his shoulder to mute the sound of my moan.

Unfortunately, my teeth in his shoulder made Nate groan, his rock-hard cock nudging against my stomach. His fingers slipped between my folds, tracing through the dampness and making me curl closer to him.

His finger pressed just inside me, and I tried to move closer, to feel him inside me, but Nate had other ideas. "You're going to come for me, *mo stóirín*. But not until I tell you to come, and you're going to be quiet. If you make a sound, I'm going to stop."

I shuddered, my hands gripping his shirt. If he didn't hurry up, I was going to take those words as permission, because I was way too riled for dirty talk.

Then he thrust his finger inside, curling it upwards, and I gasped soundlessly. He stroked me gently, but managed to hit all the places that made my body light up like the Rockefeller Christmas tree. He added another finger, stretching me, and he didn't need to pound into me like a battering ram to find my pleasure. It was like he knew me inside and out. Like he'd studied how to stroke a woman to make her come, and now he was an expert.

The idea of him practicing this technique on other women made me uncomfortable, but you know what? When he hit that G-spot like it was home base, I didn't care. Let the orgasm that was building inside of me like a tsunami be tribute to those lucky fuckers who'd come before me.

I was writhing around, my legs unable to stay still as bolts of pleasure moved down my legs. Nate stilled. "Quiet, Wren." He stopped moving, and I almost whined in protest. "Are you ready to come?"

Nodding furiously, I kept my lips welded shut so I didn't give him any reason to stop the pleasure he was pulling from my body. His palm was massaging my clit, his fingers doing something inside me that I didn't even know was possible, and it was all too much. Burying my face in his chest, I moaned my release, and Nate's hand came up to tangle in my hair, keeping me there as my pussy clamped around his fingers, trying to suck him inside me like a black hole.

I stayed there, my chest heaving as I tried to get air, for way too long. Nate took his fingers from me, and his other hand relaxed on the back of my head.

I needed to move. Needed to get the fuck off my *friend*. Hopefully, we were all having a severe case of collective delusions, and when the lights turned back on, this would all be a dream. A panty-melting, amazing dream.

But first, I needed to move. "I, uh, need to pee." I muttered the words as I was already dragging myself out of my seat faster than should be physically possible in such a confined space. With a little forethought that I'd apparently lacked ten minutes ago, I grabbed my clothes, shuffling to the bathroom and locking myself in.

Maybe if I sat on the toilet and flushed, it would suck me out into the atmosphere and I'd never have to show my face again. What had I been *thinking*?

I sat in the tiny bathroom cubicle for far longer than was polite. I ignored the knocks, muttering, "I'm in here," whenever someone got brave enough to fiddle with the lock. I needed to get myself under control. I needed to talk to my traitorous vagina and tell her that she'd already gotten us in trouble—we didn't need to go ruining the only good thing we had going on right now.

By the time I emerged, the gentle lights had come back on, and the attendants were walking down with trays of breakfast foods. The bedding had disappeared from our seats, and both of them were upright. Nate was stabbing at the small screen in front of him, like he was trying to find something that was to his liking and failing miserably.

I swallowed down the embarrassment over the fact that I'd just come all over his hand, and decided to ignore it. I'd write it off as a great sex dream and pretend it never happened. That was the responsible thing to do, right?

I sat down and forced a smile. "Are they serving breakfast already? Wow, the other half flies in style, you know what I mean?" My words were forced and upbeat, but I'd committed now. "I hope there's something other than eggs. Eggs make me want to gag." Even the smell of eggs was getting to me now. They didn't even have to be on my plate. But I wasn't diva enough to police other people's meals just yet. I just breathed in and out through my mouth and tried not to think of the gelatinous yellow goop.

Dammit, I was thinking about it now. Saliva pooled behind my back teeth, and I shook my head firmly. Talking to Nate was better than puking in his lap. He was looking over at me with those stormy blue eyes, filled with questions I definitely didn't want to answer.

As the attendant laid out my breakfast in front of me, I filled the dead space in the conversation with inane chatter. About the hardships of collecting and then re-checking our luggage. Our connecting flight from Athens to Heraklion. Getting the hire car. The fact that Nate could hide his giant ax from the eyes of humans—like *poof,* just gone.

The attendant tried to lay out his breakfast, and he put a hand out to stop her. "Can I have a breakfast like hers? No egg."

"Of course, sir. I'll be right back."

I tried not to let the warm feeling in my chest spread. If I could keep it contained, maybe I wouldn't break my own heart.

Maybe.

CHAPTER 13
WREN

Back when you were a stupid teenager, did you ever sit on a couch, drinking at some house party, feeling invincible because you'd downed three shots of your best friend's uncle's authentic Mexican tequila and felt nothing?

The obvious answer was that you were immune to alcohol, and being able to down shots like water would be your superpower forevermore. All the while, a little part of your brain was whispering that this fuzzy, happy, invincible feeling was a trap, but you were just too buzzed to care.

Later, when you stood up, you'd realize that maybe, just maybe, you should've listened to that little voice in your head, as you tipped forward, landed on your face and chipped a tooth on your friend's tiled floor?

No? Just me?

The point of this story was that when I stepped off the plane at Heraklion Airport and breathed in that warm Mediterranean air, something inside me relaxed. I felt content, warm and invincible. And I couldn't help but wonder if that was a trap.

The crushing fear that had been plaguing me for weeks disappeared almost instantly as I walked out into the warm air of Heraklion. The streaks that had plagued my vision in Boston were less intense in the golden light of the Mediterranean.

I could *breathe*. My ankles were as big as baked hams, but not even that could ruin the good vibes that this place was giving me.

So I ignored that negative little voice whispering that perhaps this was a trap.

This had to be the right decision. While the fear was gone, it had been replaced by an almost dragging feeling, invisible fingers pulling at me. The sensation wasn't bad; it was more like a sense of rightness. Like a little voice in my head was playing the hotter-colder game, and I was firmly in the warmer direction. I turned south, *knowing* that was where we had to go.

But not right now. I was exhausted. I needed a moment and a really long nap.

After collecting our luggage, we headed straight to the car hire place outside the airport. My feet ached way more than they should, considering I'd spent half a day with them up, but I gritted my teeth and pushed through. This was my idea. I wasn't going to start complaining now.

The lady behind the desk at the car hire place took one look at my pregnant belly and began to gush, coming around to rub it like I was Buddha. I stood there, eyes wide. No one had rubbed my stomach yet. Maybe Boston folks were just more aware of personal boundaries? She kept speaking in rapidfire Greek, which I had no chance of understanding.

"I'm sorry. I don't speak Greek," I squeaked out, and Nate wrapped an arm around my waist, pulling me closer to his side protectively. He didn't growl at the woman, but his face was distinctly unfriendly.

"We'd like to collect our car," he grumbled, irritation clear.

The woman blinked at him and stepped back behind the desk, her smile never dropping. "Of course. Yes. Sign here and here." She thrust a sheaf of paper at him as she scanned his passport and an international driver's license that Clio had somehow obtained on short notice.

Soon enough, Nate had me loaded into a car that was at least twenty years old, but had been well maintained. It was one of those mini SUVs, but still, Nate barely fit inside until he put the top down.

We drove in silence as I took in the ocean here for the first time. It was... beautiful. The clear blue sky made the water look even more like a glittering jewel, endless and shining. The smell of salt water in the air filled my lungs, healing something I didn't even know was wounded.

The soft voice of the GPS guided us along the well-worn roads of the town, but it barely distracted me from taking in the whitewashed buildings with broad, flat roofs, the golden grass, and the tanned people, all so different from home. The view of the beach on one side and a mountainous outcropping on the other was breathtaking.

Finally, Nate pulled through a large set of wrought-iron gates, with a huge resort rising up in front of us. "Holy shit, Nate. We can't afford this."

He just grunted as he pulled into a parking space. "I can. There's no way I'm sleeping in some shithole filled with bed bugs."

I narrowed my eyes at him. He just met my gaze and held it. He didn't blink. Didn't look ashamed. He just challenged me to be mad about it with his eyes. *Asshole.*

I huffed and opened my door. "I'm paying you back."

"If that's what you need to do," was all he said as he came around and held the door for me while I wedged my body out of the car.

I let Nate take care of checking us in as I stood in the lobby, looking around like a country bumpkin in the big city. I envied his ability to look like he belonged everywhere. Not only belonged, but his presence was so commanding that people were drawn to him. Sometimes just their gazes, but other times, I spotted people moving toward him like they were magnetized. Could people tell he wasn't human? Was that why they were attracted to him? Was that why *I* was attracted to him?

I snorted. Nah, my attraction had a lot more to do

with the fact he had thighs bigger than my waist and tattoos that I wanted to trace with my tongue.

He grabbed up the bags, our room keys in his hand, with the phone number of the concierge written across the top of the little welcome pamphlet.

I couldn't even blame her. Well, no, I could, because the fuck? Who did that? But I got that he was compelling. He was the kind of guy you dreamed about for years. The kind of man who went in the spank bank to be pulled out for decades as a "what if?" The kind of guy you'd build up the courage to shoot your shot with, just in case.

As we walked into his ground-floor room, we had a clear view over a manicured lawn and the sparkling seafoam green of the ocean. "It's beautiful," I breathed.

He hummed his agreement, flopping down on the bed. I looked over my shoulder, trying not to stare at the small strip of his lower stomach on display. Heat pooled in my belly. "Is my room next door?" I choked out. I was going to need some alone time to unpack everything that had happened on the plane.

He pushed himself up onto his elbows, his shirt stretching across his chest and making my mouth water. "I only got one room. I can't protect you in a second room."

Uh, what? "But there's only one bed."

He raised an eyebrow. "I'm aware."

"There's no couch." There was a small table, and a wardrobe that had an inbuilt section with a fridge and a microwave. The TV was mounted on the wall. The bathroom was the size of the bedroom.

"Again, I can see that."

I swallowed hard. "We'll have to share a bed." I sounded like a loser right now, but I was trying to wrap my head around the fact that I was going to have to sleep in a bed that already seemed too small to contain Nate's huge frame, with the man himself. Together. Body to body.

He sat up and walked over to me. "Stop panicking."

I wasn't panicking. Was I panicking? I didn't feel like I was panicking.

Okay, maybe a little.

Shaking his head, he wrapped his hands around my upper arms. "I promise you, we can sleep in the same bed without any threat to your virtue, Wren. I'm thousands of years old. I've learned a little restraint in that time; I can keep my hands to myself." His lips quirked upwards. "If that's what you want, of course."

I flushed red. "It's not you I'm worried about," I blurted out. I had very visceral flashbacks to humping his leg on the plane.

He gripped my chin, tilting my head up so I was forced to meet his eyes. "I'm not worried about my virtue either, *mo stóirín*. You can have what's left of it, anytime you need it." His gaze dropped to my lips, and there was an almost visceral lust in them.

My breath lodged in my lungs. "Nate…"

"You are so beautiful," he breathed. "Tell me to stop. Tell me you don't want me to kiss you, little one. Tell me this isn't what you want, and I will never touch you again, I swear it on my immortal soul."

Words lodged in my throat. I wanted him to touch me more than anything. More than I wanted oxygen.

The babies fluttered in my stomach, throwing a metaphorical bucket of cold water over my raging libido. "Nate, I'm pregnant."

He chuckled. "I am fully aware of that fact." The teasing light left his eyes, replaced by seriousness. "If this isn't what you want, just say the words, Wren, and I swear on my honor that I will treat you with nothing but respect. I'll be your friend and nothing more."

I let out a frustrated huff. Me? Not want *him?* That was literal insanity. How did I explain to him that I wasn't lithe and nubile anymore? I wasn't anyone's fantasy.

I frowned up at him. "I'm not... I'm big. And I have stretch marks now. I'm not pretty anymore, and my body will never snap back to what it once was."

He stepped away, and being proven right felt like shit. I pushed the feeling down. I wasn't an irresponsible single person anymore. I had to think of the future, not just my needs right now.

"I want you, but I can't do no-strings sex anymore. My hormones are wild, and my stupid brain will eventually construe the care as something more."

He blinked at me slowly, then lurched forward. Grabbing my face in his hands, he kissed me hard. His lips claimed mine, and I felt it right down to my toes. The golden threads whipped around us like a light-show. "I want the strings, *mo stóirín*. I want everything you'll give me."

He picked me up easily, and I could see the threads wrapping around us like golden ropes, tying us together. At least, I did until he kissed me and I closed my eyes, succumbing to the taste.

He paused, his arms still under my ass, holding me tightly to him. "Say the words one more time, Wren. Tell me this is what you want." His words passed over my skin like a shivering promise.

"I want you, Nate."

And fuck me, I didn't care what the future held, because this right here? It felt like fate.

CHAPTER 14
NÉIT

I was obsessed. This woman had wrapped her tiny hand around my heart and squeezed. She had me now, and I wanted to claim her as mine in every way she'd let me.

The feel of her tight little cunt around my fingers was a visceral memory, and if I closed my eyes, I could remember exactly how she felt, fluttering around me as she came. Fuck me, my dick was achingly hard. I was going to add epic blue balls to the ways that you could murder an immortal.

But more than my need to bury myself in her, I needed her to want me too. For the first time in so long, my fucking wouldn't be shrouded in subterfuge. She saw me completely, and I hadn't realized how much honesty had been missing in my hookups.

"I want you, Nate." Those were the sweetest words I'd ever heard, and I didn't hesitate. I dived in to capture her sweet lips in a kiss so ferocious, she might have second thoughts. Instead, she kissed me back with just as much fervor, and I growled against her lips.

Carrying her easily, I walked her back toward the bed. I could've gotten a twin room so she could have her own bed, but I was a selfish prick. I knew she wanted me, and that wasn't just vanity speaking. I was really goddamn old, and I *knew* when a woman wanted me. It was in the shy blushes, the hopeful look in her eye when I'd brought her food. It was in the way she breathed my name.

The way she came all over my fingers.

I was a selfish asshole, but I wouldn't be when it came to her. I would give her everything I had left to give. Laying her down, I started stripping her clothes from her body. She was self-conscious, but she was a fucking goddess. She looked ripe and curvy, filled with young, and it set off some primal part of my brain that just wanted to fuck her until she was pregnant forever.

Which was insane. It had been a very long time since I'd been a father, and that had been in a different millennia. A different age.

She slipped that little pink tongue past my lips, and I groaned. Pulling back, I looked down at her, now only in her panties. "So fucking beautiful," I muttered, and when her hands clenched, coming up to cover her stomach, I gripped them and pulled them above her head, holding them there with one hand. I carefully ensured that I didn't put any weight on her stomach, which was easy enough because she was a tiny little thing, even with the small belly she was sporting.

"Keep your hands there, *mo stóirín*. Don't try to hide from me." I brushed my lips across hers, then moved further down her body. Straight for her tits, like a goddamn barbarian. Still, when I sucked those dusky nipples between my lips and she moaned, I didn't think she minded overly much my lack of finesse.

She wiggled around beneath me, her fingers flexing like she wanted to move them, but she didn't. *Such a good girl.*

Moving further down, I brushed reverent lips across her stomach, hooking my fingers under the waistband of her underwear. I looked up at her. "I'm going to taste you, and then I'm going to roll you on top of me so you can ride me like a queen. Would you like that?"

Her moan said more than words could, but still, I wanted them. Luckily, she was more than happy to tell me exactly what she wanted. "As much as I want that, I've been sitting on a plane for like, twelve hours. At least let me shower first."

I laughed. I'd survived the fucking Dark Ages, when people only washed once a month. I didn't think half a day was going to bother me. But I didn't want to make her uncomfortable, or remind her just how fucking old I was.

"Is that really what you want?" I asked, my hands stroking up the insides of her thighs. "Do you want me to bathe you first?" She shook her head. "Tell me."

Her tongue came out and wet her dry lips once more. I could see her overthinking things, but I also saw the moment she decided to be brave. "I want you to fuck me. I want to feel you inside me right now."

My little queen. "Such a good girl," I rumbled, freeing her from the last scraps of her clothing. "But mark my words, I'm going to eat this sweet little pussy later, and you *will* scream for me. Got it?"

Standing, I also stripped off my clothes, and the way she stared at me made me want to preen. She looked at me like I was the only thing she could see, and this was just my shitty human glamor. Imagine if she saw the real me. The idea of fucking her in my full God form made my balls pull up. I would be too big for her, but that didn't mean the thought of her working her tight little cunt down onto me didn't make me want to bathe her in my cum before I was even inside her.

"Wow," she breathed, and I actually flushed, giving her a cocky grin.

"You can look as much as you like later, little one. Right now, I want you on top of me so I can see those pretty tits bounce." I climbed onto the bed beside her, gripping her hips, pulling her close and kissing her once more. I couldn't get enough of the taste of her. She climbed on top of me, and as her wet core rubbed over the base of my cock, it took every ounce of my willpower not to pull her down onto me. Instead, I leaned up and kissed her again, letting her grind on me until she was sliding along my cock with her own wetness.

I might actually go mad, but I gritted my back teeth

and let her move. I wouldn't rush her. This was at her pace, her comfort.

I whispered things to her in Gaelic, things I couldn't say to her in English without sounding like a maniac, as her hands pressed into my chest, her nails leaving little indentations. I *wanted* to be marked by her. Scratched and scraped. I wanted to wake up in the morning and see the evidence that I'd brought her pleasure.

"Nate," she breathed, her tone begging for something. Permission, maybe?

I was happy to give it. "Take what you want, Wren."

Reaching down, she gripped my cock and blindly notched it against her. Then she slid down, and I saw fucking stars. How long had it been since I'd been with a woman? Years? Decades? A century?

None had ever felt like this, though. This level of soul-deep perfection.

Her breathy little moan had me finding her hips and helping her move up and down my shaft. *Fuck me.* I was going to embarrass myself, coming before she'd even gotten off. Clenching my jaw, I pushed my release away, thinking of anything else but the feel of her sweet little pussy wrapped around my dick. *Anything* else. Mucking out horse stalls. The smell of the early sixteenth century. The shame of not bringing my girl to orgasm before I blew inside her.

I found her clit with my thumb and tapped it as she rode me. "Oh god," she screamed, her pace picking up, which was both a pleasure and a pain.

"Come for me, Wren. I want to feel you gush around me."

When she clenched hard, I saw stars or my fucking ancestors or something, but she did as she was told, coming hard on my cock. I breathed a relieved sigh, then pounded up inside her. *Yes.* I needed to mark her as mine inside and out, to fill her up with me so every man and beast in a hundred-mile radius would know she belonged with me. To me.

Groaning, my balls pulled up tight, and I came so hard, I saw at least ten of my past lives flash before my eyes. Her nails scraped stripes along my chest, and she screamed again.

"Nate!"

I fucking loved it. I wanted to hear her scream my name like that every day until we were both dust in the wind.

She slid off me, and I was insanely pleased with the messy sound of our bodies coming apart. Rolling us both to our sides, I held her close to me. When she whispered, "Wow," against my chest, I tried not to puff up like a peacock. But it was tough.

I tilted her head back and kissed her once more, a softer kiss that I hoped made promises to that soft human heart of hers. Promises I couldn't say out loud just yet.

"I'll go get something to clean you up." I tried not to sound super impressed with myself about that.

Apparently, I failed, because she chuckled softly. "Okay."

She looked up at me with stars in her eyes, and I vowed to myself then and there that I would do everything in my power to deserve that expression.

CHAPTER 15
WREN

The shift in the relationship between Nate and I was going to take some getting used to, especially when he wrapped an arm around my waist in the lobby and kissed my temple. My body felt deliciously sore, and I couldn't remember the last time I'd felt so grounded. So wanted. Maybe before my parents died?

No one had really needed me after that. I was the one who'd needed Mrs. Byrne, and she'd been my anchor, but I wasn't hers.

But the way Nate had worshiped my body last night, like he was the one who needed me, well, it was an addictive experience. I was tempted to blow off this stupid quest to Amourgeles and stay in bed, making love, as the warm Mediterranean sun kissed our bodies.

I sighed softly, the wind picking up the noise and whipping it away as we drove with the top down through the countryside of Crete. The further into the center of the island we went, the greener it got, the fields dotted with olive groves and white, rocky outcroppings. Hardly any cars were on the roads, and it felt a little like being free.

Nate reached over and gripped my thigh as we cruised along, and if it wasn't for the dragging feeling in my chest, I would've insisted we turn around and go back to the resort. But I couldn't ignore this feeling that tugged me further south.

Without another soul around except Nate, I could almost ignore the golden streaks in my vision. I could almost pretend we were just a couple on holiday together. That I was a normal twenty-something and not being chased by monsters. However, with every mile, the tug got stronger.

What was a whispered suggestion in Heraklion became an incessant drumbeat in my head by the time we made it to Amourgeles. It was now eating at my gut, making me feel a little nauseous.

Suddenly, it was like a heart attack, or a physical force slamming into my chest.

"STOP!"

Nate hammered the brakes, his arm whipping across my chest to hold me in place, even though I was wearing a seatbelt. I was almost out of my mind with the need to run to where the feeling was leading me. I quickly undid my seatbelt, shucking Nate's hand from my torso.

"Here," I breathed as I climbed from the car before he could get around the hood. "It's here."

He looked down the road, and in the distance, the

town itself was visible. Just a smattering of tiny, square concrete houses with flat, gray roofs, which spilled down the small incline. The paint on their walls was worn and peeling from the steady Greek sun.

Except for the building in front of us.

In front of us was a twelve-foot stone wall, the edges worn smooth by time, but the spikes lodged in the tops were shining in the sun. At the center of the wall was a single tall door with a twisted brass knocker. I could see red roof tiles just peeking over the wall. It was a fortress in the middle of nowhere.

"This place?" Nate asked hesitantly, his eyes darting around, his jaw tense.

I walked to the door, raising my hand to knock. I needed to get inside the walls. The pull in my chest was too strong.

Nate caught my hand before I could slam the knocker. "Wait. I want to look around first. It feels… wrong. I want to make sure it's safe." I dropped my hand and bit back a whine as he led me back to the car. He belted me in as I hung out the window.

He was right. I knew that, logically. Besides, what was I going to say when someone answered that door? *Oh, hi. There's a mystical feeling in my body that wants me to come inside your walls.*

What if whatever was inside there was worse than the shadow monster? Worse than the Lamia?

So I held myself still as Nate climbed back into the car and drove us further into Amourgeles. He found a *psistaría,* which was kind of like a cafe, and pulled up in front of it. A rusted pickup truck was the only vehicle outside, and there was a huge white dog sitting beside the door. A grapevine ran over the trellised porch, creating enticing shade that I wanted to curl up under.

Nate led me in, and in halted English, we ordered lunch. The woman behind the counter grinned widely, passing me a glass of milk. She rubbed her belly, and I smiled.

Nate pointed back down the road we drove in on. "The stone building. Is it a church?"

The woman's smile faltered, before she plastered a fake one back in its place. "No. Private, uh, house."

Nate gave her a charming smile, which honestly tended to fry the brain cells of anyone with a pulse, and walked outside after me. I sipped my cold milk, trying not to turn my head back up the road toward the fortress. The sun was warm but not overbearing, and I let it soak into my pale skin.

The golden threads were whipping around Nate, stronger than they normally were. I frowned and turned back to the woman in the cafe. Actually, the streaks of golden light were strong around her too. Even the dog had soft golden strands across its shaggy white fur. This town was definitely weird, and I understood what Nate meant now. I'd just been too caught up in the feeling in my chest, but there was an element of wrongness about this place.

The elderly Greek lady brought out our lunch, which made my mouth water. I was starving. No one seemed to eat a full breakfast in Crete. I'd only had a couple of pastries for breakfast, and the babies were eating through my energy stores at a rapid rate.

I dipped some fluffy bread in olive oil that didn't taste anything like the olive oil from the grocery store shelves back home. It was something else. I moaned, and Nate's eyes heated, like he was remembering last night.

Hell, now I was remembering last night, and my skin started to tingle with need.

Shaking his head, Nate stood, leaning down to kiss my temple. "I'm just going to have a look around. Don't move from this spot, okay?"

I chewed my lip. "Okay."

He raised an eyebrow. "I mean it, Wren. Eat your lunch, but don't leave right here. Promise?"

Sighing, I nodded. "I promise."

He gave me a stern look, which kind of made me want to bend over and tell him I'd been a bad, bad girl, but before I could, he stepped out onto the street with his hands in his pockets, looking like a tourist as he walked down the road, checking things out.

I watched him go and then went back to devouring my lunch. The huge white dog from beside the door came over and plopped his blocky head on my lap, looking up at me with so much longing, there was no way I could resist giving him a little piece of hard cheese.

A deep chuckle had me looking over my shoulder. A grizzled man stepped beneath the trellis, his floppy hat clutched in his hand. He said something in rapid Greek, and I shook my head.

"I'm sorry. I can only speak English."

He nodded sagely. "I was saying that he likes you."

I scratched the dog's ear. "Is he yours?"

The old man shook his head, and the dog looked over his shoulder at the man like he was interested in his answer too. "No, Cy belongs to no one. He is, er… the village dog, yes? He comes and goes as he pleases, and we all take care of him."

Cy huffed and looked back up at me with those big brown eyes full of pleading, and I gave him a piece of my meat.

The old man laughed again. "Well, we are all stupid for him. He looks up at you, and then you feed him. That's why he's so round." The man banded his arms out in front of him and puffed out his cheeks. "He needs a little less care, I think." He leaned over and scratched Cy's fur at the base of his tail, making it wag faster, even if the dog seemed slightly annoyed at being called chunky. "You're a tourist?"

I nodded, inviting the man to sit down opposite me. "Yes, we're staying down in Heraklion. My boyfriend has just gone for a stroll."

First rule of traveling: don't end up in a horror movie by insinuating you're alone in a tiny village with a weird vibe, where no one would ever find your body.

The old man smiled, and the cafe owner came out to put his own lunch plate in front of him, as well as a glass of wine. She spoke to him in rapid Greek, her eyes darting between me and the empty chair where Nate should be. The old man shrugged, and the woman huffed as she strode off.

"Your wife?"

The man snorted. "Niece."

Considering the woman had to be pushing seventy, I wondered how old that made the man. His streaks seemed almost faded, more like a bronze than a gold. "Ah."

"How are you liking the island? Amourgeles?"

I gave him a smile. "It's beautiful. Feels like coming home." I realized that was the closest description I had for the tug in my chest. Like I was so close to home, and I could feel it. But I didn't tell the old man that—it sounded absolutely insane.

"Sometimes, the gods maneuver us where we need to be, but free will has other ideas, no?"

Man, this guy had no idea. In my case, it *was* literal Gods. Or monsters, at least.

As we ate, we chatted about everything. About life on the island, about the best Greek food, about his family. He had eight children, though only one or two still lived on the island and none lived in Amourgeles anymore.

After I'd finished off the food, having fed most of the cheese to Cy the Dog, Nate returned. He cast a wary eye at the old man. "Nate, this is... I'm sorry, I didn't get your name."

The old man reached out and shook Nate's hand. "Stavros."

I smiled at him. "I'm Wren. And this is Nate." I scratched the dog's ear. "And this is Cy."

Nate's gaze ran over the man and the dog, before he nodded in greeting. He put a possessive hand on my back, as if I was about to run off with a man who must be in his late eighties, at least.

Nate continued to eye the dog, like maybe I was about to bring it home with me. Actually, that was probably more likely than me running off with the old man. Dragging his gaze back to me, he gave me a fake smile. "We should head off."

Okay then.

I pushed myself to my feet and gave Stavros's liver-spotted arm a squeeze. "It was lovely to meet you." He lowered his chin in return, his dark eyes sparkling.

Nate led me away and back to the car. The dog, Cy, trailed behind us, its nose snuffling my hand. As Nate helped me into the car, he looked down at the dog, his brow lowered. "Stay."

His voice was filled with power, and honestly, that was kind of freaky in itself. The dog didn't seem overly perturbed, however.

"What's with you and the dog?"

Nate shook his head, shutting the door so the dog couldn't get in. "It feels wrong. This whole place is just bustling with supernatural energy. I don't trust anything with you that isn't me."

My heart skipped a beat at his protectiveness, but when he climbed in beside me, I rested my hand on his tense forearm. "This is why we came all this way, remember? Neither of us thought it was going to be just a sleepy little Greek village."

He frowned harder. "I'd kind of hoped that it was just so obscure, no one would think to look for you here. I hate that we're right in the middle of their seat of power, like sitting ducks."

I could understand that. "Let's get this over with then, shall we?"

Nodding, Nate drove back up the road toward the stone wall. "There was nothing obvious about the place or its inhabitants. The fortress is old, really old, and it feels like history has been imbued into the very stone of its walls, but I can't find any hints about who might be in there."

As we pulled up outside, I drew in a deep breath. My instincts said this was what I was supposed to do. "You told me to follow my gut, remember?" I reminded him, and he muttered something under his breath that I didn't quite catch.

I waited until he'd helped me out, then strode up to the door, determined. My heart was thundering in my chest, and a cold sweat had broken out across my skin. Grabbing the twisted bronze knocker, I slammed it down three times.

Bang. Bang. Bang.

I might have hallucinated it in the midday sun, but it felt like the sound of that knock reverberated much further than it should've. It echoed around us, like we were living in a Poe horror story.

We waited, but no one came. "Maybe it's abandoned?"

He shook his head. "There are people in there."

I didn't ask how he knew, and when he pressed closer to my back, I sank into his strength. I knocked three more times.

Bang. Bang. Bang.

Finally, the handle of the door jiggled. Holding my breath, I waited as the door opened slowly. A pair of golden feet were the first thing I saw, my eyes rising further and further up, over a pair of strong golden legs, dark shorts, abs to die for, a chest so broad I wanted to sink into it, and then...

No. Fuck. No. Not again.

Not again.

I screamed, then passed the fuck out.

CHAPTER 16
TRYPHONE

The guy at the front door held the lifeless pregnant woman in his arms and growled. I knew enough about self-preservation to know that slamming the door in his face was the right move right now.

"Sorry, man. I swear to the Goddess it wasn't me." I closed it with a bang, then barred it, because that fucker was huge.

Erus, my other half, stood at the top of the stairs. "Who was it?"

I shrugged. "Some pregnant chick."

He gave me a disapproving look, and despite the fact that we were Goddess-ordained soulmates, he looked at me like it might've been mine. I mean, we'd both been manwhores in our day—me perhaps a *little* more than him. But it had been a long time since those days.

"I swear, it wasn't me."

He huffed a disapproving sound and leaped down the stairs two at a time, as surefooted as a cat. Walking over to the door, he opened it back up.

The big guy was still holding the pregnant chick in his arms, his scowl promising murder. He looked between the two of us, as the girl muttered groggily about lions.

Erus threw me a more concerned look, because from what I could tell, she was human. There was no way she could know we were Genii, with the bodies of men and the heads of lions.

It had to be a coincidence.

The guy, though… He made me pause. He was certainly not entirely human, but I didn't recognize him at all, so that meant he wasn't from these parts.

"Who the fuck are you?" he spat menacingly.

Well, that's just rude. "Uh, you knocked on *our* door, remember? I think the correct question is, who the fuck are *you?*"

Erus raised a hand to grip my arm. "My name is Erus, and this is Tryp. What can we do for you both?"

"You can put some fucking clothes on. That'd be a start," the guy grumbled beneath his breath. "You guys are Mythics?"

Now it was my turn to be surprised. Mythics was a modern way of describing what we were. Supernaturals. Legends. Storied beings. Mythological constructs made real. Immortals. We were many things, but Mythics worked for most of us.

Erus answered. "Uh, yeah. You?"

He nodded. "I am. She is not. You don't happen to be lion-shaped beneath that pretty fuckboy glamor?"

I grinned. "You think my glamor is pretty?" I fluttered my eyelashes at him. He gave me a glare which made me want to laugh, but would probably end with him waving that big-ass ax at me. "Yeah, we have lion heads."

He frowned. "She can see through your glamor," he said pensively. "She can't see through mine."

The girl twisted in his arms, and his eyes dropped back to her face, the concern etched there setting off worry in my own chest. Which was a novel emotion in itself. Mortals came and went, and outside of the townspeople of Amourgeles, I didn't really give a shit.

Erus was also frowning at the girl. "Is she okay?"

The big guy shook his head. "I don't know. She's never passed out like this before."

My other half was a sucker for a human in distress. He flung open the door, gesturing for the guy to carry the girl in. "Come, we'll go and see Teron. He'll be able to check her out." He turned back to me. "Go get Demke and bring him to Teron's chambers."

Casting one more look at the two strangers, I did as Erus asked. Racing back up the stairs two at a time, I headed to the furthest wing. Demke's rooms were slightly apart from ours; once it had befitted his station, but now? It was just because he appreciated the solitude, I think.

I ran down the long hallways until I was finally in front of the big, carved wooden door that led to his living area. It opened almost before I'd finished knocking.

"Who was at the door?"

"A pregnant girl."

Demke tilted his head at me, his frown disapproving. "Really, Tryp?"

I threw up my hands. Why did everyone think it was my fault? "I haven't fucked a mortal in, like, two hundred years. Give me a break. I have Erus. What do you, Milo and Teron have, hmm? Your hand? If anyone was going to knock up a human, it's definitely one of you three."

Demke rubbed his forehead, like he wasn't a legit God and could actually get headaches.

"Did you send her away?" It wasn't really a question. This was our haven, our fortress of solitude. We did not invite people in.

Except Erus.

"Uh, not really. She's in Teron's rooms. Or at least, she should be by now."

Demke's spine stiffened like he'd been electrocuted. "What? *Why?*" he growled.

I winced, because I was about to throw Erus under the bus and knew he wouldn't let me forget it. "Uh, the woman fainted, and then she was kind of incoherent, and you know Erus. He's such a softie for humans."

Demke stepped around me and strode down the hallway. "Find Milonos and meet me in Teron's rooms."

"Who the fuck do you guys think I am? Hermes?" I called after him. Normally, he'd come back and punch me for even mentioning the messenger God, but clearly, the fact that there was a snake in our hen house had him preoccupied.

Who the fuck even knew where Milo was? I headed down to the kitchen first. It was after lunch, so that meant it was drinking time for one of my oldest friends. He'd been slowly getting more and more listless for the last two hundred years, and I knew I was losing my friend to the ennui. He'd be two bottles of rakí deep by now, but hopefully, the draw of the unknown might give him some relief from the boredom of time.

He wasn't in the kitchen, but when I skidded to a stop in the courtyard, there was no gratification in knowing I'd been correct about him drinking. I stopped in front of him, my eyebrows raised.

"Finish your drink, Milo. We've got drama."

He raised a single brow. "Oh?"

"Yes. Strangers in the compound."

He stretched out his long legs. "Not for the first time, Tryp. Are you being dramatic?"

I leaned forward until I was close enough to breathe in the fumes of alcohol on his breath. He must've started a little early today. "One of them is a pregnant female who fainted at the door."

He reared back, his brow furrowing. "What?"

Oh, I had him. I had him *so* good. "Yep. Big belly like this and just fell over like a sack of shit, right there at the base of the stairs."

That was all Milo needed. He was on his feet, stepping around me and charging down the hallway like, well, a bull. Or a Minotaur, anyway. I danced along behind him, and despite the unknown, despite the fact that the guy with her was some kind of Mythic not from our Pantheon, this was the most excitement we'd seen in a century, maybe longer.

He got all the way to the front wall before he realized he hadn't actually asked me where the strangers were now. He whirled back around, and I smirked at him.

"Well?"

"They're all in Teron's rooms. Erus wanted to get her checked out."

He snorted an annoyed sound as he spun on his heel and walked down another hall in the maze of rooms that made up our compound.

When I got to Teron's room, the large Gryphon was standing with his hands raised, and the girl was lying on his bed, still seemingly out of it. The big guy was blocking Teron, and if I hadn't realized he was a God before, I knew it now. He'd grown even taller, his body covered in runes, and his big ax glowing. Definitely an enchanted weapon.

Demke looked like he was one threatening swing away from throwing the guy back into the great abyss, but Erus and Teron stood between the two Gods. Demke wouldn't do anything that might hurt them, even as collateral.

Still, I edged around them all to stand beside Erus, subtly putting my body between the guy and my other half. Despite what Milo said, I wasn't prone to dramatics, so when I said Erus was my soulmate, I literally meant it. We were two halves of a single soul. Not two souls meant to be together, or anything so romantic. There literally could not be an Erus without me, and vice versa.

But over the years—thousands of them, in fact—I'd come to love him so much that if we had to die, I would want to go first, because the pain of losing him would be unimaginable. Even if it was for mere seconds before I followed him into the great abyss.

The big guy seemed to take in the presence of Milo, who easily rivaled him in size, and gritted his teeth. Teron, ever the level-headed one, waved Milo back. "Stay there please, Milonos." He didn't take his eyes from the guy. "I want to help. If I can just examine the girl, we can figure out if she needs to go to a human hospital. There may be issues with the child."

"Children," the big guy grunted, like it pained him, and Teron's face got even more concerned. Even I knew enough about human medicine to know that multiple births were more dangerous for the mothers. "Fine, but they *all* have to leave." He waved his ax at us all standing around like spectators at a tennis match.

Demke shook his head immediately, which I knew he would. There was no way he was leaving Teron alone, unprotected, with an unknown Mythic. Especially one with a weapon. "No."

Teron threw him an exasperated look over his shoulder, but Demke's expression never changed. They had one of those silent conversations, and eventually,

Demke relented. I could tell, because his upper lip twitched infinitesimally.

"Milonos will stay," Demke ordered. "If you make a move to hurt Teron, Milo will break you like your bones were made from chalk."

I didn't want to contradict our leader in front of strangers, but given the look of the big guy, if it came down to it, I wasn't sure Milo could take him quite so easily.

The dude with the ax frowned harder, but when the girl moaned once more, muttering gibberish, he gave a tight nod. Demke tilted his chin at us silently, and Erus and I moved as one toward the door. Once he was away from the eyes of strangers, I could see all the questions race across our very own God's face—the same questions I had.

I didn't know who the girl was, or why she was here, but I had a feeling they were going to shake things up, and honestly, I couldn't wait.

CHAPTER 17
WREN

O

Something warm and soft was pressed against my stomach, and I stretched lazily. The feeling in my limbs could not be described. It was like waking up from the most restful sleep ever, in a bed made from clouds. I felt lighter than I had in months.

That was, until my eyes opened and I realized what was pressed against my stomach was the cheek of a man. I blinked, and the face was replaced by an eagle's head.

Blink. A man again.

I sucked in a frightened breath, but then Nate was there, his hand on my cheek. "Easy, *mo stóirín.* You're safe. This is Teron. You passed out, and he's just checking you and the babies." He muttered something about a stethoscope, but the guy ignored him.

I looked down into a pair of molten gold eyes, and something shifted in my chest. In my world. The breath

I'd been holding whooshed out, ruffling the guy's long, dark hair.

"Hello," he said softly, his voice smooth like warm wax over my skin. "Your friend here says that you can see through our glamors, so I'm trying really hard to maintain it. However, if it drops, you should know that I am a Gryphon, and therefore I'll have the head of an eagle. Please, don't be alarmed." The soft lilt of his gentle tone was soothing in a way that was hard to describe. It made my limbs languid and my eyes droopy. "My senses are heightened, given my other form, so I can hear the heartbeats of your young without the aid of a stethoscope, as your friend mentioned."

"Nate," I croaked out.

He gave me a smile that was otherworldly in its beauty. "Ah, yes. Your friend, Nate. And you are?"

I flicked my eyes over to Nate, whose face was completely impassive. "Wren."

"Wren," he repeated, drawing out the vowel like he was tasting the word. "Well, Wren, all three heartbeats sound strong and steady, so whatever caused you to faint wasn't related to the babies. Your color is looking better, and your own heart sounds strong and even. I can't test your blood pressure, though, so when you get back to Heraklion, I would suggest asking the hospital to check you over."

That seemed unnecessary. I raised an eyebrow at him. "I fainted because I saw a buff guy with a lion's head."

Teron chuckled as he pulled away. "I imagine that would be shocking to any human."

I scoffed. Not after the month I'd had. I didn't say that, though, trying to sit up but kind of hitting the bumper stopper of my stomach. I was going to have to roll onto my side and swing my legs out.

An arm pushed beneath my spine, raising me up slowly. Teron held a glass of water to my lips. "Perhaps dehydration exacerbated your shock. People who aren't used to the heat here in Crete can find it punishing after a short time."

I took the drink in shaky hands and sipped it slowly. I didn't know how to tell this guy that it wasn't dehydration making me shaky, but the weird, unexplained pull in my chest that was lurching toward him like it was alive. Instead, I just thanked him.

Nate had obviously reached the end of his restraint, because he moved toward me, taking my face in his giant hands and kissing me possessively. "You scared the almighty fuck out of me, little one."

"Sorry," I croaked sheepishly. "I'm fine." *Kind of.*

Teron got to his feet, uncoiling to his full height. He was tall and lean, his shoulders wide and his torso a dramatic V to his waist. I didn't need to be in the know about the supernatural world to know there was something different about this guy. You couldn't look at him and believe he was an average human.

No, he was the kind of guy that early civilizations would have worshiped.

I kinda wanted to get on my knees and worship him too.

"If you are feeling better, I think it might be best if we go downstairs and have a conversation with Demke in the living area. He'll want to know why a human felt compelled to knock on our door when the wards we've placed on this building should make you want to run for the closest airport just to get away."

That was definitely *not* the overriding feeling I was having right now. The more settled I became in his presence, the more the yearning in my chest evolved into a longing that throbbed considerably lower.

Nate shifted uncomfortably, and it didn't escape Teron's notice. "I promise she is safe with us. We haven't practiced ritual sacrifice in a very long time," he laughed, like he was joking. At least, I hoped he was joking.

The heat of the scowl that Nate was giving him was burning me in sheer proximity. I stood, wedging myself to his side. "I hope by a long time, you mean centuries and not weeks."

Teron smiled that blinding grin again. "Millennia. It was a different world back then."

My brain spun at the concept that both the men in this room weren't men at all, but immortals. Shaking my head, I gripped Nate's hand. "Lead the way. I'd like to get to the bottom of all this too."

Teron ushered us out of the room we were in, and I realized it was some kind of sitting room. There was a desk in the corner, and I'd been lying on a chaise lounge. The halls of this fortress were made of the same stone as the outer walls, making the whole place blissfully cool in comparison to the heat outside. The floors were a darker slate stone, covered in bright rugs. Large arch windows with white painted moldings prevented the place from being oppressively dark and dungeonlike, but still our steps echoed as the sound ricocheted around the vaulted ceilings.

I peeked through one of the windows and saw a pool in the backyard, a paved area shaded by a small stand of what looked like orange trees. The blue water sparkled enticingly, and I stared at it longingly. Who came to Crete and didn't swim immediately?

Teron turned and ushered us into the central part of the home. A big stone arch was rendered white, and through the arch were large glass doors that led out to what I assumed was the back patio area. The sitting room was flooded with light, which meant that I saw every single one of the monsters before me in stark, crisp technicolor.

There were two lion-headed men, though they were both wearing shirts this time. Their faces flickered back to human quickly, and I could see the one I met at the door looking a little guilty now that his features were something I recognized. And what beautiful humans they made, golden gods in mortal-looking bodies.

Beside them was the largest man I'd ever seen— even bigger than Nate.

No, not a man. I swallowed hard as he stared at me from a bull's head. Large horns curved gently from his face, his broad nose looking velvety soft, a gold hoop through the septum.

"Concentrate, Milo. I don't want to scare her any more than necessary," Teron chastised gently, and suddenly, the bull's head was gone, and in its place was a strong jaw and a pair of piercing blue eyes the color of the Aegean sea.

The guy lowered his chin. "Apologies. It's been a while since we've met anyone who can see through the glamors quite so easily."

I turned to the last man in the room. This one didn't have any glamor, but he still made my knees shake. The raw power coming from him whooshed over me, shining so brightly that I squinted against it. The golden streaks spread from his body like fireworks, and I sucked in a breath. I wanted to touch him.

No, I wanted to rub my body all over his, like a cat marking its territory.

A pain pounded in my head from staring at him, and I closed my eyes against the lights completely.

A warm hand wrapped around my wrist, making Nate growl with disapproval. Teron made a soothing noise, and I wasn't sure if he was trying to appease me or Nate. "What's wrong, Wren? Why do you look like you're in pain?"

I chewed my lip, squinting at him. "He's too bright."

"Bright?" he questioned, and I screwed up my nose. How did I explain my visual hallucinations to complete strangers?

Luckily, Nate answered for me. "She describes seeing golden streaks of light around people."

Teron hissed out a breath. He looked over his shoulder. "Erus, get me your sunglasses." One of the lion-headed guys disappeared and returned quickly. He stood in front of me, threading the shades over my ears until they sat perched on my nose. He was really very pretty, with his shiny brown eyes and the small dimple in his chin that I kind of wanted to stick the tip of my tongue into.

The sunglasses were wonderfully dark, and my headache relented almost immediately. I smiled softly at the man—er, man-lion?—in front of me. "Thank you."

He gave me a gentle nod, and I resisted the urge to lean into his body.

Teron slapped him on the back. "Indeed. Thank you, Erus. I think it's best if you start at the beginning, Wren."

The bright man grunted his agreement. "Why would an American be in Amourgeles?"

I sucked in a deep breath. This would be the moment they decided I was crazy.

Well, maybe not, considering the animal heads.

"An Oracle told me that if I didn't come here, to Amourgeles, that I would be murdered and so would my babies. When the Lamia turned up on my doorstep, I decided that even if the Oracle was crazy, she might also be right."

The big bull-headed guy—Teron had said his name

was Milo—sucked in a breath. Even Erus looked perturbed.

I risked looking over at the big, overly bright guy. I could tell he was the leader, because everyone else was shooting looks in his direction as well, as if waiting to see what he would do or say. He crossed tanned arms over a broad chest, his almost-black beard just this side of scruffy. With the darkness of the sunglasses, I could look at him with minimal wincing.

"Explain."

Hooboy. If I *had* an explanation, I wouldn't be here. But I went right back to the beginning and hoped they'd understand, and maybe, just maybe, they'd have some answers too.

CHAPTER 18
DEMKE

Exile had its benefits. There was something soothing about knowing the days would be the same, that we were the lords of our domain, the most powerful beings on our little island paradise. But after thousands of years, it also led to an ennui so great, it threatened to suck you down into a darkness that you'd never be able to rise from. Not much ever changed. Days blurred together like seconds, weeks like hours, centuries like years.

But in all the time we'd been in exile, I could honestly say, we'd never had a situation quite like this.

The little human kept darting her eyes in my direction, one hand protectively on her rounded stomach. The God behind her—because there was no doubt in my mind that's what he was—hovered behind her protectively, keeping us all in his vision. He was a bloody God; I could tell that too. It was written in the violence of his aura.

Before she could start, I stared at him. "What Pantheon are you?"

He tilted his head at me, his eyes narrowed. I stared back. If we were going to have a battle of dominance, I wasn't going to lose in my own home. "Celtic," he told me, his hand flexing around the handle of his giant ax.

I nodded. Given the runes in his tattoos, that tracked. I pushed my luck. "Battle God?"

He curled his lip. "God of War. Néit."

The girl sucked in a breath and looked up at the man I'd assumed was her lover, given how he curled his body protectively around hers. Did she not know she was being protected by an ancient war God?

Interesting.

The God of War raised an eyebrow in my direction. "It's polite to introduce yourself in return." His voice was menacing, but I was beginning to wonder if that was just the natural pitch.

"Demke, Minoan God of Renewal." I pointed to Teron. "The Great Gryph." I pointed to the two lion-headed men. "Erastus and Tryphone. They are Genii." The woman, Wren, opened her mouth to ask questions, but I interrupted before she could get the words out. There would be time for questions later. First, I needed answers. I pointed to Milo. "Milonos. The Divine Bull."

"Divine Bull?" she asked before I could continue, and I gritted my back teeth.

But it was Milo who answered. "Fancy name for a Minotaur. Which is just the human way of saying a bull-headed Demigod. *The* Minotaur was actually my cousin. Long story." He smirked at her, and for the first time in a century, I realized I was seeing my longtime friend and confidante almost sober. As supernaturals, it took a serious amount of dedication to be drunk all the time, but it felt like that was the only thing Milo had been dedicated to in a long time.

She was frowning and nodding at the same time. She had long, dark hair and skin so pale, it looked like milk. Her eyes were the color of the sea before a great storm. She was beautiful, if nothing else. But all temptations sent our way had been beautiful.

Sucking in a deep breath, the girl pointed to herself. "Wren Mahone. Goddess of coffee."

Néit snorted a laugh, and I got the impression she was making fun of me. I couldn't be sure, though—it had been so long since anyone had dared to tease the God of Renewal.

Tryp laughed. "I don't think we have a Goddess of Coffee. I vote we make it canon."

Erus nudged him with his elbow, trying to keep his easily distracted lover on track. Some days, I looked at their closeness with envy in my heart. What would it have been like to go into this isolation with a lover, someone to keep me warm in the darkness of the night?

That old pain of loss, like a gaping hole in my chest, made me impatient. "Now we have introductions out of the way, I believe you might need to go further back in your explanations, human."

She blinked in my direction again, her face annoyed,

like I could turn down the imaginary lights that only she could see.

Teron also threw me an irritated expression, his tone soft as he asked the same thing I did, but in a gentler tone. "Before the Oracle, when did you notice things starting to change?"

She bit her lip, and I wanted to suck the full, pink flesh between my own. I might have kept my face neutral, but inside, I balked at the random thought. Where the hell had *that* come from? I hadn't felt desire in… too long to remember.

"I started to see the streaks about five months ago, I guess? Just one or two, like when the sun hits your window just right. Then it was more and more, until I went and saw a doctor. I thought I had a brain tumor." She huffed a laugh that didn't sound particularly mirthful. "What I actually had was a bad case of pregnancy."

"The father?"

"I don't even remember getting laid."

Tryp groaned. "Man, that has to suck. Imagine getting knocked up and not even remembering getting off. Unless…" He paused. "You didn't get frisky with any swans, did you? Maybe a cuckoo?" He shot a grin at Milo. "Or a bull?"

I knew what he was getting at, and it was a valid question, even if he was making it sound like a joke.

Wren, though, looked at him like he'd lost his mind. "You're asking me if I fucked a swan? Am I getting this right? And what the hell does a cuckoo even look like?" Tryp went to answer, but she waved a hand at him.

"No, I don't want to know. I haven't fucked any animals."

"Would you like to?" Tryp teased, letting his glamor slip on purpose, because the guy was a whore, despite having a sexual partner.

Erus rolled his eyes as he picked up Tryp's line of questioning. "Did you stand in any golden rain? Perhaps eat some funky-looking lettuce or fruit?"

Tryp chuckled. "Golden rain. Heh."

She shook her head like we were crazy, but then stopped. "Actually, I helped an old lady pick up some fallen fruit, and she gave me an apple. It wasn't funky, I don't think. Maybe abnormally delicious? That would have been just before the lights started." She frowned. "That's insane, though. It was an *apple.* I've eaten hundreds in my lifetime."

The Celtic God behind her sniffed angrily. "Fucking Greeks. Fucking golden rain and poisoned fruit. The hell is wrong with you people?"

Anger lit up my veins. "We are Minoan. We aren't part of the Greek Pantheon." I looked at Wren. "We can't know for sure if that was what it was. I can tell you if your children are Demigods, however. I am the God of Renewal, and therefore fertility. It's in my wheelhouse, as you would say."

"How?" she asked hesitantly.

"I would just have to be inside you." I'd have to fuck her. An inconvenient way to discover divinity, but the old powers really enjoyed fucking.

"Inside me how?" she breathed. "Like poke a finger

in my ear, inside me? Or, like, your dick inside me kind of inside me?"

Tryp coughed, hiding his mouth behind his hand.

"The latter," I answered calmly.

The big God pulled his ax. "No fucking way. Over your dead body," he threatened.

Wren's lips were parted, and I could see the rapid rise and fall of her chest. Her pupils had dilated, her tongue dipping out to wet her bottom lip. She was imagining it right now, and given the way her pupils were blown out, she liked what she was daydreaming about. She wanted me; that was easy to see.

Still, she grabbed Néit's wrist, the one hefting the ax, and lowered it back down to his side. "Thank you, but I'll pass. I can wait until they're born to see if there's anything I need to know about them."

I shrugged, like the idea of being inside a woman after all this time wasn't appealing. No, that was wrong. Not inside *a* woman. Inside *this* woman.

There were women in the village who came and went, but I hadn't desired any of them in a long time, outside the basic needs they fulfilled. Until now. Until her.

I didn't like it. It felt like a trap, especially now that I suspected that she was perhaps another shackle from Olympus. Still, I couldn't stop myself from saying, "The offer stands."

Milo was sitting across from her, the large mass of him seeming to consume half the room. "Tell us what happened after the apple incident. Anything else stand out?"

She went back to finding out she was having triplets, which made the hairs on my arms rise. Three was a magic number in the Mythic world. I didn't think the fact she was carrying triplets was coincidental.

Her eyes welled up as she told us about some kind of shadow monster attacking her, and the death of her landlady. A tear rolled down her cheek, making me clench my jaw. Her pain was like sandpaper against my skin. The creatures sounded like Verserpents, and that made the whole thing even more suspicious.

Still, I had to ask. "What makes you think it's the Greek Mythics?"

Néit snorted. "Other than the Oracle and the Lamia?" Compelling evidence, I guess, but both of those beings tended to be unruly, making decisions without any regard to a higher authority.

Wren shrugged. "I guess I don't. I just know she said I should come here, and then this feeling in my chest pulled me to Amourgeles. To this place."

I met Teron's eyes over her head, and his face was filled with the same confusion as mine. Still, our downfall had begun with ignoring the warning of a Delphi Oracle. I wasn't about to make the same mistake twice.

I stood and walked out of the room, heading to the library to see if there was anything in those dusty old tomes that might give any insight into this human's situation. Perhaps we could figure out what those visual hallucinations were exactly, though I already had my suspicions. I dared not tell the girl yet, or even breathe of it to my friends. My brothers.

Because if I was right, then the Ouroboros had turned once more, and it spelled uncertainty for us all.

Because if I was right, that small, waifish woman sitting in my living room was seeing life threads, and that spelled turmoil for the whole world.

Demke just stood and left. He didn't say a word to me, or to his friends. He just left. I looked over at Teron, who watched him leave, but didn't seem surprised.

"We'll look into what it all means, Wren." His golden eyes bounced between Nate and I. Or should I say, Néit. I'd known he was some kind of immortal, but I really, really hadn't known he was the God of War. The same guy who took me to my OB-GYN appointments. Who'd driven Mrs. Byrne around like Miss Daisy. That guy was an ancient God of War.

Shaking my head, I tuned back into what Teron was saying. "I think you should both stay here, at the compound."

I resisted the urge to snort. I wasn't so caught up in the Mythics and supernatural plots that I was going to voluntarily lock myself inside a fortress with a bunch of guys who had animal heads. But before I could politely decline, Nate was lifting me to my feet. "No."

I frowned at him, because while I agreed, I was more than capable of speaking for myself. "What he means to say is no, *thank you*. We're staying in a resort down in Heraklion. We'll come back and visit before we go home, though, just in case you've found something."

Teron looked back over his shoulders at his friends, and they seemed to have some kind of silent conversation, before he nodded. "If that's what you wish. Though I would strongly suggest you stop and get a quick check-up at the hospital, on your way back to the resort. Just to be on the safe side."

Erus leaned over and whispered something to Tryp, but I couldn't hear the words.

I climbed to my feet under the scrutiny of five sets of eyes. "Okay, I will. Just to be on the safe side," I promised.

Nate maneuvered me out of the room, and with an innate sense of direction that I sorely lacked, back through the fortress and right out to the front gate. Milo, the Minotaur, followed behind us. He unbarred the heavy wooden door at the base of the stairs and stood aside. He was frowning, but didn't stop us from leaving.

Despite the ominous noise Nate made, Milo reached out and grabbed my arm. The feel of his hand on my skin was like being electrocuted. I felt it down in my *soul*, which was really fucking weird. His lips parted as he stared at the point where our bodies touched, his eyes flying up to meet mine. I guess I wasn't the only one having a bizarre physiological response to innocuous contact.

He let out a shaky breath, and I watched the golden cords whipping around his body, slightly brighter than normal, tangling around my fingers. Looking back up into his face, I was kind of relieved to see he was in his human form still.

"Promise you'll come back if you run into any trouble. Crete… Well, it's ours, but I can't guarantee it's completely safe. If you need us, call us." Sliding his hand down my forearm, he wrapped my fingers in his own, slipping me a piece of paper with a number written on it.

I wasn't sure if the streaks were finally getting to me, or if I'd just lost all self-preservation, but the words were out before I even thought through the consequences. "Can you show me once more, so I know I'm not insane?"

He frowned harder. "Show you what?"

"Your real form."

His eyebrows rose high, like they were trying to escape into his hairline. "This is as much my real form as the bull."

He sucked in a deep breath, his barrel chest pushing out impressive pectorals. The streaks brightened, then faded slightly, and before me was the same man, except bigger somehow, broader if that was possible, with the head of a bull. His neck was thick and muscular, which made sense considering his head was fucking huge.

Covered in short, soft fur only slightly darker than his golden skin, the very end of his nose was shiny and black, a golden hoop looped through his septum. Horns as long as my arms shone in the late afternoon sun, and I desperately wanted to run my hands along them.

Unable to help myself, I lifted my hand and ran my fingers beneath the underside of his head, only able to just brush his jaw with my fingertips. He stooped lower so I had better access, and I didn't breathe as Milo watched me intently with eyes that had doubled in size —no longer vivid blue, but darkening almost to hazel, like the color had been diluted.

I traced up over the side of his blocky head and wrapped my fingers around the base of his left horn. He hissed, reaching up to grab my wrist. "Easy there." The sound of Milo's voice was deeper coming from the bull mouth. How fucking insane was that?

I flushed red, horrified. "I'm so sorry. I didn't realize they might be painful."

He snorted, quite literally, like a bull. "Painful isn't how I'd describe the sensation."

At that, Nate snatched me back toward his body, basically picking me up and marching me to the car before I could so much as collect my thoughts. Or realize that I'd basically given the Minotaur a horn job.

When I looked back over my shoulder, Milo was still standing outside the wall, watching me. He had a soft smile on his face as I climbed into the SUV.

A few yards away, I noticed the dog from the cafe sitting at the base of the wall. Another smaller dog was beside him, this one looking far more scraggly and very obviously a stray. I waved at them. "Bye, Cy!"

I lifted my hand in Milo's direction too as Nate roared away, making pale dust fly up in a cloud behind us.

I'D KEPT my promise to Teron, sitting in the waiting room of the hospital in Heraklion until my ass went numb, just for the doctor to take my blood pressure, do a fetal heartbeat scan, and declare me fit and healthy. He prescribed lying on the beach and plenty of water, and to avoid caffeine, which I was already doing.

It was dark and late when we made it back to the resort, but the kitchen was still open. Nate ordered an entire banquet of food while I had a shower. He'd been quiet on the way home and while we sat in the waiting room of the hospital. He didn't seem mad—more pensive, I guess.

I wondered what he thought of everything, but I was too nervous to ask. I was a little scared to confess the pull of the men in Amourgeles. I was a little worried that he'd drop me on their doorstep and wash his hands of me and the drama I represented.

As warm water ran over my body, I tried to come to terms with everything that I'd discovered today. I tried to slot the puzzle pieces beside each other, but kept coming up with an abstract collection of nothing. Even now, I felt my body leaning toward Amourgeles, like I was trying to be closer to the town, to those men, like even just a couple of inches was a relief. It was starting to scare me, feeling out of control of my body once more.

I also thought about Nate, and the fact he was the God of War. I could vividly remember his hands gripping my thighs as he ate me out this morning, while whispering things in Gaelic I couldn't understand, but which my heart clung to desperately.

I was breaking my number one rule when it came to Nate—I was getting attached. But when he held me so gently his arms, fucked me like my pleasure was the only thing he'd ever desired in his whole life, it did something to my heart that there was no chance of resisting.

"Wren, the food is here!" he called from outside the bathroom door.

I rested my head against the cool tiles of the shower, trying to pull myself together. Turning off the water, I slipped on one of Nate's shirts and a pair of boyleg underwear. It was getting hard to drag them up my thighs now. I was going to have to start going commando if I got much bigger. Which I would. It was so hard to conceptualize the fact that I was only half way through my pregnancy when I was already this huge. That I'd get even bigger.

The bathroom door opened, and the worried face of Nate was in front of me. "Are you okay?"

I gave him a tight smile. "Sure, I'm fine. I'm coming."

"You've been in here fifteen minutes since the food

arrived. I was worried," he said soothingly. He rubbed his hands down my arms. "You're shaking."

My face screwed up as I looked down at my hands. I *was* shaking. "Huh. I hadn't noticed. It's probably low blood sugar. Let's go eat."

One thing Crete had in abundance was damn good food. As I sat on the bed, Nate spread all different foods around me so I didn't have to reach, like I was some kind of fertility deity and he was paying tribute with carbs.

He leaned against the bed, his own plate loaded down with dips, pita and some kind of hand-size pies that looked comically small in his fingers. I did begin to feel better after the food, but the trembling continued. I sat on my hand so Nate couldn't see.

"So, are we going to talk about how you're the God of War and didn't tell me?"

He rolled his eyes at me. "I was *a* God of War. There are a lot of us rolling around. Mythics like nothing more than a good bloody battle."

"You weren't going to tell me?" I tried to keep the note of betrayal from my voice, because I had no real reason to feel that way. He hadn't promised me his truths. He hadn't promised me anything.

He shrugged. "I haven't been the God of War in nearly three thousand years, *mo stóirín*. That God died on the battlefields of Moytura. That God was exiled from the Emerald Isle. The man made his way to the Americas. The man is who you know."

"He just happens to be bathed in runes and knows

how to handle his ax?" I joked, trying to break the sadness of his words. There was pain there, and three millennia was a long time for a wound to fester.

He stood, grabbing the plates from the bed and tossing them haphazardly onto the table beside us. Then he crawled up over my body and kissed me softly. "My ax isn't the only thing I know how to handle," he purred, and my whole body clenched with need.

"Prove it?" I teased.

Boy, did he prove it. Twice.

CHAPTER 20
WREN

I woke up sweating. My body felt both hot and cold, chilled by rivulets of sweat that felt like ice as they slid down my forehead into my dampened hairline. My legs were tangled in Nate's, but our torsos were as far apart as I could get.

Every part of my body felt like it was vibrating. My heart felt… weird.

"Nate," I whispered. "Nate, wake up."

He was on his feet, his ax in his hand, before his eyes had even opened. "What's wrong?" he rumbled, his eyes searching the dark corners for intruders. But there was nothing here that wanted to harm me, except my own body.

As I shook my head, I realized some of the moisture on my face was tears. "I don't know."

"The babies?"

They felt fine, and I couldn't even explain how I

knew that. The pain was definitely coming from my limbs, not from my womb. "I think they're fine. This... I don't know." I made a keening noise, getting to my feet and moving toward the door. As I walked over to it, the pain eased. "We need to go back."

"Back where?" Nate asked, sounding more rattled than I'd ever heard.

"Amourgeles. The compound." I groaned, my shaking hands fumbling with the door lock. "I need to go back. It's like I'm being dragged back there by my insides." I slammed the flat of my hand on the door. "Please, Nate. Please, I need to go back."

He was nodding, throwing on his clothes. "Okay, little one. Okay. Let me just pack our shit up."

He rushed around the room, his face worried. Luckily, we hadn't really unpacked, so it only took minutes for him to gather our things from the bathroom and stuff them in our bags. But those minutes felt like an eternity as I leaned back against the wall and groaned. Every muscle in my body ached. Nate's shirt clung to me, sticky with sweat.

With the bags in one hand, he ushered me out of the room and down the darkened hallway. I felt like I was suffocating, and as we stepped into the warm night air, I sucked in a deep breath. We hurried to the car on silent feet, the light breeze drying the moisture that was filmed on my face.

The sea air soothed something in me, but not enough. My muscles felt rigid as I climbed into the front seat, while Nate quickly tossed our bags in the back. He peeled out of the parking lot and onto the darkened roads of Heraklion.

"Are you sure you don't need to go to the hospital?" he asked, like we hadn't been there only hours earlier.

I couldn't explain to him how I knew that the only thing that would help was going back to the compound in Amourgeles, because I really didn't understand it myself. I just *knew*. I felt like a junkie who needed a fix, like there was a fist wrapped around my heart, squeezing.

So I shook my head. "Just take me back."

A part of my brain that wasn't feverish knew this was unfair on Nate, especially when I saw the tense line of his jaw and the strain around his eyes.

I curled into a ball on the passenger seat and breathed through the ache as we drove slowly toward Amourgeles. Even though I wanted Nate to go faster, I knew he wouldn't. It was the middle of the night, and the roads were unfamiliar. I wasn't so far gone that I'd put the babies at risk by suggesting it.

Still, every minute of that trip felt like torture.

There were no other cars on the roads, and the village was completely dark. The large wall loomed in the distance, and finally, I could breathe slightly easier. My body eased its giant cramp, but the anxiety in my chest doubled.

I tried to get out of the car, but my legs felt weak. Nate scooped me up in his arms, striding to the door at the base of the wall and thumping on it so loudly, I wouldn't have been surprised if he'd woken the whole village. He pounded on it until it sounded like distant thunder.

I wriggled in his arms, and he lowered me to my feet, his arm tightly around my waist so I was propped against his body, just in case I did anything as audacious as to topple over.

Finally, the door was wrenched open by one of the two guys who looked similar, but different. Erus, I think. Definitely not the one who'd opened it the first time.

"Nate? Wren? What's wrong?"

With the door open, something came over me. It was like something else had possession of my limbs as I pushed past Erus and climbed the stairs two at a time. I ran down the halls, though I didn't know where I was going. I only had a feeling that pulled in my chest. I needed something, and I knew it was this way.

So close.

I already could feel the yanking sensation easing, like the world's most uncomfortable game of Marco Polo. I ran past the shocked face of Tryp, hesitating slightly beside Teron's rooms. Another set of stairs had me going down, down, down.

Close. Close.

A huge door stood in front of me, and I knew it was there. Relief was behind those doors. Pushing it open with strength I didn't know I possessed, I launched myself into the darkness beyond. It was a bedroom coated in shadows, no windows, just a huge four-poster bed in the middle of the room. There was a lump in the center of the bed, gently snoring, and just the sight made me sigh with relief.

Almost there. Almost.

I climbed into the bed, shifting around the blankets until I could find skin. Only touching would help ease the fever that was wracking my body. I knew it in my soul.

Milo rocketed up in bed, his naked chest almost colliding with my face as I climbed up his body. "Wren?"

The first touch of my skin on his was like the best painkiller in the world flooding my body. Muscles that had been pulled taut in my body relaxed, and I sagged. My jaw cracked as my teeth unclenched. But still, not quite right. Needed one more thing.

"Shift. Please shift. Change. I need..." What? What did I need? This was craziness.

Milo stared at me with wide eyes, but he dropped his glamor, and then the bull was in front of me. I climbed up his body, curling up on his huge chest like a cat, tucking my face beneath the huge line of his blocky head.

I sighed as the rest of the tension left my body. As endorphins flooded my veins, my brain crashed, and I let go of my last grip on consciousness.

. . .

Voices filtered in and out of my hearing, making the swirling darkness of sleep slip away.

"Tryp woke up the doctor from the next town over and raided his practice. I'll get what I can get shipped over from the mainland as soon as possible."

Something squeezed around my arm, and I opened my eyes, blinking slowly, because wading out of sleep seemed harder than usual right now. I looked directly into Teron's golden eyes.

"We have to stop meeting like this, Wren Mahone." His smile was soft and reassuring, and I found myself smiling back.

I looked over at the blood pressure cuff wrapped around my bicep. "I feel good now. Probably don't need that," I slurred. I was on my side on the warmest bed ever, even if it was a bit hard.

Actually… it was *too* hard.

It all flooded back to me, and I realized I wasn't on a bed. I was on a broad, inhuman chest. "Oh *shit*."

Embarrassment had me trying to move, but two big hands landed on my hips, keeping me in place. "It's okay. Stay until the blood pressure machine finishes its reading."

I looked up at Milo, my cheeks flooding with heat. I'd basically assaulted this guy. I'd climbed his body like a tree and just gotten comfy. I hadn't even given him an explanation, just forced him to drop his glamor.

His face was still that of the bull, the soft puffs of breath from his nose displacing the sticky hair that was hanging lankly around my face.

"I'm *so* sorry. I don't know what came over me. It was like I was on drugs or having a mental breakdown or something. You can, uh, shift back if you want."

"If that would make you more comfortable," he murmured softly, shifting back to his human form, although his chest was still wide enough that I didn't really move at all. "Don't be embarrassed. It's been a long time since a beautiful woman has barged into my room and climbed into my bed," he joked, and I flushed even redder, if that were possible.

Teron tsked at us. "Stop. You're messing with the blood pressure reading when you tease her like that." Finally, he unwrapped the cuff from my arm. "Now that you're awake, I'd like to check you out properly, if I could."

Milo was currently human-sized, which meant he was slightly shorter, so when I climbed off him, my thigh moved across, uh, certain parts of his anatomy that it probably shouldn't have. Hard parts of his anatomy that made him hiss through his teeth when I brushed against it. I chanted an apology while trying to look anywhere but at the people in the room, quickly scooting to the end of his bed.

Teron's eyes sparkled with amusement. I tried to focus on his lips and not his eyes. No, wait, that didn't help, because he had such a pretty mouth. A cupid's bow top lip, and a slightly more plump bottom one. He had lips made for kissing.

I'd look at the center of his forehead instead. *Yeah, that's much better.*

He held up a pen light and shone it in my eyes, humming softly as he tested whatever it was you tested with a blinding pen light. "Your responses all seem good."

"Are you a doctor?" Man, if he'd been my general practitioner, I'd be out there licking doorknobs and doing adventure sports, in the hopes I'd break something.

He chuckled. "Not officially."

Milo snorted, a definite bullish sound, even in his human form. "Only because you can't go to school and get a piece of paper." He stood up, his body uncurling until he was standing just there, wearing nothing but tight boxers and a hard-on. My eyes went wide, and I looked back at Teron, hoping he couldn't read the dirty thoughts on my face.

"What Milo is trying to say is that medicine is a passion of mine, and I have stayed up-to-date with the latest research and practices, as a hobby essentially. Sometimes, I will help the villagers if they can't make it down to Heraklion to the hospital." He raised a single dark eyebrow. "I have a lot of time to fill with many hobbies."

I met his golden eyes, and a little part of me longed to know every single one of the things he was passionate about. How old was he? Did he have a wife? Could he fly?

The door creaked open, and then Milo's room started to fill with huge bodies. Too many bodies. Nate came in first, his face completely unreadable. Erus and

Tryp came next, both shirtless and disheveled, and finally Demke, his expression completely blank.

Milo snorted again. "Guess it's a party in my room today."

Demke stepped forward, his eyes skating right over me to look at Teron. "Is she healthy?"

The big Gryphon stretched up to his full height, rolling his shoulders. "There's no medical reason for last night's episode that I can find." He looked down at me, as if he realized it was rude to speak about my health like I wasn't even here. "Your temperature, blood pressure, your cognitive responses—they're all fine. Milonos said you felt chilled when you, er, entered his bed, but that might have just been the night air. Perhaps it was something more. I have ordered equipment from the mainland to monitor the fetuses better, and it should arrive in the next couple of days, but I think they are fine. Physically, you are in good health."

I looked between him and Demke, then over at Nate. He looked both relieved and worried simultaneously, which shouldn't be possible, yet there he was.

Demke, however, looked stormy. "I was afraid of that." I was perfectly healthy; how could that be a bad thing? "Come. We have a lot to talk about." Demke looked past me. "This affects you too, Milo." There was barely restrained anger in his tone, and I couldn't understand what I'd done to offend him so badly.

Broke into his house.

Kind of assaulted his friend.

Okay, maybe I'd be pissed too.

Milo gave the God in front of me a quizzical look. "Me?"

Demke's eyes dropped back to mine, and there was a coldness in them that made me shiver. "It seems that the human has bonded you."

What the fuck did *that* mean?

CHAPTER 21
MILONOS

When you'd lived as long as I had, you saw a lot of religions come and go. Some stuck around, but most disappeared in the blink of an immortal eye. However, maybe this "new age" religion of crystals and manifesting was onto something, because one minute, I'd been dreaming about the pretty little human, about impaling her on my dick while she screamed my name. The next minute, I was waking up to the woman herself crawling into my arms.

It wasn't until I'd felt the ice of her skin, the way she was shivering against me like she was frozen, that I'd snapped out of the lust haze I'd woken in.

The big guy had been close behind her, as were Erus and Tryp, and those three being in my room had definitely chased away the last of the fantasies.

I'd wrapped her in my beast, warmed her body with mine, and by the time Teron made it into the room, she'd stopped trembling. That hadn't stopped him from ordering Tryp and Erus into town to collect medical equipment.

Néit had tried to gently pull her off me, but she'd clung to my body like a barnacle, even though she was unconscious. Eventually, he'd stepped back, looking heartbroken. I was glad she hadn't been awake to see that expression. I might have only spent an hour in her presence, but even I could tell she thought the sun shone out of this guy's ass.

So Teron had taken her vitals, and they'd left her there, sleeping on my chest. I hadn't been able to go back to sleep, but those five hours when she'd slumbered soundly in my arms had been the most peaceful rest I'd had in centuries. She'd soothed the beast, and that feeling of contentment buried itself into my chest, wrapping around my soul.

I should be scared. What if she was another trap? Instead, I felt at peace. If she was a carefully laid assassin, then at least I would die happy.

Back in the present, our fearless leader was *pissed*.

"Snap out of it," Demke barked at me in our native language. It was long forgotten by the humans of today. Not even scholars could decipher its written form. "She has bewitched you."

I shrugged. "Not on purpose, Dem."

Once upon a time, I would have called him my King. But those days were centuries gone, and now, he may be a God, but we all sat on the same pedestal, equally cast aside and forgotten. It was no pedestal at all, really.

He frowned at me, then shifted his focus back to the woman in question. Her cheeks were still a little pink. *Good.* She'd been far too pale earlier.

She met Demke's furious gaze with her own, which was ballsy. People had supplicated themselves at his feet for centuries, rather than meet his eyes. But not this little firecracker; she met and held them like she was the Goddess, only a slight wince telling me that he was still "bright" to her.

"What did you mean by bonded?"

Demke sighed, and I noticed he was looking old. Not physically old—none of us would ever look older than late twenties, but the weight in his eyes felt heavy. "I think that perhaps the lights you are seeing are the threads of fate."

I hissed a sound that wasn't even remotely human. The threads of fate? That wasn't... "How?" I gasped.

Everyone looked shell-shocked. Even Wren's protector looked like he'd been suckerpunched.

Only Teron didn't seem surprised. "I'd wondered if that was what it was. You've confirmed?"

Demke shook his head. "No, not really. But with the evidence presented, it seems almost irrefutable, don't you think?"

Wren waved a hand. "Okay, now for the human in the room? What the fuck are the threads of fate? And what does that have to do with Milo?"

I got the expression on Demke's face now. The last few turns of the Ouroboros had not ended well for us, or those we loved. We'd been forced out of our world and relegated beyond the annals of history, right into pits of obscurity.

I'd seen three turns of the Ouroboros, and had no wish to see another.

But here she was, the tiny little catalyst, and something inside me reared its head. An urge I hadn't had in so long. The urge to *protect*.

"The threads of fate affect us all. They weave the patterns of history, of mortality, of our kind. They come from a power higher than any God or Goddess, and they are gifted and taken away at their whim. The current wielders of the threads of fate are the Moirai. Humans know them as The Fates. The Maiden, The Mother, The Crone."

"Bitch One, Bitch Two, and Bitch Three would have been better titles," Tryp grumbled, and I had to agree. They'd screwed us hard in their time holding power.

"Before Clotho, Lachesis, and Atropos, there were the Norns from the Norse Pantheon. Before them, there was another trio. And another before them. Every time the snake bites its tail, the higher power resows the ability to weave the threads of fate, and the old Fates lose their powers."

Wren had gone pale, her hand reaching out toward Néit, and I tried to push down the jealousy. She might've unintentionally needed me, but she relied on him. There was no cause for this feeling of envy in my chest.

He came to her, of course, sitting on the couch beside her, pulling her tightly to his body like he could protect her from Demke's words. "What are you saying?" she breathed.

Demke looked like he was giving her the worst news, and in a way, he was. "I believe you are carrying the three new weavers. The Fates. I think that's why you're being attacked. The Greek Mythics are trying to hunt you down to preserve their power for a little longer, and to do so, they need the new Fates out of the way. By killing off the new weavers before they are born, the power gets reseeded by the higher power again and again. Because until the new Fates are born into the world and take their first breaths, the ability to see and weave the threads remains mostly with the old Fates."

"Unless those old Fates die," Teron added, his eyes filled with heavy meaning.

I breathed through my teeth. *Fuck. Fucking fuck.* It was the best word invented in the last five hundred years, and encapsulated my feelings about this moment perfectly.

It was a death sentence for this human. A death sentence for her babies. The power of the Greek Mythics was that there were so many of them. Polytheistic religions were always harder to topple than the monolithic ones, and those fuckers did it best, running roughshod over every religion and adapting it to their own, until they also fell out of favor two thousand years ago.

However, there were enough believers around that they'd maintained some of their power, including the ability to weave fate. They held enough sway through recent history that it had taken this long for the Ouroboros to reach the end.

They were selfish, murderous bastards. Wren didn't stand a chance. The idea made me want to shout at the moon like a mournful wolf.

She sucked in a shuddering breath. "And what about this bond with Milo?"

"I think, somehow, your threads and his have tangled together, and now he is yours."

"Mine?" she repeated.

"His life is entwined with yours. Your fate is his fate. As is that of Néit." Demke looked like he wanted to spit the words like poison from his body.

Wren shook her head. "Impossible. I don't have any golden threads. Maybe I'm just a blank spot and that's why they want to kill me? I can't be all that. I can't—" She started to breathe heavily, and Néit pulled her onto his lap, stroking a hand up and down her back.

"It'll be okay, *mo stóirín*. I won't let anything happen to any of you."

Teron looked at her sympathetically. "It's my belief you can't see your own threads, Wren, but if you live and breathe, they are there. We all have them: humans, Demigods and Gods alike." He gave Demke a pointed look.

"So what he's saying"—she lifted her chin at Demke —"is that I'm screwed, and I've dragged Nate and Milo down with me, all because I ate a piece of fruit?"

Tryp looked unusually solemn. "Welcome to being a Mythic, babe. It makes no sense."

Words trickled away, and only Wren's panicked breaths and the soft friction of Néit's hand running up and down her spine broke the silence.

Finally, she seemed to get herself under control. She looked up at Demke, her jaw tense and her eyes blazing with determination. "So what do we do?" There was still fear there, but her hand rested over her stomach. She was determined, for her young, if not for herself.

Demke raised an eyebrow. "We?"

I shot him an aggravated look. "Yes, fucking *we*. When have we ever just stood by and let an innocent woman die?"

Erus huffed. "The Bronze Age? Women and children died at the drop of a hat back then."

I growled at him. "You know what I mean, Erastus. Besides, my fate is tied to hers now. Would you so easily cast my friendship aside, after four thousand years?" I pinned Demke with a stare. "Just roll over and let us—let *me*—fall to the people who fucked us over in the first place?"

Teron rested a hand on my shoulder. "Of course not, brother. Demke is just making a point. Even without the prophecy of the Oracle, we would not let Wren be harmed." He gave the others a hard look. "Besides, the Ouroboros has turned, and perhaps this could be the

Age where we are unwoven from the web completely. We cannot go into oblivion without a struggle. It is not our nature. At least, it's not mine."

He was taunting Demke, who'd become more and more apathetic over the years. As each cycle came and went, marked only by death and rebirth, he'd lost more and more of himself. Teron might've seemed confident that Demke wouldn't hang me out to dry, but I wasn't so sure anymore.

Demke sucked in a breath. "We'll help, the best we can. You'll have to stay here, in the compound. It is warded against other Mythics." He glared at Néit, and I wondered how Néit had made it through the ward. Maybe it was because he'd had Wren in his arms?

"I can't stay here forever. I have to go home. I have appointments, and the babies..." Her voice trailed off, the panic returning.

I found myself edging closer and closer to her seat. I tried to inconspicuously touch her skin, but I should have known better. As I wrapped a gentle hand around her ankle, sitting at her feet, the eyes of all my brothers took in my position.

Fuck it. I had no regrets. I was tying myself to her voluntarily, and they could make of that what they wanted.

"It isn't safe for you to go home. We can't protect you back in America. We can protect you here," I told her as gently as I could. "Teron has more knowledge trapped in that giant head of his than all of your specialists combined. I promise, whatever happens, we'll take care of you all." I looked up into her pretty face. "Trust me."

Her eyes were big and damp as she stared down at me, and I saw Néit's hands flex where they sat on her hips. But he didn't contradict me, perhaps because he knew we were right. He didn't have to like it, but right here with me?

Nowhere else in the world was as safe.

CHAPTER 22
WREN

Somehow, the decision was made that we would stay. And I meant we, because there was no way I was staying without Nate. If he'd insisted that we head back home, then that's where we would've gone. I might've had to kidnap Milo as well, because that painful tugging in my chest last night wasn't something I was in a hurry to experience again. But Nate had agreed to stay, and I wasn't too proud to admit that I was relieved.

Erus led us through the house to the wing where we would be staying. House was the wrong word; it was far too large for that. It was almost like a castle, but not. A fortress might have been the best description for it, since it was huge and made of stone. Maybe once upon a time, it might've even been considered a palace, but the idea that I was staying in a palace made me feel weird.

"The only wing we have spare is one that once

belonged to someone else…" Erus trailed off as he pushed open the door, and I could see why. This wasn't a room, for one thing. It was a full suite, including a sitting room and private bathroom. It was decorated almost entirely in light blue and white, making it look like the room was set amongst the clouds. Tiny animal motifs ran along the walls of the room, and all the furniture was covered in large drop cloths. I didn't need to see under them to know that it would all be finely made and probably crazily expensive antiques. Whoever had lived in this room had been someone seriously important.

That made me feel really fucking weird. "I don't want to pry, but the person who lived in this room before me, she was…?"

"The Goddess. Our Goddess," Erus said, his voice choking up. "Actually, she was more of a reflection of our Goddess. She was stripped of her powers a couple of millennia ago, then eventually just faded away." He let out a shuddering breath. "It was hard. No one has lived in this suite since then. Tryp comes in to redo the motifs every hundred years or so, in her honor."

He pointed to the mural, a tree with different animals and birds perched in the branches, including goats, which was kind of amusing. A dog ran along the exposed roots. The Goddess stood to the left, wrapped in snakes, with a bull wrapped in ropes near her feet, like a sacrifice.

Beside her, two lion-headed men poured liquid into a well from earthen jugs. On the other side, a man stood, wreathed in vines. Even with the primitive style of drawing, I could tell it was Demke. Beside him stood a Gryphon, large and proud. I couldn't see Milo in the motif anywhere.

Erus bustled around the room, removing the sheets to uncover heavy wooden furniture. As he uncovered the bed, a cloud of dust flooded out around us, and he screwed up his nose. "I'll go and pick up another mattress from Heraklion today. I don't even want to think about what might be living in that mattress and how bad it would be for you and the babies."

He led us to two doors to the left of the room. "There's an attendant's room through here," he said, opening one door into a smaller suite that was still bigger than my apartment back home. "The door locks on both sides, you know, if you want to keep someone out." Erus flushed, turning his golden cheeks a little pink. Closing the door, he opened the next one. "Your bathroom."

I stepped inside the beautifully tiled room, its large sunken bath big enough to fit the defensive line of a football team. On the wall to the left, a shower head poked out from the tiles.

There was no doubt anymore; this place had definitely once been a palace.

Erus stepped back into the main part of the bedroom. "I'll leave you guys to get settled in. Lunch will probably be in an hour or so. Demke cooks."

I scratched my head, feeling awkward as hell. "I

could cook too, if you'd like? I'm not great, but I don't want to feel like I'm freeloading."

Erus gave me a lopsided grin. "I'm sure we'll think of something." He hesitated, then shook his head. "Demke wouldn't say this, but we're glad you're here. Milo… Well, he hasn't coped well with being anchorless, I guess. We were worried he'd be the next to fade away. Tying your fates together is a blessing, even if we do lose him in the end. At least it won't be a slow death, where we have to watch him turn into a ghost before our eyes."

I didn't know what to say to that, and Erus didn't wait for a response. He just strode out the door, pulling it gently closed behind him. I flopped down on the chaise lounge, putting my head in my hands. My life was out of control.

I looked up at Nate, guilt eating me alive. "I'm sorry."

He shrugged. "I'm not." He sat down beside me, and luckily the chaise was built sturdier than modern furniture, because it didn't even groan. "Milo wasn't the only one suffering from immortal ennui. I had no purpose, and now I do. I'd also like to avenge Zelda, if I can."

My heart clenched at the thought of Mrs. Byrne, the first casualty in whatever supernatural fuckery was going to follow me around from now on. Rage at the injustice of such a good person being killed for what, some mythical power grab? It burned through my chest. "Me too."

Nate pulled me into his arms and kissed me softly. "It'll be okay."

I shook my head. "You can't know that."

"I can. I'm a fucking God, *mo stóirín*. I'll make it so."

He sounded like a toddler throwing a tantrum, but something inside me lit up like the golden threads I saw wrapped around him. Teron's words about not being able to see my own threads made me wonder if I was equally as bright, wrapping him as tightly as his threads wrapped around me.

"Come on, I'll run you a bath in that monstrosity they call a tub. They must have to drain a lake to fill that thing," he grumbled, but led me into the bathroom. He ran the taps, and when it was full, I descended the steps until I could sink into the huge pool.

The hot water parted around my body, and when Nate slipped in behind me, I laid my back against his chest. He wrapped an arm around my body just below my breasts, and I floated there in peace, for however long it lasted.

WHEN WE EMERGED from our suite, Milo was pacing in front of the large glass doors. As soon as he saw me, his face lit up like he'd seen the first sunny day in spring. "Wren! We are eating outside beneath the trellis." His feet ate up the ground between us. "Feeling better?" He stopped when there was not an inch of space between us. Apparently, we'd moved past personal bubbles. I wanted to be mad about it, but being this close to him made me feel content.

I nodded. "Much better, thank you." I looked over my shoulder at Nate, who was giving us one of those neutral looks I knew so well.

With a huff, he stepped around us. "I'll meet you outside." I reached out and squeezed his fingers, and he threw me a wink.

Swoon.

Looking back at Milo, I raised an eyebrow at the amused expression on his face. "He's a protective friend," he murmured.

"Lover," I corrected, because we were going into this —whatever this was—with all our truths out on the table.

If I'd thought Milo would be upset by the idea that Nate was my lover, I was obviously mistaken. He just grinned. "Understandable."

"Milo…" I started. Fuck, how did I tell a man I was sorry for catching him up in something I didn't even understand, let alone mean? "I didn't mean to—"

He placed his finger over my lips. "I don't want your apologies, Wren. We'll figure everything out. Now, come and eat."

He leaned forward and kissed my forehead, like it was the most natural thing in the world. The way my insides melted was directly at odds with my god-given what-the-fuck-o-meter. My head and my gut were at war, but one of those had already gotten me in trouble, and it wasn't my gut. So I leaned into his lips, trusting the contentment that washed over me.

He let out a small noise of surprise, then wrapped one of those tree-branch-sized arms around my shoulders and led me outside.

The pool in the backyard was sparkling invitingly. The stone deck had a couple of loungers and umbrellas around it, as well as one of those covered ottomans, which made me want to curl up like a cat on it with a good book.

Off to the side was a trellis covered in a leafy grapevine, creating an enticing shady area. A long wooden table sat beneath it, covered with food and large jugs of what looked like fruit punch.

Tryp was leaning back in his chair, the two back legs holding his weight precariously as he grinned at me. "Little Dumpling, are you feeling better?"

Erus reached over and pushed him backwards, making him land on the ground with a thud. "You don't call a pregnant woman a dumpling, dumbass."

I reached down to grab Tryp's hand, not that I had a snowball's chance in Hell of lifting him off the ground. A little shock ran up my arms, and I laughed. "It's okay; he isn't wrong. I'm more round than I am tall at the moment."

Erus was frowning down at Tryp, who seemed impervious to his censure. "He still doesn't have to say it out loud. Tryp has always been bad at watching his tongue."

Erus wasn't wearing a shirt, and honestly, I was having a hard time not drooling. Tryp was wearing one of those tanks with gaping arm holes that showed your nipples, not really covering anything.

"You haven't ever complained about how I use my tongue before," he purred at Erus, and there was heat in his gaze as he looked up at the other man. Erus raised a single eyebrow, but there was a curl to his lips that told me he was vividly remembering exactly how Tryp used his tongue. They were looking at each other like lovers.

Oh shit... Well, I guess that made sense. They *were* lovers.

I went to step away from Tryp before Erus got the wrong idea. That was when I noticed Tryp's threads wrapping around my arms, and I jumped away with a yelp. Surely it didn't happen that easily, right? Surely it wasn't that easy to bond someone?

I shook my arm, like the golden streaks were actual ropes that might fall off, but nothing happened. If anything, they curled tighter around my arms, climbing higher and wrapping around my torso too.

"Oh, no, no, no. This can't be..." I looked frantically between Tryp and Erus, who were both watching me with wide, confused expressions. "I don't think... I'm sorry!" Teron was in front of me, reaching toward me, but I scrambled backwards. "Don't touch me!" I shouted, tripping over my feet. Only Milo's sturdy body behind me stopped me from ending up on my ass.

Teron lifted his hands. "What's wrong?"

My frantic eyes bounced past him to Demke, whose frown told me he'd already guessed. "I think I just bonded with Tryp."

CHAPTER 23
WREN

Someone gasped, but my eyes were locked on Demke. Disappointment contorted his face, and I wanted to shout that it wasn't my fault. I hadn't meant to do it.

Teron stepped into my line of sight, cutting off the staredown Demke was giving me. "What makes you think that?" He reached to place two fingers against my wrist to check my pulse, but I stepped away again.

I looked hard at the golden threads this time, really searched them out, now that I knew they weren't random, that they meant something. Tryp had thin threads floating around him, with at least one touching every single person here. But the threads that ran from him to me were like ropes in comparison to string. They banded around my body so tightly, it was a wonder they didn't strangle me like a boa, curling one over the other like a braided rope.

I looked at everyone else—except Demke—and

really took notice of where their threads led. Nate's were wrapped firmly around me, with very little of his light touching the others. They swirled over my rounded stomach, and I knew he was invested in my babies as much as me.

Milo had one thick rope, as wide as my wrist, wrapping up my arm like a serpent. Teron had a soft, small streak coming toward me, but it was thin, wispy. The same as the ones to the guys. I knew that meant he wasn't bonded to me. That was good; I didn't want to examine why it sent disappointment coursing through my veins.

I looked away from his threads, back up at his eyes. "Because his threads are wrapped so tightly around me, I can almost feel them," I muttered miserably.

Teron made a thoughtful noise, looking at Tryp like he might hold the key to it. "And Erus?"

I frowned. I hadn't touched Erus at all, as far as I could remember. But when I looked at his threads, they spiraled around Tryp and then around me. Tryp didn't have several threads—like Milo, he had only one. The other one was Erus's.

"I don't understand." I didn't understand *any* of this. Milo rubbed my back, and I realized he was holding me softly against his front. I met Nate's concerned expression and resisted the urge to ugly cry in frustration. Why couldn't life ever give me a moment to catch my breath?

"They are two halves of one soul. That means if one's fate is entwined with yours, they both are,"

Teron said matter-of-factly, but his eyes were taking me in, like he was trying to count my heartbeats without touching me. I wondered if he could actually do that.

Why wasn't I bonded to him? He'd touched me a lot. His whole head had been on my stomach at one stage. I was pretty sure I'd touched him too, but his threads were barely there.

"I still don't understand anything." Despondency rose up in my chest to replace the fear and confusion.

Milo cuddled me closer, and that warm comfort slid over my body again. The Milo effect. "We'll figure it out."

Fucking fuck. As much as I tried to resist, my eyes dragged to Erus and Tryp. They stood together, Tryp looking pale and Erus looking concerned. I let out a shaky breath. "I'm so sorry. I didn't mean to."

Erus stepped forward, and all my muscles froze. I wouldn't blame him for screaming in my face. I wouldn't blame him for throwing me out. I'd just stolen his lover and given both of them a death sentence.

I looked down at the ground, at the sandy-colored pavers, at the small ants scurrying across them, each with a tiny flicker of a golden thread that I hadn't even noticed until now. How could ants have a fate?

Soft fingers beneath my chin lifted my gaze up. I stared into the brown eyes of Erus, waiting for censure or even hatred. Instead, there was only compassion warming their depths.

"Come and eat. There's time to fret about this later."

His thumb stroked my jaw almost absently. "You couldn't have known."

"You might die."

His smile was mirthless, twisting up one side of his pretty, plump mouth. "So be it. It is long past our time." His hand moved down to my arm, and he nudged me gently toward the table. "Everything's better with food. Normally, I'd say with a little rakí, but that's not going to work, considering it's Milo's brew and therefore strong enough to put hairs on your chest. For you, we have grape juice."

He sat me down in the middle of the table beside Nate before moving over beside Tryp. Teron lifted the jug with the deep red grape juice and poured me a tall glass. It was cold, the glass condensing immediately as it hit the warm Aegean air.

Milo laughed, sitting down heavily next to me and pushing his cup toward Teron. "I might have grape juice today too."

All the guys turned to look at him, their faces various shades of disbelief. Were guys not meant to drink grape juice? Teron filled Milo's glass with the sparkling juice, and the table fell back into silence.

Until Tryp grabbed a tall, thin bottle that was sitting open on the table. "Well, I'll drink Milo's glass for him. Goddess knows I need it." He poured a couple of fingers of the clear alcohol, downed it in one gulp, then repoured another, raising it. "*Yamas!*"

The guys all lifted their glasses, and repeated it back. Nate lifted his wine, screwing up his nose.

"*Sláinte.*" He took a sip and sighed. "What I wouldn't give for a whiskey right now."

Milo tapped his glass against mine softly, looking happy, though I had no fucking idea why. "Cheers, little one." He put his glass down and started piling food onto my plate.

Teron bopped his hands with another set of tongs. "No cheese. It's unpasteurized out here. Not good for pregnant women."

Milo looked at him like he'd just suggested oxygen was detrimental to my health. "No cheese? What's she going to eat then?"

Teron just rolled his eyes. "There's more to food on this island than just cheese, Milo." He shook his head. "Try the dolmades. Demke has perfected them over the years."

Milo piled six onto my plate, which was way more than I could eat, especially when he added pita, dips, some kind of meat, grapes, cucumber salad, and more bread.

The guys chatted casually, like I hadn't just sucked two of them into the tangled web of my fate; they discussed their investment portfolio, someone from the village whose daughter had just become a doctor with help from Teron, and the sale of land on the beach to the north to human investors.

Nate had his arm around my shoulder, and I leaned into his body, soaking in his warmth like it was a balm for my frazzled nerves. Milo somehow looked lighter than he had the day before. The day I'd met him.

I had only met these men *yesterday.* Holy shit, this was insanity.

Milo picked up a grape, holding it to my lips as he chatted with Demke. Unsure what to do, I took it between my teeth and crunched, the sweet, warm juice bursting into my mouth. The grapes were amazing, and I could see bunches hanging from the vines above our heads, bees and insects darting from cluster to cluster.

"Cy is hanging around too," Milo said conspiratorially, like the presence of a stray dog meant something.

Demke raised an eyebrow. "Where?"

"At the front wall. He was there when Wren left yesterday. He's already gathering strays."

I thought about the large white dog that I'd shared my lunch with. He didn't look neglected, but surely he'd prefer a warm house and regular meals. "Does Crete have an animal rescue? Maybe they could find Cy a home. I'd take him back to the US with me, but I'll have enough to worry about, I think."

Tryp threw back his head and laughed. "That dog already has a home and a territory. He has the whole village wrapped around his finger."

"Paw?" I corrected, and Tryp laughed harder.

"Yeah, paw. Don't tell him you want to keep him, though—he'll never leave you alone."

Erus looked amused, while Milo huffed an irritated sound. I was missing something here, but I couldn't tell what. Demke just rolled his eyes. "Keep an eye on him. If it gets too out of control, I'll go and speak to him."

I looked up at Nate, who shrugged. Maybe he could

talk to animals. Far less strange than having a lion's head, probably.

Erus turned to me, his eyes soft. "You should tell us more about yourself. We know very little, except that you spoke to an Oracle and that you're pregnant. What did you do before this all started?"

I wanted to give him some warmhearted story about how wonderful my life had been to this point, but honestly, it made sense that I was somehow mixed up in a Greek tragedy.

"She's been on the earth for barely twenty years—how interesting could it be?" Demke sneered.

Milo tensed beside me and shot Demke a look that promised violence if he didn't watch his tone. It was an expression that looked a lot like indigestion.

On my other side, Nate stiffened, putting his drink back down on the table. He eyed the men around the table with barely restrained disdain. "Perhaps we should go back to the rooms so you can get some rest."

I did feel tired. Creating three people was exhausting.

I gave him a wan smile. "Okay." I looked around the table. "Thank you for lunch. It was delicious," I said to Demke, my voice polite. I ran a hand across Milo's shoulders, and he leaned into my touch.

I needed time to digest all the revelations of this morning, and I intended to do that while snuggled in the safety of Nate's arms.

CHAPTER 24
ERASTUS

As soon as Wren left, the vibe of the table changed. It didn't help that Tryp was well and truly on the way to being trashed and that Milo's eyes followed her until she disappeared into the house.

It also didn't help that something lurched in my chest, compelling me to follow her, and it took an awful lot of willpower to squash it down. Even then, the urge sat there like a weight, rippling over my skin and whispering in my brain to go to her.

The compulsion hadn't even been this bad with the Goddess. I'd wanted to be with her all the time, but out of devotion, not because the threads of fate were tugging around me like I was caught in a fisherman's net.

"Well, that was interesting," Teron said, sipping his drink.

Demke growled beneath his breath. "Interesting isn't the term I'd use, old friend."

"The girl didn't mean it." I was already jumping to her defense, though I knew in my heart that even if I wasn't now tied to her, I'd feel the same. She'd looked distraught at the idea.

Giving me a haughty look that he'd perfected so well, he took a sip of his drink. "Purposeful or not, she's pulled you deep into her web. Even now, I can tell you want to leave and go to her."

Teron was giving him a sharp look, but I couldn't deny his words. I was saved from replying by Tryp's forehead hitting the wooden table top. "I just want to fuck her."

I rolled my eyes, stroking my fingertips down his muscular back. "You wanted to fuck her before your fates were tied."

"Didn't say I didn't." He wouldn't meet my eyes, and our connection told me that he wasn't quite as dismissive of what had just transpired as he'd like to pretend.

Shaking my head, I looked back at our leader. Demke had guided us from death more times than I cared to admit over the last few Ages. "So, what do we do now?"

"Teron and I stay the hell away from her," he grumbled, but Teron merely squinted an eye at him.

"I'm not going to do that. She needs medical observation. I can't do that from six feet away."

Curling his lip in a sneer, Demke stared down his oldest friend. "I'm not going to lose you too."

The mirthless smile on Teron's face was filled with

pain. "You think I would wish to stay on this plane of existence without my closest companions, my family? I'd rather go back into the tapestry with them than suffer an even lonelier existence without them."

Demke's eyes burned, but he didn't try to dispute Teron's words.

I posed the question to Demke about what we would do, but I knew that despite the fact he was our leader, I had a new purpose now. One that had its hooks in my soul and wouldn't relent until she was safe.

Was it weird to feel relieved? To have a purpose once more? A new Goddess. I shied away from the thought. No, not a new Goddess. I'd had one of those and I didn't want another. Wren could be something new to me, perhaps something more than anything I'd had before.

I bit through a warm grape, letting the juice pool on my lip. "We should fortify. Strengthen the wards. Put out a call to the people who watch the edges of our territory, in case other Pantheons or the Fates try their hand at entering our territory once more."

We weren't going to be naive the way we were once before. We wouldn't trust their words again. Their "honor." We'd lost everything by being too trusting of their intentions. Never again.

Demke waved a dismissive hand. "Do it. I will protect you with my dying breath. This you never need to doubt." Us. Not her. I gritted my teeth, but the reasonable part of my brain fought with the yearning in my chest.

Shaking his head, Teron downed the rest of his drink. "I must go make some calls. Our literal existence hinges on the health of her and the babies. I will give them the best possible care I can." He stared down Demke as he said the words, the challenge not even veiled by his normal genial personality.

Demke stared back, and for the first time, I wondered if Teron would shirk Demke's control and fight him for leadership of our little ragtag family. Teron had never been a part of the natural order of our Pantheon. He'd sailed onto our shores in a time long ago, and stolen the heart of the Goddess. She'd absorbed him into our world, into our lives, and when the people of Crete had seen him, they'd worshiped him as a God too. He was from a long-dead race, no longer even remembered, let alone thought of.

Much like us.

Demke didn't drop his eyes, and I wondered if they really would fight. But while his gaze never moved from Teron's, his words threw up a white flag. "Of course, old friend."

Teron disappeared into the house, and then there were four. Milo looked antsy, but bright-eyed and sober for the first afternoon in decades. Even if we died, that would be worth risking it all. The alcoholism wasn't the problem; it was that he used it as a crutch to stave off the ennui.

Now there was Wren, and while that mightn't be healthy either, it was all we had.

I looked at Tryp, who seemed oblivious to the

tension in our group and was now drinking the rakí straight from the bottle. I no longer needed to worry for Milo, but apparently, Tryp was ready to take his place.

Grabbing the bottle from him, I slid it back up the table to Demke. "I think you've had enough," I murmured to my other half. My lover. The one person I would burn the world for over and over again. Wrapping an arm around his waist, I hoisted him to his feet. "Let's go sleep off what will probably be an impressive hangover, shall we?"

Tryp nodded. He didn't say anything. Didn't weigh in on the tension that was thrumming through our group. He just staggered his way into the house. He must have thrown back a bottle of rakí over lunch, because we didn't usually get that drunk that quickly. Especially not Tryp and I, who were basically forged in sacrificial wine.

We made it to our wing, and I helped him into his room. We might be partners but everyone needed their own space, and that was especially true when you had to be with the other person every day for centuries.

Tryp pulled me into his room, and I dutifully caught the clothes he was throwing off haphazardly. Placing them in the clothes hamper, I shook my head at the absolute chaos of his room. We really were two sides of the same coin; my room was clean and organized, because it made my mind calm. Tryp lived in a room that wasn't dirty, but it was chaotic. Stacks of books sat beside random instruments he'd tried and discarded. Clothes lay strewn over pieces of furniture, and I'd be surprised if any remained folded in the armoire.

But mostly, his room was filled to the brim with art supplies and half-finished paintings. Objects he thought were interesting that he might want to paint sat in crates beside portraits that he'd been unhappy with and smeared with red paint.

He was a perfectionist, and sometimes he'd fall into a depression and attempt to draw the Goddess once more, trying to recapture her face from memory. It never worked. While I could remember how she'd made me feel, I could no longer remember her face. Just the rough portrait of her etched on the mural in the room now occupied by another woman.

"Are we being unfaithful to her?"

"The Goddess?" I asked, honestly surprised. Tryp had never been a very devout follower. No, that was unfair. He'd loved the Goddess with a fire that burned so hot, I'd sometimes wondered if we would both burn out right along with her. A lot like Teron, though, his devotion had been for the deity herself, not for the pomp that eventually became her religion.

I sat down on his bed, dragging his body toward mine. "No, Tryp. I think we've been the most devout of followers, most faithful of lovers. For years, we've loved no one else." I swallowed hard. "But she's been dead and gone for over a thousand years. She no more exists now than the temples she was worshiped in. She is dust. Wren is real, here, and she needs us."

His shoulders heaved as he sucked in deep breaths. I

lifted his chin, so he was forced to look at me. "She would want us to do this; we both know it. She would want us to protect Wren, to get long overdue vengeance for our betrayal. More than that, she would probably like Wren. And until we're woven back onto the same fabric as her, we're not betraying the Goddess. We are honoring her." The words were as much for me as they were for him.

He flopped down onto his back, his fist curled in my shirt, and soon enough, I was spooned around him. "I'm sorry, Erus."

I kissed his full lips. Just a whisper of a kiss. "If I don't blame Wren, I certainly don't blame you."

He rested his forehead against my chin. "I'm sorry that I always give you less than you deserve."

An odd feeling twisted in my chest like a serpent. "Regrets are for your deathbed, Tryp. Until then, you have time to turn it all around." I kissed his smooth face, untouched by time. "But you don't have to apologize to me, my love. Never to me."

He was already snoring lightly, and I smiled against his skin.

CHAPTER 25
WREN

I'd heard horror stories about how sick women got when they were expecting multiples, and I wasn't sure if it was the supernatural aspect of this pregnancy, or if life had just decided not to kick me in the crotch for once, but I'd been relatively free of morning sickness in the second trimester.

Golden threads, however? I had those in abundance.

Exhaustion so intense that I sometimes didn't think I'd ever get back out of bed? Also yes.

But spending hours hugging the toilet bowl? Thankfully not.

So I knew the swirling feeling in my gut wasn't morning sickness. Instead, it was guilt making me want to puke.

It had also made me hide in my wing of the compound through the rest of yesterday, feigning exhaustion once again. Nate had stayed with me, and when Milo had dropped off dinner for the two of us last night, he'd hung around a bit, soothing that prickling feeling in my chest a little.

He'd talked to Nate about figures from myth like they were real people. Alexander the Great. How hot Helen of Troy had been. The resurgence of the Norse Pantheon just because of some superhero movies. It was freaking bizarre.

When my eyelids had gotten heavy, Nate had tucked me into bed, then stepped aside when Milo came over and kissed the top of my head, a gesture that could have been construed as caring or as something more, depending on how much you chose to overthink it.

And I chose to overthink it a lot. For most of the night.

I'd eventually cycled from Milo to Tryp and then Erus, then around to Demke. I couldn't get past the flash of absolute devastation that had quickly morphed to anger on his face when I'd blurted out that I'd bonded Tryp.

I deserved Demke's ire. They had been living happily out here, and I came stumbling in through their gates like a madwoman, stealing the lives of his best friends. I would legit be furious in his position. In fact, I would have booted myself out hours ago.

Which meant in the cold light of day, I was restless, hungry, and guilty as fuck. It was causing insane indigestion. Or maybe it was just the heel of one of the babies pressed straight into my guts causing that sensation.

Nate grabbed me around the waist, halting my pacing —which was actually more like the furious waddling of an outraged penguin—and dragged me down into his lap. "Relax, Wren. You didn't mean to bond them, and if they have a problem with it… well, I still have my ax, and we'll see how immortal they really are."

How he knew what I was worried about already was kind of disconcerting. I mean, it was pretty obvious to me, but really, I had a thousand things to be worried about. They ranged from The Fate Of The World Was In My Womb, right down to God-Monsters Wanted To Eat Me. So I mean, it was pretty eerie he just happened to know my stupid brain had decided to fixate on the fact that I'd bonded my life unintentionally with two more Demigod beings. Now if I died, they would too.

I frowned at Nate. "What if my life is tied to theirs now too? What if they trip down the stairs, or choke on an olive, and I die?"

Fuck, how hadn't I thought of that before? I should have asked more questions.

His jaw went tight. Guess neither of us had really thought about that. "I don't think it would work that way. You're the anchor." I didn't like the uncertainty in his voice. Maybe that meant that if I went to Hell, they were all coming with me. Not particularly reassuring right now.

There was a soft knock on the door, and I was a little

surprised to see Teron. "I thought you'd be avoiding me like the plague."

He gave me a tight smile. "You and Demke seem to hold similar beliefs, but I'll tell you what I told him: I would never give you substandard care, just to protect myself. I've lived thousands of years. I've forgotten more lifetimes than I remember. If helping you brings that endless cycle to a stop, then I won't be mad about it. I will go with a smile, knowing that my life ended the way it began, by contributing something to humanity."

I stared at Teron. He was so freaking beautiful. Full lips. Bronze skin. Golden eyes that burned into mine. He was so obviously otherworldly. But more than being beautiful, he was kind, and that was hell on my emotional walls.

Swallowing hard, I inhaled a shaky breath. "That's stupid, but thank you."

He snorted out a laugh. "Yes, on that, you and Demke agree again." He lifted something in his hand. It was an honest-to-god doctor's bag, which made me smile. All he was missing was a white lab coat. Actually, I was pretty sure I'd seen a porno that started just like this. "I thought I'd just take your vitals, just so I have a baseline for my records."

Shrugging, I went and sat on the bed. "Sure."

Nate watched Teron with a bored expression, but his eyes tracked him like a predator. He mightn't be standing over him with an ax this time, but he wasn't dropping his guard either. Teron acknowledged him with a tilt of his chin, and having the two of them in a room raised the atmospheric temperature by several degrees.

Warm, soft fingers gripped my wrist as Teron counted my heartbeats. "I thought you might both have questions about the whole Fates thing. I'm not an expert, but I can give you the basics, along with my educated guesses. This isn't really a topic where there are many experts." He paused. "Well, there *are* experts, but they aren't people you'd want to track down and ask questions, if you know what I mean."

"Because they're the ones trying to kill me with monster snake women?"

He winced, but nodded. "Exactly." He pulled out a blood pressure cuff, wrapping it around my upper arm. We both watched the numbers rise and fall, but his face was almost professionally neutral. "A little high, but that's to be expected. Nothing that I'm too stressed about yet." He pulled out a stethoscope and placed it on my back. "So, questions?"

I looked at Nate, who was leaning forward in his chair. Despite his words about me being an anchor, I just needed to be sure. If not for me, then for the babies. "If one of the guys chokes on a grape and passes away, would that mean I'd die too?"

Teron chuckled. "We're eternal, Wren. I can't even count how many grapes we've choked on in the many lifetimes between us. We're hardier than that. Someone would have to behead us with great purpose to kill us in that manner, and we are more than capable of fending off most attacks." I didn't miss the quick slide of his eyes to Nate. "And even if that weren't true, I don't believe that the death of any of your bonds would result in you dying too. The thread would just snap between you; you're held too tightly to the mortal plane. It would be unbelievably painful, however. Like the feeling that drove you into Milo's bed, times a thousand. You may wish for death."

Well, that was basically what Nate had said, but fuck, Teron wasn't sugar-coating it for me. Like a phantom limb, I could feel the ache of an imaginary loss in my chest.

I chewed my lip as Teron hovered close to my face, checking my temperature. "And I really have no choice in who I bond with?"

Teron's hands stilled, his eyes dropping to mine briefly. "Yes and no. Fate won't bond you to someone you won't need. But you can choose as well, I believe—the way you chose the God of War over there. Or maybe he was chosen for you." He shook his head. "You can never really know. Whether you fall in love with someone because your heart desires them, or because a higher being decided you needed them, is a mystery you may never know the answer to.

"However, you have a choice, because there is *always* a choice. If you want to break the bonds, there would be a way. I just don't know what that way is right now…" He trailed off, as if it pained him that there was knowledge he hadn't obtained yet. "But I can research it if you'd like."

Did I want to break my bonds to Erus and Tryp? To

Milo? I looked past Teron to Nate. Did I want to set him free? Every part of my soul rebelled at the thought. Selfishly, I couldn't let him go now; I was way too attached. But the others? I barely knew them. Surely if I could break the ties between us, without hurting either of us, I should. Right?

My heart gave an irregular thump, and my gut churned. I hated the idea. How could I hate the idea already, when I barely knew them?

I was shaking my head before I even came to a conscious decision. "There are more important issues at hand." Well, that sounded like a douche thing to say. "Unless the others want to find a way to sever the bond. I, uh, am not opposed to keeping the threads, if they don't feel trapped."

I didn't know you could verbally dig yourself into a hole this deep, but here I was, halfway to Australia with my words.

Teron pulled back. "You have Milo forever now. I wouldn't even bother asking. He hasn't been this happy in"—he shrugged, like he couldn't remember the last time Milo was happy—"maybe ever."

How could that even be possible? He was thousands of years old, if their stories were to be believed.

"And Tryp and Erus?"

Teron's lips curled in amusement. "You'll have to ask them, but I think you'll find that they'll be more in line with Milo's thinking then Demke's." He straightened back to his full height. "Everything looks good. The ultrasound machine should arrive later today. I managed to find someone to put it on a supply boat this morning, and one of the townspeople will collect it this afternoon. I'll feel more confident once I can see what the fetuses are doing. I'm limited with the equipment I have right now."

I couldn't believe I was even considering having my babies on an island in the middle of the fucking ocean, to be delivered by a guy whose head shifted into an eagle's if he didn't concentrate hard enough.

In all honesty, sometimes I wasn't convinced this wasn't some grand coma delusion. It would be far more logical than my life now. But there was something reassuring about Teron, about how he made me feel. If I'd come across the ocean on a gut feeling, clearly I was going to have to commit to trusting it for everything, and my gut said that Teron wanted what was best for me and the babies. I didn't understand it; however, that didn't mean I wasn't grateful.

"Thank you."

He gave me an indecipherable look, and I could see the golden threads of his life force straining toward me. I leaned further back, dodging them like they were snakes and not lassos of commitment.

At this point, I'd probably prefer snakes.

Not that I didn't want Teron. Hell, my vagina had gone rogue and wanted them all. Right now. Together. Separately. Propped upside down like a reverse wheelbarrow. She wasn't fussy; she just *wanted*.

No, it was my pesky brain that ensured Teron's threads didn't wrap around my arms or throat, because

I wasn't ready. Did I think it was just a matter of time? Absolutely. Someday, I might drop my guard and add the handsome doctor to my merry band of unintentional—and probably unwilling—bondmates.

Until then, I'd give him a chance to survive this bullshit.

CHAPTER 26
TERON

The library had always been the place I was most at peace. Surrounded by those soft leather spines and the scent of yellowing paper, well, there was hardly a place on earth more soothing than a library. I'd once seen the Library of Alexandria—I'd sat in it as a temple of learning in amazement, feeling like I'd come home.

I'd mourned its loss for centuries. In fact, even thinking about the knowledge lost over the squabbles of men made me inordinately pissed off. They'd really put themselves back a few centuries in learning, and for me, that was unforgivable. But I'd given up caring about the foibles of men a long time ago. Politics hadn't been my problem in centuries, and I wasn't in a hurry to change that, despite our current predicament.

The answers I was searching for were probably in the ashes of that building. That was the real frustrating part about the world following the burning of Alexandria.

We'd done our best to store invaluable tomes from around the Mediterranean here in Crete, especially after the monolithics came into power. We were a pagan religion, after all, and everyone knew that to rise to power, you had to obliterate the identity of the people you were conquering. We protected what we could, and I tried to remember what I couldn't. Sometimes I wrote it down in the old language, just in case anything happened to us, but humanity would need someone to decipher that too.

For the first time in an age, the library here didn't give me peace. It wasn't giving me the answers I needed to reassure Wren, and I found that more frustrating than I wanted to admit. I wanted to tell her that it would all be okay, give her a step-by-step account of events to expect.

But no such checklist existed.

I thought about the small, waifish thing that seemed to be shrinking under the size of her stomach every day. She'd been here for four days now, and we all hedged around each other like wild animals sussing out new predators in the territory. Except Milo. He'd thrown himself into caring for Wren like it was his only purpose in life.

Once, caring for a Goddess *had* been his only purpose. All our purposes. I shook my head at those old thoughts resurfacing. Wren wasn't a Goddess. She was just a woman who'd gotten caught up in something she shouldn't have. Her only fault was being too nice.

The ultrasound machine had been caught up at the sea port, due to an industrial strike, so it had been delayed arriving, but should be here any moment now. I'd spent all my time reading obstetric texts and journals about the dangers and monitoring of multiple births. By the time they were ready to be delivered, I would ensure that I knew everything there was to know about any eventuality.

She would still need to go down to the hospital in Heraklion, and I hated that idea already. But I would be with her, and if anything happened, I wouldn't hesitate to flex my powers and take over.

I nodded at the plan I was forming, closing the book in front of me and standing to flex my shoulders. I wanted to fly, stretch my wings, maybe do a lap around the islands to assure the Gryphon inside me that our territory was well defended.

He'd been restless since they'd arrived, and I didn't fool myself by pretending I didn't know what that sensation in my chest meant. I just wasn't ready to admit what it could be. Not now, when the future was more clouded than it ever had been before.

Unlike my brothers, who *were* their animals—their human forms merely glamors of themselves—I was dual-natured. I shared my soul with the Gryphon, and we shared the body we both possessed. He was wise and surprisingly good-natured, so he was happy to let the man walk around primarily. Even he knew the time of flying the skies freely as a Gryphon had long passed. He didn't like it, but as I said, he was wise.

When we'd left the deserts of our homeland and come to Crete, the world had already been changing. Our territory had once ranged from Persia to Egypt, but the Gryphons had been all but eradicated. The people we'd had, the riders we'd carried, were all gone too. The magic we'd possessed had gone back to the earth; all that was left was two forms and no purpose.

Alone, my Gryphon and I had flown across the Aegean, and I'd become enamored with the Goddess, who believed in life and death and renewal. I'd fallen in love with her so completely that her death had almost killed me too. If I hadn't had the Gryphon, I may have just faded away with her.

But while the Gryphon had loved the Goddess, thought of her as part of his flight, he hadn't loved her with his whole soul.

Which made his feelings since Wren's arrival more concerning. He'd been pushing at the edges of my control, anxious to be out. He was grouchy and discontented, but he'd given me too much control over the centuries, so I was able to hold him back. His emotions, which I'd always been able to read like my own, were wild and anxious.

In short, I didn't know if she was his mate or if he wanted to murder her. And that was terrifying. But I couldn't keep him locked away forever either.

A knock at the wall door reverberated through the whole compound. It was part of the ward, but if the person who knocked had bad intentions, it would zap them halfway back to the ocean. I assumed it was the townsperson who was delivering the ultrasound machine, so I made my way down from my wing toward the front room. Usually Erus or Tryp answered the door. They were the least... *other* of us all. So if it was just a tourist with seriously broken instincts, they'd send them on their way easily enough.

When I walked into the front room, Milo was hefting a giant crate heavily wrapped in plastic through the doorway, like it weighed nothing. "Where do you want it?"

I looked around the formal living room. This would do as a temporary med room for now. We never used it; it wasn't as if we held lavish parties or ever entertained at all. I'd bring in one of the chaise lounges that sat in storage, and that would be enough.

"Here is fine. Thank you, Milo."

He set it carefully down, eyeing the crate. "Do you, uh, need help setting it up?"

Goddess, no. Milo was not the most gentle creature when it came to things that needed finesse. He'd built the wall outside with his bare hands. He could bench press a car with ease. He could fight like no man I'd ever met before. But he could not gently piece together medical equipment.

"It should be fine, brother. Could you tell Wren that the equipment has arrived and should be ready in about an hour?"

Milo grinned at the idea of seeing Wren, nodding and all but skipping away. His happiness was something I hadn't thought I'd ever see again, and even if I didn't think she was the Gryphon's mate, I would protect her with my life just for that.

It took me a little longer than I thought to set up and calibrate the machine, and I ran through the instructional videos a couple of times. However, by the time Wren knocked on the doorjamb, it was all set up and ready to go.

Was it odd to be nervous?

My Gryphon huffed inside my head, and I hushed him. "Wren, come in." I waved her over to the long piece of furniture I was using as a bed. It wasn't really a convenient height, but it would do. "I just finished setting it up."

Unsurprisingly, two steps behind her was the God of War. The Gryphon grumbled at his presence, but seemed to take it in his stride. Again, that confused me. If the Gryphon thought Wren was his mate, he wouldn't take the connection of Néit so easily. He could be a possessive fucker.

I wasn't particularly surprised that Milo, Tryp and Erus followed. They'd been creeping around each other, but there was no doubt the bond was getting stronger. She'd described it like a pull, and apparently, with the bonds being so new, the pull meant they had to be at her side all the time.

She was probably going to lose her mind if she didn't get some space. No matter how bonded, everyone needed alone time to reset.

Again, the Gryphon grumbled, but didn't protest. I

grinned past Wren at my brothers. "I see we have an audience today."

Wren rolled her eyes, though she didn't seem overly put out. "I can't blame them. Their entire futures hinge on these three."

I frowned at her words. "That doesn't give them any rights over you. If you want them out, I'll make them leave." The Gryphon's growl rumbled up my throat before I could swallow it down.

She sat down in front of me with a heavy sigh, rolling her shoulders. "It's fine. I don't mind them being here."

As if to fly directly in the face of her words, Demke appeared. Their eyes clashed, and I waited for her to protest, to ask him to leave, or send me an imploring look or something.

Instead, she just tore her eyes from him and smiled tightly at me. "Let's get started." She laid down and pulled up her oversized shirt—which I was fairly sure belonged to Milo—and the rounded expanse of her stomach became center stage.

I squirted some of the cool gel on her stomach, then a little more on the wand. I was happy with the quality of the ultrasound; it was top-of-the-range technology, and I was long past justifying how I spent my money. Besides, once Wren gave birth, I could anonymously donate it to the hospital in Heraklion.

"There isn't a hospital on the mainland missing this piece of equipment, is there?" she asked, her eyes focused on the screen as I got my bearings.

Shaking my head, it didn't take me long to find the first baby. "No, this is brand new. I was just thinking we could donate it once it's no longer needed." Taking a still image, I checked the measurements. "Okay, baby number one." I really wished I could have her files from her normal doctor, but I had no medical standing to request them. Maybe I'd get Wren to request them, and hopefully they could email them over as soon as possible, both so I can adequately judge Wren's care, and because I was insanely curious.

"Wow," she breathed as the image rendered. A 3D recreation of the baby's face appeared on the screen, and while he looked a little like the clay monsters which appeared out of the Persian desert four thousand years ago, I knew he was perfectly formed.

The more concerning part of that statement was the *he*.

"Do you want to know the sex?" I choked out, trying not to spoil one more thing for Wren, when really I wanted to ask Demke what he thought the baby's gender meant for our theory about the Fates.

The Fates had *never* been male. They were always a trio of females. Had we been wrong about this whole thing?

"Uh, I think so. I've had enough surprises this pregnancy."

Milo laughed, but his eyes were locked on her face, not on the screen at all. I looked between Demke and Néit, because they'd understand what I was trying to tell them with my next words. "You're having a boy."

Milo's eyes snapped to the screen, so maybe he knew what I was trying to say too. "What?"

Wren's face folded into a confused frown. "Why do you all look so freaked out?"

Néit squatted down beside her easily, which was quite a feat, because the guy was huge. "It's nothing bad. Just historically, the Fates have always been girls. Women. That means either Teron is wrong reading the ultrasound, Demke is wrong about the threads of fate, or the Great Weaver has decided to mix things up."

I raised a brow at him. "I'm not misreading the ultrasound." I managed to keep the snippiness out of my voice... mostly. I looked around for the next baby, finding him easily. Yep, another him. "Another boy. But he looks healthy and strong." From what Wren had told me about how far along she was, and what her OB-GYN had said, they looked like they were growing well.

I searched around for the third baby, who was a little more hidden, but I found him eventually. Still perfect in every way. Still another boy.

Three boys. What did that even mean?

Meeting Demke's eyes, I found him as equally at a loss as I was.

Had we been completely wrong this entire time? And if we were operating under the wrong conclusion, what did the Greek Mythics want with Wren?

CHAPTER 27
WREN

I had a lot in common with a yacht that had run aground as I laid out beside the pool the following day. Regardless, I felt more carefree than I had in months. Something in me had relaxed once I could see the babies, their unique little faces, and know they were okay.

I wasn't sure why them being boys had freaked everyone out so much, but if Demke was wrong and they weren't the future Fates, then I was ecstatic. Hell, I'd be thrilled if they were just ordinary kids, mortal with no divine calling. Not Demigods, or Oracles, or any other mystical thing. That this had all been a giant misunderstanding. I would even take the huge blank spot about their parentage and go back to just assuming it was some random hookup in a gross club bathroom.

I was clutching at straws, but until I had confirmation, I was going to live in hope that they would have normal lives, where the most aggravating thing that would ever happen to them was people repeatedly saying, "Oh, gosh, you're triplets!" for the rest of their lives. And where no one tried to kill them with Greek monsters.

I mean, there was one surefire way of finding out, but I wasn't going to fuck a guy who hated me just to get a little peace of mind. Not yet, anyway.

My pale skin tended to burn pretty easily, so I rotated on the sunbed like a rotisserie chicken, trying not to cook one side too much.

"Have you been in yet?"

I looked up at Milo, who was standing so his handsome face was silhouetted by the sun. My heart thudded in my chest as I looked at him, a completely ridiculous response.

I shook my head. "I was worried I wouldn't be able to haul myself back out again." And that I'd sink like a rock to the bottom with all this extra weight. It was an old-school pool that was essentially just a hole in the ground, equally deep all the way around, with small ladders on all four sides to climb out.

Except I had this fear that I wouldn't be able to heft my stomach all the way back up the ladder and I'd be stuck in there forever.

Milo threw back his head and laughed, the mid-morning light making his sun-kissed hair glow like a halo. "I'll come in with you, if you like. You look overheated."

I hesitated, but only briefly. The water did look amazing, and I could almost viscerally imagine what it would be like to float weightlessly. It was too tempting to ignore, much like the man in front of me.

Seeing me strain to sit up in a poor imitation of a crunch, Milo took pity on me and helped me to my feet. Walking backwards, he balanced precariously on the edge before letting himself fall backwards into the deep blue water, the splash coming out like a wave. It splashed right up to my thighs, and I let out a girlish squeal that I hadn't even known I possessed as I danced away.

Popping back up out of the water, he looked like a merman, and my breath caught in my throat. God, he was so fucking beautiful.

"The water is perfect," he laughed, and I gave him the stink-eye for soaking me. I was in a tiny bikini that hadn't always been tiny. My boobs were huge. Like, freaking massive. I'd only ever dreamed of tits like this, and if I could run, I'd be a little worried that they'd fly right out of this top and I'd flash the entire household.

Milo swam over to the edge of the pool, looking up at me like temptation personified. "Come in, Little Bird. I'll catch you if you jump."

There was no way I was jumping in the water—I'd end up drowning us both. Instead, I sat on the edge and then gently fell forwards, turning onto my back immediately.

The bliss... It was something else. My body felt weightless for the first time in so long, and I couldn't hold back a contented sigh. I'd always been a little ass-heavy, and the extra weight in my torso wanted to drag me down, but Milo was there, his hand resting softly beneath my spine, even though the salt water was keeping me buoyant.

"This feels so good," I moaned, and he slowly moved us toward one of the built-in seats along the side. He boosted himself up onto the seat, then just sat there, his long arm holding me up, letting me float. He didn't talk, didn't try to draw me closer or push me away. He just let me be, and after ten minutes, my body completely relaxed. Muscles I hadn't even realized were tense finally let go.

The sun beat down on my face, and I didn't worry about how I was probably burning to a crisp in the sun, or if my tits were succumbing to gravity and giving me epic boob spillage out the side of my bikini top. I thought of nothing but the relaxed feeling in my limbs and the warmth on my skin. The babies moved and shifted around, obviously enjoying me being relaxed too.

"We'll have to fence this area off soon," Milo said softly, more to himself than me I think. "We don't want any accidents." It took me a while to realize that he was talking about putting up a pool fence.

I hadn't thought about what it would mean after the babies were born. Would I be stuck here on Crete? What about Nate? He'd want to go home, right? His life was in Boston. His career. Mrs. B's house. His friends. My friends. All on the other side of the ocean.

I couldn't stay here, but the thought of leaving was like a knife through the heart.

I felt betrayed once more by my fate. Everything was so out of control. Tears welled in my eyes, and I internally bitched about pregnancy hormones, even though I sneakily suspected that perhaps it had nothing to do with hormones and everything to do with the fact that I'd been dealt a really shitty hand.

Milo wrapped his hands around my waist and pulled me closer to his body. "Hey, what's wrong? We don't have to do it now or at all, if that's not what you want. It seems a little dangerous, but you're their mom —you know best, right?"

I knew jack shit.

Turning my head into his shoulder, I sucked in a few deep, calming breaths. "No, you're right. If there are toddlers around, we should fence it off. I just hadn't thought about the fact that some of us will have to uproot our lives, and none of us even asked for this to happen."

Milo pulled me onto his lap, his hands wrapping around me so I was plastered to his front. It was so nice, it was beginning to become an addiction.

"No one asked for this, but I think maybe I was silently praying for it." I looked over my shoulder at him like he was crazy. "Not this exactly, of course, but something. I needed a purpose. Someone to adore. Something other than the endless days and hours, waiting to fade to nothingness." He pushed the hair out of my face. "It was what we were all doing, and you need to put the idea that you've somehow doomed us from your mind. We were already doomed—you just gave us something to fight to live for."

His golden threads whipped around like arcing electricity, and I couldn't help but lean forward to brush my lips over his. They were warm and smooth, and as he deepened the kiss, I sighed into him.

His fingers flexed on my sides, and he shifted me so my thighs were either side of his hips. He didn't pull me any closer, didn't grind up into me, even though the extremely hard evidence of his arousal was sitting right there against my stomach. He was leaving the pace up to me, and if I didn't already adore this man, that would have cemented it for me.

He tasted every part of my mouth, like he was obsessed with how I tasted. His hands began to roam, and when I didn't protest, he groaned and undertook his exploration with a singular focus. Up and down my spine, around my ribs, over the curve of my hips, like he was mapping me completely.

I pressed myself tighter around him and ground down on that giant rod he called a cock. We both gasped in unison, because *holy shit*. The other thing they didn't tell you about being pregnant was that everything felt *more*.

Milo's hands fell back to my hips. Now I'd made the first move, he was happy to help me grind on him. But I wanted more. So much more.

Reaching between us, I slipped my hand beneath the waistband of his shorts and grabbed his cock. Seriously,

I could barely get my hand around it. His head fell back against the tiles of the deck, and he moaned.

"Wren, I can't... Your hand feels so good fisted around me like that." He grunted as I stroked him a couple of times, up over the fat head and back down again until he was panting. "I want you to tell me what you want, how to please you. My cock is yours. My mouth, my tongue, my fingers—they're all yours. Use me."

Holy shit.

"Undo the strings on my bikini," I ordered between kisses, and he was eager to comply, undoing the bows on my hips without looking. My bikini bottoms floated away, and then there was just my naked bottom half and his shorts pushed down to his thighs in the water. "Slow and easy," I breathed, and I pushed his cock still in my hand toward my entrance.

His jaw was so tight, I thought it might shatter, but he definitely did it both slow and easy, each agonizing inch down his cock taking an eternity. I felt so full as I stretched around him. It felt nearly impossible, but I wasn't going to stop, because it felt so fucking *right*.

"Milo," I whispered, panting now as he thrust up the final few inches and was fully seated inside me. It was more than a physical fullness, though. I could feel him deep in my very soul right now.

He moved me up and down his cock in short, sharp movements, until my walls relaxed around him, and then he dragged me back up his cock. Honestly, it was a wonder there wasn't a rest stop halfway up. It was that big.

Then, I shit you not, he held me up and fucked me with just the first couple of inches of his cock, hitting my g-spot like he was playing *Where's Waldo?* and could find that son of a bitch first time on every page. It was like magic.

Screamingly good magic.

"Milo!" I came around him, and he grunted as he held me still. The soft breeze made my nipples pull tight in the afternoon sun. Normally, I would be worried about who would see, but how could I care when my brain was flying so high, it was like I was on drugs?

"I want to fill you up, but if I come in the pool, the guys will murder me. And if they murder me, I won't be able to make you scream my name again and again." Taking a few deep breaths, he lifted me off his cock, and I mewled pitifully. He spun me so I was facing away from him, my back to his chest so he could kiss across my shoulders and spine. I wiggled my ass against his hard cock, and he groaned. "Ah, fuck it. Worth it."

Notching himself back against my entrance, he thrust up inside me once more, and I gasped, the oxygen leaving my lungs. The noise he made wasn't even close to human.

Slow and gentle, he fucked me with a precision that was honestly impressive. "Wren… Little Bird… You feel so good. I don't ever want to stop." I didn't want him to stop either, as he kissed and licked the salty water from my skin. "Come for me one more time. I want you to milk me dry."

He reached around and flicked my clit, making me moan and shake as I came once more. If we had neighbors, they'd have been scandalized. Worry wanted to sneak into my brain, but I pushed it away, especially as Milo's big hands came up to clutch at my breasts, massaging them as his thrusts got wild. Still gentle, slow and easy like I'd asked, but his strokes were becoming a little less rhythmic and his thrusts slightly more wild.

He was losing control, and I loved it.

"Wren!" One arm wrapped around my ribs while the other hand landed on my hip, pressing me tight against his chest as he came in hot ropes inside me.

Panting in my ear, he whispered soft words in a language that I didn't understand. He nuzzled his face into my neck and breathed, and I didn't need to know the language to understand the feeling behind the words. He was thanking me. Promising me something with so much fervor, it made my chest ache with joy.

And then I thought about Nate, and my happiness plunged into ice. What had I done? I'd just cheated on the one man who'd stood by me without any promise of anything at all.

I pushed down the panic that was trying to rise up inside me. "Milo?"

"Yes, Little Bird?"

"I need to go to the bathroom."

Standing, this gentle giant of a man helped me

uncurl, jumping out of the pool and grabbing me a towel before lifting me out gently. He wrapped it around me, using the corner to wipe some of his release from my thighs. "Sorry. I made a bit of a mess."

I let out a choked laugh and tried not to burst into tears. Turning, I raced back toward my suite, desperately hoping I didn't run into anyone. Not Teron, or the guys, or Demke.

Most of all, I hoped I didn't run into Nate, because how was I meant to look him in the eye after this?

CHAPTER 28
NÉIT

Wren hadn't been able to look me in the eye for most of yesterday afternoon, going to bed early and staying there. I had my suspicions that it wasn't heat distress causing her to hide away in her room, but a different kind of distress. I knew what she looked like when she was freshly fucked, and I'd seen her down in the pool with Milo, floating in the water. It didn't take an Oracle to know that they'd progressed their relationship.

It should make me jealous, I knew, but honestly, I felt content that there was someone else who could ease her burdens.

I had to go and tell her all this, of course, but first I wanted to call home. I hadn't heard from Clio in a week, which was kind of strange. Normally, she sent me three memes a day, as if I was someone who could give a damn about memes. Most of the time, I didn't get the pop culture references anyway. Like the one with the pink frosted donut, surrounded by chocolate donuts? What the hell did that even *mean?*

Lifting my cell to my ear, I gently shut the door to my suite that butted onto Wren's. It was early, so I didn't want to wake her up just yet. The phone rang and rang, and I was beginning to worry, until the call connected to what sounded like a club.

"NÉIT!" Clio yelled, forcing me to move the phone away from my ear. "I WAS BEGINNING TO THINK YOU'D FORGOTTEN ME. ONE SECOND, I'LL MOVE SOMEWHERE QUIETER!"

There was a shuffling noise, and the sound of laughter and shouting drunk people. After some quick mental math, I realized it was about midnight in Boston.

Finally, the sound of blaring house music was replaced by the steady thrum of traffic and Clio's voice once more. "You still there?"

"Yeah."

"What can I do for you? Because I have a hot little thing who looks like Selma Hayek on the dance floor, and I was about to help her recreate the snake dance from *From Dusk Till Dawn.* She was going to be Selma, and I was going to be the snake," she teased, but I knew she was fucking with me, because who the fuck was Selma Hayek?

"I don't know what that means," I huffed. I also didn't want to tell her that I was worried about her. We had a dynamic, and I wasn't about to upset it after a couple of thousand years.

She laughed down the line. "Did you call because you missed me?"

I rolled my eyes. "Of course not. I wanted to know if you had any further news?"

She sighed heavily, and there was a level of gravitas to the sound that made my spine tingle. "It's turmoil here, Néit. I don't know who the fuck your girlfriend is, but there are monsters turning up in the city in droves, and everyone seems really pissed. Territory disputes have turned violent, and the wards around your house are working overtime." She lowered her voice. "It's not just that. Gods and Goddesses I thought faded into the abyss have turned up looking for your girl. Old Gods, Néit. Older than us. The legends of our legends."

The actual hell is going on right now? "Any word as to why she's so important?"

Clio let out a growl. "No, but word on the street is that Atropos threw an epic Greek hissy fit and killed off a bunch of humans in a power plant explosion. The Fates said it was the will of the threads, but the underground is humming with discontent."

Well, at least that confirmed that Demke and the guys were partially right. If Atropos, the oldest and deadliest—literally—of the Moirai was angry, it could be because they knew we were here, in the relative safety of Crete.

Or it could have nothing to do with Wren, and they were just throwing a tantrum, which they liked to do occasionally. No one was more dramatic than the Greeks; they'd literally coined the word.

I was silent too long, and Clio—who was always too astute, hence why she was the mouthpiece of our Pantheon—picked up on my unease. "Do you know something?" There was none of the laughing Demigod in her tone now. She was all politics.

"I might."

"Do you and Wren Mahone need help?"

It burned me that the answer was yes. It tore at my pride that despite who I was, I couldn't protect her by myself. "Yes."

The silence on the other end of the line told me that Clio was just as shocked. It wasn't often she was rendered speechless. "Now? Are you in immediate danger? Do I need to come over there?"

Fuck, what a question that was. I was so out of my depth right now, I wasn't convinced I'd see danger before it was burying a sword in my gut. "I don't think so. Besides, the Minoans aren't ready for you." I didn't think anyone was ready to come face to face with the wild battle maiden that was Cliona. "You're more valuable where you are, Clio. We're okay for now."

She made a rude noise in the back of her throat, and I'd known her long enough that I could imagine her face as she did it. "I'm still going to make some calls. Get some people on standby." She was well connected, but the idea of her calling anyone I could think of off the top of my head made anger light up my veins.

"No one from the old country, Cliona." They would kill Wren without thought for the machinations of the

Fates; they'd do it to punish me for things that had happened before human memory.

"*Obviously*, Néit. I'm not an idiot. You call me if you need me, okay?" When I didn't say anything, she huffed. "Say it, you big, dumb, stubborn-ass baby!"

I couldn't help the chuckle that rolled past my lips. "I'll call if I need help."

"Good. Give my love to Wren. She's too good for you."

Even if I wanted to dispute that, she'd already hung up. I turned over what she'd said in my mind. Why would the ancients be crawling out of hiding now? Whatever the reason, it meant that things were even more dangerous for Wren, and it probably meant we were right about reaching the tail. There would always be a large group of Mythics who were reaching their final turn, falling fast into obscurity. Maybe we wouldn't be re-weaved in the next age of men. Me included.

Sighing, I looked out the window at the Minoans down in the courtyard. I still didn't know how I felt about any of this, whether I should trust them or if they were the enemy, but I was outnumbered and outgunned. Wren trusted them, and more than that, their lives were now tied to hers, so I had to give them the benefit of the doubt. Milo was a nice guy, and Teron seemed to care about Wren and the babies' health, but the rest I knew far too little about to be complacent.

Wren was still hiding out in our rooms, and I

decided enough was enough. Knocking on the door frame, I strode in. "Are you feeling unwell, *mo stóirín?*"

She huffed something under her breath. I wasn't sure what it was, but I couldn't hear shite through the blankets. Lifting the heavy quilt, I slid into the bed beside her. "Wren? What's wrong?"

Her eyes were big and glassy as she looked at me, her nose pink like she'd been crying. "I slept with Milo."

My jaw flexed at the idea of sharing my Wren with a bunch of strangers, but the poor woman already looked guilty enough. I could ease this burden. "Did he hurt you?" Her head whipped back and forth so fast, it was a wonder she didn't injure herself. "Was he really bad? I mean, I thought what he lacked in finesse, he'd make up for in size," I teased.

She frowned. "You aren't mad?"

I pulled her body into mine. She was soft and warm, and I wanted to hide us beneath these covers forever. "He is tied to your soul, *mo stóirín.* It seemed almost inevitable that you would eventually have sex. I understand the draw he must feel to you almost viscerally." I kissed her cheeks, her puffy eyelids. "If he feels half of what I feel for you, then there must be an ache deep in his chest when he can't hold you in his arms."

She let out a shaky sob, and I stroked her back, just letting her shudder and sigh against my chest, keeping her close and safe. She gripped my back tightly. "I thought you'd be mad. I felt so… disloyal afterwards.

Like you'd asked me for so little, and I couldn't even give you monogamy."

I kissed the words from her lips. "You've had so little happiness, I would never begrudge you this. I can share." Only a small lie. I *could* share; that didn't mean I ever had. But for Wren, I would try. "I talked to Clio. She said that big things are happening back home. I'm glad your gut told us to come to Amourgeles. Even if it means that you're not just my Wren anymore, at least you four are safe, healthy and finding small amounts of joy where you can."

She kissed me softly again. "I don't know if it was fate that tied you to me, or if we would've ended up here either way, Nate, but I'd choose you every single day."

"In a thousand years, there has been no other quite like you, Wren Mahone. I choose you as well." And I'd choose her for a million more.

CHAPTER 29
WREN

Growing some lady balls, I dragged myself out of my bed and went to face the rest of the house's occupants. As I walked out onto the deck, Milo looked up at me with big, sad puppy-dog eyes. I guess I'd hurt his feelings by taking off like a scalded cat yesterday, and that made me feel even more terrible.

Pushing down my guilt, I tried to come up with something to say to him that was better than *you dicked me so good, I had an existential crisis.*

I could feel the heat of Nate's body at my back, and I looked over my shoulder at him. He just lifted his chin, making something inside me relax. I strolled over to Milo and sat on his lap, kissing him soundly on the cheek. I could feel the weight of the stares from Erus and Tryp, from where they sat over on the other side of the pool.

"I'm sorry. I didn't mean—" Milo placed a finger over my mouth to stop my words, then replaced his finger with his own lips. The soft kiss had a world of feelings.

"You don't have to be sorry. I thought I'd rushed you. I thought I'd ruined everything and that you regretted being with me."

I snuggled into his massive chest. *Gah, this guy.* It was hard to imagine I'd only known him a week—my soul felt like I'd known him for a lifetime. Several lifetimes, even. "Not a single regret." I leaned up and kissed him once more, and he gave a shuddering sigh of relief.

"Thank fuck, because I can't look at the pool without thinking about you screaming my name, and getting hard." He stood up, still holding me like a baby, and strode to the other side of the pool. As we got closer to Tryp and Erus, my chest got lighter and lighter. It wasn't painful being away from them, like it had been with Milo that first night in Heraklion. More like when all three of them were together in the same spot, it felt like the sun was shining softly on me and everything was all right.

Happiness. That was the feeling.

Milo plopped me down on the lounger between them, and Tryp snuggled closer, rubbing his cheek on me like a cat.

"Sorry," Erus muttered. "He's been dying to scent mark you since you bonded."

I flushed pink, but smiled goofily. It was like that happy, tipsy feeling you got after a half glass of good wine. "And you?"

He grinned. "I'm better at restraining myself," he teased, though maybe he was chastising his errant friend. Boyfriend? Lover? Twin? Man, this was getting kinda weird and very mythological, I guess. They hadn't exactly been known for keeping the family lines distinct.

"You guys aren't actually related at all, right?" That was probably a completely inappropriate thing to ask, but I kinda *really* wanted to know.

Tryp looked up from where he was running his cheek on my shoulder. "Goddess, no. I'm far too handsome to be related to this guy."

Erus rolled his eyes. "We were created to be the opposite sides of the same coin. I was born into a high-class family, he was born into one of the poorest. He is brave and brash"—Tryp snorted in derision—"and I am careful and considerate. But the one thing that anchors us both is that I love him more than anything or anyone in this whole world. Including our former Goddess." The *including you* hung in the air, and I was pretty okay with that. "We share the same *soul.* It is hard to express that kind of relationship to anyone else."

I nodded, because I could only imagine. Actually, no, I couldn't. The concept of a soul was such a weird idea to me. I mean, as a society, we talked about souls, but I'd always just assumed it was a human concept we used when teaching young children how not to be psychos, or to explain why music made us feel the way we did.

Until recently. Obviously, now the idea of a soul was probably fundamental to my continued existence.

Erus was looking longingly at his other half rubbing on me. Tryp was pressing his body to my stomach now, and it should feel weird, because I mean, it *was* fucking strange. These guys were completely unknown to me a week ago. They had lion heads, for fuck's sake. But instead, it just felt nice, felt right, like I was being claimed.

So I lifted an arm and waved Erus closer. "Do you want to…?" I waved a hand in Tryp's direction. The relief that flashed across Erus's face made my heart clench. He leaned against my chest and rubbed his cheek in short, sharp motions on my clavicle.

Despite their closeness, their hands remained in respectful positions, though maybe I wouldn't have minded so much if they'd wandered a little more. I looked up at Nate, who was still on the other side of the pool, sunglasses over his eyes so I couldn't tell if he was watching this display or not. Was this okay? I knew he was okay with Milo, but this felt intimate in a different way.

He didn't barge over here and yank me back into his arms, so I just had to trust that if he had a problem, he'd tell me. He wasn't exactly a wilting flower. He was a fucking God of War.

Still, I raised an eyebrow at him, and he gave a tiny hand gesture that I took to mean *it's fine.*

Tryp flopped back with a contented sound. "Finally. I've been dying to do that for days." He winced. "Sorry.

I just meant to do your cheek, but once I started, I couldn't stop."

Reaching out, I stroked my fingers through his golden hair. Maybe that was too intimate too? Trying not to second-guess myself at every turn, I continued the motion, and when my fingers scraped against his scalp, he actually purred. Or a strange, gurgling noise deep in his chest that might have been a purr.

It actually shocked me into stilling. "Uh…"

Erus laid back and laughed. "That was a good noise. I think Tryp likes your stroking."

"So it really was a purr?"

He shook his head. "We can't purr. But we can make, like, a happy thumping sound in our chest when something feels good."

So fucking strange. "Do you have any more lion-ish traits?"

"I like to fuck from the back—does that count?" Tryp laughed, nudging my fingers with the top of his head again. I went back to scratching his scalp, and he swallowed down the noise he'd made before. It was kind of cute.

Erus rolled his eyes at his lover. "In answer to your question, not really. We are far more man than beast, and other than scent marking, a slight possessiveness, and the odd noise, we don't really possess that many qualities to the creature whose visage we share. We aren't lions. We are Genii. It's different."

Tilting my head at him, I tried to remember what he

looked like. I'd only seen their other forms in flashes, right before I keeled over in shock. "Can I see again?"

Tryp lifted his head to look down at me. "Will it make you faint? Because I think the God of War might thump me if I make you pass out once more."

There was a grumble of agreement from across the pool that let me know that Nate was indeed paying attention to what was going on.

Shaking my head, I grinned at Tryp. "It's fine. I'm expecting it now. Besides, I've seen Milo in his full bull glory. I'm becoming desensitized."

A look passed between the two Genii, but Erus nodded, pulling back a little from my body. I tried not to pout at the loss of his warmth.

Then, beside me, was a gloriously beautiful man with the head of a lion.

Holy shit. Holy fucking shit.

Although the size of his head didn't change, just morphed into the face of a lion, his mane was huge and flowing. And so fucking glorious. And the eyes in that lion face were still Erus, watching me with cool intelligence as I lifted my hand to his face, brushing my fingertips through the soft fur on his face. He tilted his cheek hard into my hand, rubbing it firmly against my skin.

Scent marking me again.

Tryp huffed. "If I knew I could mark her in my lion form, I would've waited."

I turned and looked at him, my eyes wide as I

laughed. I was stroking a half-lion man now. What even was my life?

Tryp obviously took my expression to mean I wouldn't mind him scent marking me *again*, but as a lion this time. "Really?" Nodding, I laughed at his whoop of joy.

He was slightly darker than the light golden coloring of Erus. The light and the dark. That big lion head was stroking all over my body once more, starting at my hands and moving up my arms. At my shoulder, his huge tongue came out and licked my pale, freckle-spotted skin. I squealed. It was rough, like a cat tongue, but huge.

Erus huffed. "Keep your tongue to yourself, Tryp."

Tryp made a low grumble. The kind of sound that would never come from a human mouth. But his next words would. "He didn't say that when I was tonguing his balls the other night," he whispered in my ear, and I made a choking noise. That sensation on any kind of private part sounded awful. Like sandpapering your testicles.

I was saved from replying by his furry cheek rubbing against mine, and I got a face full of mane. But with his smooth, muscular chest pressed against mine and Erus on my other side, it was like being in a sexy sandwich. A fully clothed sandwich; at least for now. My body didn't really want to listen to my head when it said fucking a lion was weird.

I owed Eleanor Heber from the seventh grade an

apology. Simba really did deserve his place in the top ten sexiest cartoon characters of all time.

CHAPTER 30
DEMKE

The girl was everywhere. In the halls, by the pool, on the laps of my best friends. In a few short weeks, she'd taken over the compound, and worse, over our lives. Like an icon of fertility, she was round and beautiful, and my dick betrayed me every time she walked past.

She was snuggled between Erus and Tryp outside, and I was watching them creepily through the window, like a ghoul in my own home.

"Doing some research, brother?"

I jolted, turning to see Teron, my oldest and best friend. Trying not to look guilty, I fixed my face into its usual mask of apathy. Teron had that small smirk on his face that told me he knew me better than I would've liked in that moment.

"Yes, I'm trying to work out how to break the soul bonds, if it comes to that. There must be something in these dusty old tomes." The library was Teron's pride and joy. He'd gathered each of these texts lovingly over the years.

He moved toward the large wooden table that sat in the middle of the room. "I'm afraid that even if you did find a way to break those bonds, none of them would choose to take the path. They are quite enamored with the little human."

They weren't enamored. They were obsessed. "If she falls, I won't lose them." It was a declaration. I vowed it to the universe, the words flying in the face of the Great Weaver themself, but I didn't care. I couldn't take any more losses.

Shaking his head, he gave me a sympathetic look that set my teeth on edge. "Demke, if she falls, it won't matter if you break the bonds or not. We are all screwed. Us, them, the world. I believe we all hinge on her and those babies."

He sat beside me and picked up one of the books I'd been reading. It was on the Fates and the turn of time by a hermit heretic several thousand years ago. The pages were fragile and beginning to crumble, but the information inside was still legible. The fact that some of these texts still existed at all was a testament to Teron's care—and the fact he made us all use gloves to read anything older than 1956.

Pointing to the pages, he raised an eyebrow at me. "But you know that, don't you? You know she's important to us all—not just emotionally." There was gentle chastisement in his tone, and I resisted the urge to roll my eyes.

We'd always been like this, Teron and I. While there'd been a certain amount of reverence from the others at one time or another, as their Goddess's Consort, or as a God myself, Teron had never genuflected to a single person in his life. He had held himself apart, not quite my equal, but not my subordinate either.

He had loved our Goddess, but he hadn't worshiped her. He loved and respected me, but as a man, not as a God.

"I understand she's important, Teron."

He was still shaking his head. "She's more than important, brother. She's our final chance at retribution. She's the world's chance for a fresh start."

"She isn't—the infants are," I argued. Semantics, but if I put Wren on a pedestal now, I worried she'd never come down.

He gave me a disappointed expression and sighed as he turned to the books in front of me. "I've never heard of male Fates. Do you think they are something else?"

"Or nothing at all," I protested, but I didn't believe that. Not really. It was all too coincidental. There was something Mythic about them, of that I was certain. I just didn't know if they were the Fates, as suggested, or something more.

There were so many unknown factors. I hated it. I'd

become complacent in our exile, and this much uncertainty was driving me crazy.

Teron grabbed another book from the stack I had in front of me. "We both know that she isn't nothing." With that, he pulled on some gloves and gently opened the book in front of him, leaving me to chew over the problem once more. We sat in silence as we searched book after book for answers.

The Oracle had sent her here, and we wouldn't make the mistake of ignoring an Oracle again. I needed to work out how to protect my friends, and yes, that meant protecting the girl.

"You know, you could always reach out to—"

I shook my head immediately. "No." I shut down the very idea before Teron even whispered it onto the wind. There was only one God who was as pissed at the Fates, and the Greek Mythics, but I would cut out my tongue before I asked him for help.

Teron snorted. "Stubborn." But that was it. He didn't argue or contradict.

We went back to work, and I got progressively more annoyed by the lack of information we possessed. One thing was becoming increasingly obvious, though: there were no male Fates. Not since the first recorded turn of the wheel. That didn't mean that there never could be. Occasionally, the power was even vested in a single deity. But that deity was always a woman.

I sighed and closed the book. It was hard to predict the pattern, and it wasn't for a nearly obsolete God like me to know. "It's going to come down to a fight, isn't it?"

It wasn't a question, not really. As soon as she'd walked into the building, the signs were there. She had altered our destiny as soon as she'd swooned at Tryphone's feet.

Closing his book too, Teron met my eyes. "Yes, my friend. It will come to a fight. Perhaps the most important fight of our eternal lives. Are you okay with that?"

Surprisingly, I was. We'd had an eternity of nothingness. A purpose was already doing us good. However, I wasn't a warrior God. Teron was a warrior. Milonos. They were built to defend and defeat. I was created for what came after.

I nodded. "I've come to terms with the fact that things will change. My head knows that this is our chance. This is a cause worth fighting for."

He raised an eyebrow. "And what does your heart say about the pretty human?"

My heart? I was purposefully ignoring it. And my body? That traitor strained toward her every hour of the day, like it knew that my only purpose was to protect her and then fuck her into the next century. I couldn't let myself get close, though, because it would spell the end of me. One of us had to keep a cool head when it came to the human.

"My heart is firmly locked away in the prison of my chest where it belongs," I told Teron, the sound of the chair scraping on the wooden floorboards making me wince as I stood. "I will be the faithful hound that destiny has cast me as, but I won't fall in love with her like the rest of our brothers. I will keep a clear mind for us all."

Teron had the audacity to chuckle at me, and I glared. Striding out of the room, I stomped down to my quarters like a petulant youngling. Wren's laughter drifted up through the open windows, and I gritted my teeth.

She was everywhere, except one place. I opened the heavy door to my quarters, moving through them sightlessly. They hadn't changed in a thousand years. The same heavy wooden furniture. The same coverings. The same tapestries on the wall and copper wash bowl in the corner. It had been the same for centuries upon centuries.

The broken pieces patched, but never changed.

Walking to another heavy door, I stepped out to the walled courtyard beyond my rooms and sighed as the warmth of the earth surged up to greet me. Surrounded by the small copse of fruiting trees, I let my toes sink into the soft clover grass. I spent a lot of time tending this garden, and it had become more of a shrine than a courtyard at this point. A place I could escape from the constant temptation.

Removing my clothes, I knelt down in the grass and let life seep back into my bones. I might be a forgotten God, no longer worshiped by many humans, but the townspeople were sometimes enough to rejuvenate me for a moment.

The energy of the nature around me, the soft

budding of the trees—it all meant something to me. And yet my body still strained toward Wren. My dick throbbed as I thought about her, making me grit my teeth. She called to me; I could admit that to myself, even if I couldn't admit it to Teron. She was so beautiful, with her open face and plush lips. Full breasts. The curve of her fruitful body.

Growling at myself and my hard dick, I reached down and gripped it, biting my lip hard in annoyance. I could hear the soft music of her voice, even though her words were lost in the distance.

I let my hand travel up and down my cock, and I groaned, throwing my head back and closing my eyes. I imagined it was her hand around me, gripping me just right, sliding along me with the perfect amount of speed and pressure.

My moans echoed off the stone walls, and I pumped faster. In my mind, it wasn't her hand but her tight little body sucking me inside her as I thrust, wild and free for the first time in so long. I imagined her whispery little moans, the way those puffy pink lips would wrap around my cock like an embrace. The hooding of her eyes as pleasure made it hard to keep them open. Her mouth opened in a little gasping O.

Fuck.

All too soon, my balls were pulling up and I was shooting my seed across the clover lawn, feeding my release back into the earth. Slumping back onto my heels, I grunted angrily at myself and turned my face to the sun. Cold air whipped off the mountains, making goosebumps spread across my overheated skin.

Slowly, I stood, pulling on my clothes. This was as much as Wren could take from me, because I'd meant what I said to Teron. I wouldn't give her my heart. I'd given that away once and almost died for the pleasure.

I wouldn't hurry to make that mistake again.

CHAPTER 31
WREN

I was surrounded by limbs, and realized both Tryp and Erus had climbed into bed beside me last night. They seemed to seek comfort from me, and if I was honest, I got the same amount of comfort from them. They soothed the panic that seemed to live permanently in my chest.

My stomach suddenly gurgled. *No. Wait.*

I sucked in a gasp as one of the babies kicked. I slapped a hand over my stomach, trying to find the place, and then there was another kick, but higher up, like it was a different baby who'd just learned kung fu from his sibling. They'd been moving around for a little while, but this was the first time it had felt like a real little foot was trying to wedge its way around my body. The first time I could feel it from the outside too.

Erus lifted his head. "Are you all right?"

I grabbed his hand and dragged it over to my stomach. "They're really kicking!"

Holding still, his wide eyes watched my stomach, his fingers wrapped around the now large curve of my stomach. I looked how some women looked at full-term, my stomach bulging out like I'd swallowed a watermelon.

The babies kicked again, moving around, and it felt like they were trying to find space inside me. Erus's eyes got even wider, and a grin broke out across his face, stealing my breath. He was so impossibly beautiful, the most perfect of all of the Demigods. They were all attractive, but Erus looked like a Greek statue, a physical embodiment of the ideal of beauty.

I realized Tryp was awake as he burrowed beneath the blankets to press his face to my stomach. I was beginning to learn that if Tryp could touch something with his face instead of his hands, he would. It was like he wanted to be as close to the sensation as possible. He'd always kiss my cheeks and temples instead of a friendly pat on my arm. He'd rest his cheek on top of my head instead of hugs. He slept with his nose pressed somewhere to my body instead of his arm around me.

And when the baby kicked now, it kicked him right in the face. *"Oof."* His laughing voice was muffled somewhat by the blankets, but I still laughed, especially when he emerged back to flop back on the pillow, his eyes sparkling. "Strong kicks. Definitely little warriors."

Happiness. That was what being pressed between these two felt like. A bubble of happiness that just surrounded us.

Tryp looked over at me, and something more than

happiness was in their depths. Heat made his eyes molten, and I felt my breath catch in my throat. He leaned forward and brushed his lips across mine, just a whisper of a kiss, then pulled back. "We should get out of bed. We're taking you to town today."

I gasped. "Really?" I looked between the two of them, both nodding.

"Yes. We have to pick up some supplies, and we can take you for lunch. Soft launch you to the locals. Demke has to talk to the town leaders too, in case anything happens."

In case their town got invaded by mythical monsters who wanted to kill my babies. It sounded insane.

Erus stroked my arm gently. "It'll be okay, Wren."

I gave him a tight smile. I had to believe that too, or I'd go insane. I almost wanted to keep the babies inside me so they were safe and secure, and as the weeks counted down to their due date, my worry only increased.

As if they sensed I was spiraling, Tryp brushed his lips over mine again. "So tense, Dumpling." He rubbed his cheek against mine. "Would you like Erus and I to help you relax?"

There was no way that was anything but a sexual proposition. I looked at Erus, and he was gnawing on his bottom lip, his eyes hopeful.

The answer was obviously yes. Hell yes, even. Now that I'd talked to Nate and he'd seemed, well, not cool, but accepting of the bonds and sex thing, I had nothing to feel guilty about.

But still, I hated the idea that they might be doing this against their will. "Is this what you really want? It's not the bond muddying your feelings?"

Erus looked surprised, while Tryp outright laughed. "Babe, I've wanted to climb between these thighs since the day you fell at my feet. Please let me eat you out, until you're completely convinced that I want nothing more than to fuck you." He paused. "Except maybe for Erus to fuck you while I watch." His eyes lit up. "Or for him to fuck me while I fuck you."

I groaned and let my head flop back onto the pillows as I imagined what he was describing. *Holy hell.*

Erus leaned close. "Would you like that?"

"So much."

He sucked my bottom lip between his. "Us too. Unfortunately, Tryp is right, and we don't have time to do everything we'd really like to do right now..." He trailed off, like he was imagining all those things too. "But we do have time to make you feel really, really good."

Tryp disappeared beneath the blankets, and I felt him tug at my sleep shorts. "Do you think he'll be able to breathe down there?" I asked Erus, who just laughed as he leaned up on his elbow, kissing my jaw and down my neck.

"I once made him choke on my cock for a solid seven minutes. Trust me, he'll be fine."

Sweet baby Jesus, these guys are going to be the death of my vagina.

Pulling my sleep shirt up over my chest, he found

my nipple and sucked it into his mouth the same moment Tryp found my clit. The sensation was… indescribable.

"Oh god," I gasped, and they took that as like a starting gun for their tandem act with only one finish line in mind—making me come like I'd never come before. Tryp's hands spread me wide and he was eating me out with wild abandon. I couldn't see him at all below the blankets, and somehow, that made it more wild. Every sensation was a surprise. Every tongue swirl around my clit, every time he thrust an impressively long tongue inside me, was as thrilling as it was shocking.

His other half, however, was doing his best to worship at the altar of my breasts. He sucked and licked them, scraping his teeth over one side while rolling the other in his fingers, and somehow he was in perfect synchronization. It was as eerie as it was mind-blowing.

I gripped Erus's hair in my fist, holding him to my chest as I rode Tryp's face. "I'm so fucking close. *Please*," I begged. I didn't know how they could read my body so well, but Tryp thrust three fingers into me as he moved his mouth back to my clit, and Erus went back to kissing me messily as he lavished attention on my nipples.

I came on a high-pitched, gasping scream, my thighs locking around Tryp's head, grinding against his nose in short, sharp movements.

When my whole body relaxed, I flipped off the blankets, hoping he was still alive down there. He leaned around the mound of my stomach, his cheeks glossy and pink, and a wide grin on his face.

"I've missed this," he said dreamily, his head resting on my thigh.

Erus slumped down beside me, cuddling me close to him. "Me too." He kissed my temple. "Thank you."

I shook my head. I'd never been thanked for letting someone go down on me before, but I was here for it. "You're welcome?"

Tryp chuckled, his cool breath blowing on my over-heated core. He squeezed my thighs happily, and I didn't think he was anxious to return to his pillow.

"You okay down there?"

I felt more than heard his answer. "Yep. I might never emerge from between your thighs."

Erus laughed. "You're going to have to, because in about three or so months, it's going to get kinda wild down there." He kissed me once more. "Want to have a shower with us and watch me blow Tryp for a job well done?" he asked me lightly, and I was nodding before he'd even finished.

Hell yeah, I did.

CHAPTER 32
ERUS

I couldn't see the golden life threads that Wren could see, but in this moment, I could *feel* them wrapped around my heart, leading directly to her hands. What we'd done earlier had shifted something fundamental in my chest. And judging by the longing way that Tryp was staring at her, in his too.

Who was I kidding? If I felt this soul-deep connection, it was metaphysically impossible for him not to feel it too.

We were walking into Amourgeles, and it had been a long time since the townspeople had seen us all together. Maybe never in the lifetime of some of the younger inhabitants. We used to come to town once a year to celebrate the solstice, leaving before the moon was high, but that had fallen away in the last fifty years or so. We'd said goodnight to the old traditions, no longer trying to resurrect them for people who had science and technology and no longer believed in the mythical.

But sometimes, when we came to town en masse like this, even the most skeptical of believers could feel the shift in the air. We weren't normal; no one could look at us and think we were. Which was why Demke had decided it was a good time to land on them, before the evidence that the mythical was real came in the form of a Hydra or something. We were much more palatable than a many-headed snake.

It was the middle of the day, so the village was pretty much empty anyway, since most of the inhabitants drove down to the larger towns and cities to work. Some even lived on the mainland and only came home for the weekends now. There wasn't a lot to keep young people on this island, and I couldn't blame them for that. There was a whole world out there, easily traversable, and the island life was dying out as quickly as its senior citizens.

However, those who were still in town stopped and stared, or came out of their homes to gawp. Demke led our little precession like it was one of the grand parades of a time that had crumbled into dust.

I could see Cy watching from the shadows. Demke was going to have to do something about that, but not today.

We made it to the *psistaría*, and Helena, one of the locals who stayed and worked on the island full-time, came out to greet us, her smile welcoming. Well, until her eyes fell on Wren, and then she gasped.

I could see her struggling with her words, like she was trying to find the correct reverence while asking her questions. "She is an American tourist," was what came out in Greek.

Demke nodded. "Yes."

"Her country will look for her."

Most people would never have been subject to the imperious glare of a God, but Helena was about to get the VIP treatment. "They will not. Wren is here for her protection, but outside of that, her movements are none of your business."

The woman in question looked at them, hard. She knew her name, though, and she wasn't an idiot. She knew they were having a terse conversation about her.

With a nod, Helena waved a hand at the table outside. In English, she said, "Please, take a seat."

I led Wren over, holding her elbow gently. Demke remained where he was. "I am going to see Stavros." With that, he turned and left.

Stavros was the unofficial leader of the town, but I was fairly sure it wasn't an elected role. He was just an elder, and I was fairly sure he was related to at least seventy percent of the island's population. However, he was respected, and the people listened to him. That was good enough for us.

Tryp pulled the seat out for Wren, and we all found our places around her. Néit sat beside her, though, glaring at the rest of us, daring us to argue about his right to be beside her. As if we ever would. We'd learned to share a long time ago.

Teron didn't take a seat. "I am just going to speak to Eladio—he's the village doctor," he added for Wren and Néit's benefit. "I need a few things that can only be obtained through traditional means."

He meant drugs. He needed drugs, in case something happened to Wren and he needed to medically intervene. The idea of her going into labor scared the shit out of me. I was tied to her now, as was Tryp, and childbirth in humans was a dangerous endeavor at the best of times, let alone when there were multiples.

As if she sensed my anxiety, she reached beneath the table and wrapped her fingers in mine. She smiled up at Teron. "Do you want us to order you anything?"

I didn't need to be one of his closest confidantes to know that Teron was becoming more and more smitten by Wren. The smile he gave her was one filled with tentative warmth. "No, thank you. I don't know how long this will take. I'll order if you're still here when I get back." I saw his fingers flex against his side, like he was desperate to lift his hand and stroke her face. Instead, he turned to Milo. "Walking around town is fine, but if she is tired or uncomfortable, straight home, okay?" he said sternly, before softening his features as he looked back at Wren again. "Exhaustion is a real factor at this stage. I don't want you to push yourself too far."

She shrugged. "Okay." She was a beautiful, amicable soul, and so far hadn't told us all to go screw ourselves. She definitely had the patience of a saint, with all the overbearing supernatural beings in her life.

With that, Teron left, and she leaned against Néit's bulging bicep. "He isn't wrong about the exhaustion. It's nice to be out, though."

Helena appeared with a bunch of food and laid it all around the table, including a glass of milk for Wren. She was stiff and kind of wary, which was okay. We had that effect, even without Demke here. Milo was still a huge guy, and a lot of humans found him physically menacing. I mean, he was basically a marshmallow if you knew him. But coupled with his "otherness," it was disconcerting. I was fairly sure that Tryp and I, with our sometimes synchronized movements, could also be unsettling.

Wren was the only one here who was just sunshine and happiness. Or at least, it felt that way to me.

Milo pushed the food toward Wren. "Eat. We still have places to go after this."

She picked up some bread and nibbled it. "We do?"

"Uh-huh," he said, smiling widely, looking at her with a look that could only be blind love. That would have worried me a week or so ago, but now, I totally understood. Fate had pushed us into her arms, but it was Wren herself that had me enamored.

We talked about other things while we ate. Normal things. Things Milo had read in baby books. Stockpiling formula, just in case pumping wasn't enough, or Wren decided to mix feed. Fencing the pool. Baby names.

An hour passed, and I could see Wren start to flag a little. We needed to move if we were going to finish our errands and not risk exhaustion.

Full and content, I walked into the cafe to pay Helena. Pulling out an even hundred, I passed it to the woman who was still eyeballing us. She pushed it into the cashbox, but met my eyes directly. She had some balls, I'd give her that.

"She is safe, yes?"

"From us? Yes. I would protect her with my life. From others? No. She is being hunted. You need to be safe too. Maybe tell the boys to stay on the mainland for a little while?" Helena had two sons, who each had large families that came to visit occasionally. We didn't need any collateral in a war I knew was coming. "Maybe you and Stavros could go visit them?"

Helena nodded once, frowning, and I walked back outside. I tried not to think about what could be coming, and the effect it would have on the village, or even the island as a whole. I wasn't going to borrow trouble just yet. The wards could hold.

Wren was cuddled into Néit's chest, and he looked growly, though he was tolerating Milo running his hand up and down her back.

I pointed to the left, and we all wandered further down the dirt sidings of the road. Wren looked around. "I haven't seen Cy. You think he's okay? You don't think he's been hit by a car or anything, do you?"

I snorted. "I doubt being hit by a tractor would hold him down. But I saw him earlier napping beneath the trees at the top of the hill." There were even more strays with him now.

We stopped outside a warehouse made of repurposed tin that looked about as rundown as it could possibly be while still standing. Milo knocked on the tin, and a tiny woman in dirty overalls appeared. She looked warily out at us, but not in an unwelcoming manner. Like Helena, she just wasn't used to us all at the same time, and definitely not with a heavily pregnant human in tow.

Tryp grinned at her, his affable face enough to put anyone at ease. "You can put down the hammer, Sophia. We're just here for the things we ordered."

She looked between us. "Did you bring the truck?"

He frowned at her. "We can't carry it between us? We're very strong," he said, winking at Wren, making her roll her eyes.

Sophia snorted, leading us through to the back. Whenever we needed things shipped to the town, Sophia and her husband, Myron, let us use their warehouse. They were builders, but there wasn't a huge call for it out here, outside of patching old places and making furniture. Occasionally, they'd do a whole new place, but most of the time, people who weren't locals would get one of the bigger firms from the city to do new construction.

So acting as a halfway point for us let them bring in some extra passive income. It also exposed them to us a lot more than the average townsperson.

Sophia threw open the door to the storage room, and I gaped. It was packed full. Tryp turned to stare at me, like I was the one who'd gone on a shopping spree, but I just shrugged. It hadn't been me.

We both turned to Milo, who was grinning unapologetically. "What? I forgot I ordered so much. Online shopping is deceptive. It kept leading me to more things we might need. Besides, it's fun."

Who would have thought that a nearly seven-foot Minotaur would enjoy online baby shopping?

I looked quickly at Wren, who was still gaping. She looked panicked, and I knew it was time to get out of here before she had a real freakout.

Looking over at Sophia, I gave her an appreciative nod. "You're right. We'll come back with the truck. Thank you again for receiving all of... this." I gave Milo a stern look, but he just grinned, bending down to whisper something in Wren's ear. Her face softened. Sweet-talking bastard—who knew he had it in him?

I only had to take one look at his face to know he was head over heels in love with her. And if I knew anything about humanity, I suspected she might be a little in love with him too.

CHAPTER 33
MILO

Tryp and Erus had returned to the warehouse the following day with the beaten-up truck we kept out the back of the compound. As I unloaded boxes and boxes of things, I felt only minorly guilty that I'd gone so crazy.

She still looked like she was adrift, and I hated it. I wanted her to moor herself to me, knowing that I was a safe port for her. And that started with providing for them. Making her laugh. Making her happy.

I knew I was feeling too much too fast. Teron had warned me that I was overdoing it, that I was just as likely to scare her away with my attention as make her feel safe. But for so long, I'd lived in a vacuum of darkness—years upon years of nothing, with no purpose, and no future but hoping that the end would come sooner or later.

When she'd turned up, a small spark had flickered in the depths of my abyss, and I'd found myself moving toward her like some kind of ugly fish in the deep trenches of the ocean, searching for the light. When she'd chosen me first, it had given me a duty, a reason to be the best man I could, to drag myself from the ennui that had insulated me from feeling for so long.

My life had shifted in that moment, and it had been a constant war about doing what would make her comfortable, and throwing myself at her feet in supplication.

However, now, as we stared at all the boxes, she didn't seem particularly happy. Grateful, and a little overwhelmed, which I could understand. Even I was overwhelmed, and I'd bought most of this stuff. There were a few things in here purchased by the others, but only I'd gone overboard.

Guilt grew in my chest, and I couldn't resist the urge to wrap an arm around her shoulders and hold her tightly to my side. The thought that Teron was right, that I would make her run away with my attention made me panic slightly.

"Don't stress, sweet one. I'll construct everything. You just have to relax over there on the couch and give me directions. I can even do it without a shirt on," I said with a lascivious wink, earning a laugh that spread through my veins like a drug.

I was addicted to that sound. It was my opioid of choice.

She wrapped her arms around me, and I bundled her up close to my chest. I wanted to lift her into my arms and drag her back to my bed where I could worship her, but she was tired. I wasn't going to add to her exhaustion.

Well, maybe I could just lick… *No.* Her needs came first.

So I nuzzled her cheeks, smelling Tryp on them—the fucker couldn't go five seconds without scent marking her—but I found I didn't mind at all. I loved them. I loved her. It was right.

"Are you mad at me? I promise, I did this because I wanted to. I wasn't trying to buy your love. I'm excited about the babies' arrival."

She let out a choked noise, and I pulled back, looking down at her large, tear-filled eyes. Had I said something wrong?

Brushing her hand across her eyes, she sniffed. "I'm fine. Sorry. I just realized I don't think anyone has been excited about the babies coming into the world, until you. Worried. Stressed. Fearful. But not excited. Not even me." I frowned, and she continued. "I'm excited to hold them, but I'm also so fucking scared, Milo."

Ah, this woman. "Don't cry, Wren. You're breaking my heart." I kissed her cheeks. "Want me to make love to you? It'll stop your tears, and hopefully make you happier."

She laughed, squeezing me tighter. "You make me happier, Milo. Thank you for being excited."

I lifted her easily into my arms and carried her toward the bed. "I can tell you that I'll protect you all with my life. I can tell you that I'll love you and all three babies with my whole heart and soul. I can tell you that you make me happier than I've been in so long. But I think it's best if I show you all these things... with my tongue."

She giggled and buried her fingers in my short hair. "Show me, my love." Her words were like an injection of happiness straight into my heart, resurrecting that battered old organ and making it pump once more.

MY EYES SNAPPED open in the darkness of predawn. I sent out my senses, trying to work out what had woken me. Wren tossed and turned uncomfortably, but she did that every night. Being heavily pregnant meant she was being used as an arena in the fight for womb space going on inside her, which didn't often lend itself to restful sleep.

The urge to shift was strong. I looked over at Néit, who was sleeping on the other side of Wren, and his eyes looked back at me. "Something's wrong," he said softly, trying not to wake her.

I nodded. Slipping from the bed, I looked out the window. The darkness of the moon set made the landscape dense with shadows. My instincts were telling me there was something out there, though. I searched and searched until I saw a flash of movement. It could just be Cy and his unruly pack. But it felt like something else.

Another flash of movement on the other side. Nothing had tripped the wards yet, but they were circling.

"We're under attack. Wake Wren," I murmured. "Take her down to my rooms below the building. I'll get Tryp and Erus to come and guard her." Néit was a warring God. He wouldn't babysit. He'd fight.

On this, we could relate. I was no God, but my purpose was to protect. Demke was a rejuvenation God. Of life and fertility, but what people always seemed to forget was that energy was a finite substance. You could only have new life with death, and he was more than happy to dispatch the energy of the unworthy back into the universe. Teron's Gryphon was... terrifying in battle.

No, the only ones of us who didn't particularly relish a good fight were the Genii. Tryp and Erus could and would fight, but they were made for more hedonistic pleasures. Drinking, fucking, partying. They'd been designed as playthings. Bringers of joy and merriment. They would protect Wren with the ferocity of their lions, but they didn't enjoy killing.

Néit didn't argue, gently waking Wren as I rushed from the room. I wasn't surprised to find Teron's Gryphon already walking the halls. He freaked me the fuck out, even after all these years. The Gryphon and Teron weren't the same person. The Gryphon was something else, and even though I'd say we were friendly, I knew he tolerated us only because Teron loved us. The Gryphon didn't feel one way or another for us.

I bowed my head at the regal creature who stood eye to eye with me in this form. He was huge. His eagle eyes looked at me appraisingly, the long talons on his lion paws scraping gouges in the slate flooring. "We're under attack."

He tilted its head at me, then nodded.

"Néit is taking Wren down to my rooms beneath the building. She'll be safest there."

The Gryphon lifted the feathers around his neck and shook them out. That could have been an agreement with my decision, or it could just be a reaction to the mention of Wren.

When I'd asked Teron recently if his Gryphon might be an issue regarding Wren's safety, he'd snorted. "*Your* safety might be more of an issue when it comes to the relationship between Wren and the Gryphon."

Between his words that day, and the slightly haunted look on his face, I'd made an educated guess that it meant the Gryphon liked Wren. Mate-liked Wren. Though Teron had never said as much.

Now, I was beginning to think I was correct. We needed to sort this out now and quickly. "I love Wren. I will lay my life down to protect her. I know she's your... mate." I hesitated over the word, in case he decided to gouge me for my audacity, but he just tilted his head at me. "But she's my mate too. She'll need all of us."

The Gryphon's golden eyes watched me for so long, I began to sweat. Finally, he inclined his head, and I resisted sighing with relief. Instead, I smiled. "Glad we've sorted that out. I'm going to wake Demke and the others. Do you want to fly out and see what dares to step foot into our territory?"

He made an angry snapping sound at that, his outrage clear. I hurried around him, down the hall to Demke's wing. Thumping hard, I yelled, "We're under attack."

But then the wards went off, waking the whole house. Rushing to Tryp and Erus's quarters, I found them already stumbling out the door, half asleep.

"Down to my rooms. That's where Wren is. Protect her. Soothe her. The stress is bad for the babies."

They didn't ask questions. They just ran.

Demke strode into the hall, fully dressed with a sword in hand. He looked like a bloodthirsty God of old, his power whipping around the room. It would be a good reminder for these fucking Mythics to know *exactly* who they were fucking with. That we wouldn't give her up.

That we would fight for what was ours, and this time, we wouldn't lose.

Néit appeared at the same time as the Gryphon flew back in the window, and if I hadn't been watching, I wouldn't have seen the normally unflappable God of War actually looking surprised. He cleared his throat and stepped around the Gryphon, and over to us.

Demke stopped him. "This is Teron's Gryphon. He's not Teron. You should treat him with respect, or he'll bite your head off in a rather permanent manner," Demke informed him.

Néit bowed to the beast, and to my surprise, the

Gryphon lowered his head in return. *Interesting.* I'd unpack that at another time.

The Gryphon looked over at Demke, and they were clearly doing that ESP thing they had. Eventually, Demke nodded. "The Gryphon thinks this is just a probe attack. Checking our weaknesses. Six lower-level monsters, including some Verserpent and other little night demons. Nothing as powerful as the Lamia, or any of the Old Gods that Néit's contact mentioned. He said Cy and his pack have already torn apart one of the night demons."

Néit's jaw tensed, and his ax glowed as he grew twice his size, the runes on his chest beginning to grow. "No survivors."

Demke nodded and looked at me. "No survivors," I agreed. I walked over to the weapons that still hung on the wall like this was medieval times, and palmed my favorite mace. "We'll probably have to put these in the armory or something when the babies come," I muttered to myself. "I'll take the south."

We all took a direction, splitting up. Feeling the cool weight of the mace, and the unnatural stillness of the air as I stepped into the courtyard, I went out to defend the woman I loved.

CHAPTER 34
WREN

I paced around Milo's underground suite, anxiety making my skin feel too tight on my bones. I'd been tossing and turning all night, and when Nate had woken me, my body had reacted immediately with panic. He'd hustled me down to Milo's bedroom and waited with me until Tryp and Erus arrived.

Then he'd kissed me hard and disappeared back upstairs, but not without shutting the heavy wooden doors. Erus had barred them after him, making the anxiety ratchet up another notch.

What if they were out there being hurt? Would I feel it? Would I know if they were in trouble, or in pain?

Tryp came up behind me and wrapped his arms around my body, stopping my trek back across the room. "It will be okay, sweetheart. Please, come sit."

I let him lead me to the bed, sitting stiffly on the side. I had to distract myself, or the what-ifs were going to kill me. I couldn't deal with the unknown.

"Why is Milo's room underground?"

Erus sat beside me, reaching down to grip my hand, threading his warm fingers between mine. "He's a Minotaur. They were all born in the tunnels of the Labyrinth, deep underground. The story got a little muddled as the old religions of Crete were subsumed by the Greek Pantheon, but ever since the original Great Bull, they all lived in a labyrinth beneath the island. He feels more comfortable down here beneath the earth, even after all this time."

I chewed the inside of my cheek. "Muddled how?"

"You know the story of Theseus and the Minotaur? With the golden ball of thread?"

Man, I was going to have to brush up on my mythology. "Vaguely?"

Tryp huffed a laugh from the other side of the room. "It's all bullshit anyway."

Erus nodded his agreement. "Well, the quick version is that Athens was sending children from the mainland as sacrifices to some imaginary carnivorous bull beast, because their city was struck with plague and famine. Of course, it wouldn't be mismanagement by their own rulers, but some kind of divine punishment." He rolled his eyes. "Anyway, they did this for years, and we'd get these boats of scared kids, feed and clothe them, and they'd just live on the island. Most of them were orphans and paupers plucked off the streets, who had no urge to return home to poverty. The Goddess would give them homes, and if they were young enough, parents. A lot of the island's residents are descendants of the Athenian sacrifices.

"Anyway, after a couple of decades, Theseus decided to be the hero, too stupid to know that they were the reason these kids were being shipped off. He came over, declaring he was going to kill the great Minotaur of Crete. Except the Minotaur was actually Prince Catreus, who could shift from man to bull, like Milo can. The prince introduced him to the Goddess. The Goddess showed him their 'sacrifices'"—he did air quotes—"some of whom were old and gray, with families. Theseus fell in love with Princess Ariadne. Between them, they all decided to conquer this stupid myth, stop the damn sacrifices, and Theseus returned to the mainland with Ariadne as his new wife."

I blinked at him. "So no one was slaughtered?"

His face shuttered then, and I could almost feel his residual pain. "Not that time."

Swallowing hard, I wrapped my arm around his waist and laid my head on his shoulder. "Are there other Minotaur left?"

Erus shook his head. "Just Milo."

Something bad had happened, that much I knew. I wanted to know everything about these guys, about how they came to be, how they'd ended up here in their isolation.

But not now, while they were up there fighting for me. Dying for me, even.

I *hated* this.

The haunted swirl of Erus's eyes was like a knife in

my chest. Erus, sensing my discomfort, pulled me deeper onto Milo's giant bed. "Lay down, Wren. We won't know until it's all over." I settled down onto the bed, and his arm reached out and cupped my stomach, rubbing in tiny circles. The babies kicked out against his palm, and he chuckled into my hair.

We didn't speak, and the silence around the room, around the whole building, felt thick enough that I was wading through it. Tryp stood by the door, the last sentinel of my safety. Even though he was shirtless, leaning against the stone walls with ease, I knew from the way his hand rested on the pommel of a huge sword that he was ready to lift it in a fraction of a second. There was also a large dagger strapped to Erus's thigh, and I felt so safe and protected, it was almost a relief.

"They're holding their own, my love. The walls haven't been breached, or we'd have heard the ward alarm. Between them, they have more battle experience than all the human history books combined. It will be okay."

I nodded, turning on my side and burying my face in his warm chest. I trusted them, but it might only take one lucky swing to destroy my world forever.

FORTY-FIVE ETERNITY-FILLED MINUTES LATER, I'd moved on to counting every rough-hewn stone in Milo's wall, still ensconced in Erus's comforting arms. When there was a thump on the door, Erus sat up, eyeing the door, and Tryp lifted the sword, holding it as easily as I might hold a pen.

"It's me." Milo's voice came through, but the guys didn't seem any less wary.

"Too many mimics. Gotta check if it's really him," Erus told me quietly, before calling out, "What happened the first time you made homemade rakí?"

I could hear Milo sigh through the door. "I made it too strong and passed out in the olive grove at the back of the compound."

"And?" Tryp prompted.

"A scorpion climbed up my shorts and stung me on the balls, making them swell."

Erus smirked. "Seriously, like the size of balloons. Massive testicles."

Tryp was giggling like a girl as he opened the door. An unimpressed Milo stood there, glaring at the guys, but I could see Nate over his shoulder, and he looked amused. If he was smiling, it had to be okay, right?

I was off the bed as fast as I could—with a little assistance from Erus—and across the room in a flash. I made it to Milo first, but even as I was wrapped in his arms, I reached for Nate, dragging him closer so I could touch him and make sure he was okay.

Milo kissed the top of my head, then gently passed me to Nate. "It's okay, *mo stóirín*. Everyone is fine. The threat was minimal," he said softly, brushing his lips across mine. "Come back up and we'll all debrief together."

I nodded and followed him, the solid warmth of

Milo at my back as we walked up the stairs. Finally, I could breathe easier.

I was unsurprised to see Teron in the sitting room, holding a blood pressure cuff and a stethoscope. He looked fine, but Erus had said he would fight as the Gryphon. I found it hard to imagine that this gentle man turned into a giant bird-lion, but I'd seen his glamor drop enough to know it was true.

Milo sat on the couch and pulled me onto his lap, nuzzling his nose into the back of my neck with a happy sigh. I held out my arm, and Teron dropped into a squat beside me, strapping the blood pressure cuff around my bicep.

"You're okay?" I asked him softly, and he looked at me with those molten gold eyes.

"I'm fine."

"And the Gryphon?"

There was a deep rumble in his chest, the sound not in the least bit human, and Teron cleared his throat. "The Gryphon is also fine. He, uh, wants me to tell you that it wasn't even a hardship for him to eradicate the demons, and that he could have taken them all single-handedly without assistance from anyone else."

His cheeks were pink, and it was kind of adorable. Milo was silently laughing beneath me, and I had the feeling he was enjoying Teron's embarrassment.

Erus had explained that the Gryphon and Teron were two entities that shared a body. His wasn't a glamor; it was an actual form. What did I say back to a Gryphon to let it know I appreciated it?

"Tell the Gryphon that I know he's a fierce hunter, and thank him for coming to my aid."

Teron nodded as he checked my blood pressure and noted it down. Then he listened to my stomach. His jaw was tense, and I got the impression he was conversing with the beast inside him. *So weird.*

"Everything sounds good, though your blood pressure is a little high, which is to be expected. We'll take it easy over the next couple of days."

I nodded, and Demke sighed, leaning back in his chair. I always thought of it as *his* chair, because it was a high wingback that looked a little like a throne. "I think we are long past the ability to make any promises of normalcy for a while. This attack was a probe—that much was obvious. And the fact that so many demons of darkness got this close to the compound is concerning. Tighten the island wards, Erus. Block anyone with any ill intent for now."

Erus nodded, and I realized once again that I knew hardly anything about them.

Teron cleared his throat from where he now sat cross-legged on the ground. "It's because the wards are only made to block our neighboring Pantheon, and the Verserpent aren't part of the Greek Mythics. They are creatures of the underworld, a shared domain."

"Then we ban everyone who isn't us," Milo rumbled.

Demke shook his head. "We will soon need assistance from others, and I don't want to be trying to untangle wards when we need help the most. But we can plug up this problem and hope it gives us a little more time. Until the babies are born, at the very least. The power will pass and no matter what the Fates wish, there's no getting it back. Even if they kill the infants, the power will never pass back to them."

I shuddered at the thought of the Lamia eating my babies. Of those nightmare creatures getting their hands on my children. A whimper passed my lips, and Milo held me tighter. "No one is getting to you, or them," he swore to me.

"I don't want to lose any of you either. Maybe I could hide somewhere they won't look."

There was silence around the room, until Demke stood. "Wren, walk with me?"

CHAPTER 35
DEMKE

The Gryphon had done a thorough sweep of the surrounding area in the darkness and declared it safe, and I trusted him with my life. Cy and the pack would also keep an eye on the grounds and village, both day and night. Somehow, this diminutive woman had earned their loyalty.

She had that effect. Even I felt protective of her now, and I'd done my best to ignore her existence completely. It was the weave pushing us together, destiny trying to tie us in knots to complete whatever it decided we needed. Who knew which Fates had set this in motion. The ones who were in power during my birth and rise to Godhood? The Norns? The Moirai? That was the thing about fate; sometimes it left you with more questions than answers.

I led Wren over to the tapestries that hung on the wall, depicting battles and wild monsters, fantastical creatures and brave heroes. They looked like picture books, but they were our history, and I kept them here as a reminder of what failure could mean: to my people, to my friends, and to me. This one in particular was painful for me to look at, even after all this time.

"I don't know how much the others have told you about how things were… before."

She wet her lips, looking up at me with those soft eyes and shaking her head. "Uh, not a whole lot. Just little bits here and there."

I nodded, because I understood. No one wanted to drag up ancient history, especially when it was painful. "Before, we were the deities in a reasonably simple faith. We all worshiped the Goddess, even me." I'd loved her too, but it was in the way a blind man loves the sun. Before her, there was no one and nothing but darkness. "She was a beautiful, benevolent Goddess who believed in feasts, plenty, and very few sacrifices. She had this tiny island domain, with the humans and the Minotaurs, who all prayed to her. She didn't want to expand her reach. She just wanted to look after her people."

And me.

"When the new Greeks overthrew the old, we didn't worry too much. They went west and took Italy, and we thought they'd continue that way. They had an appetite for war and games, and we just… didn't. We were floating out here in the middle of the ocean, geographically close but too small to conquer. We met with the big ones, Zeus and some of the other Olympians, including Hera, and he and the Goddess came to an agreement. We would let his people come and go, and he wouldn't try to subsume us.

"The Fates were with him, all the time weaving and seeing, and seeing and weaving." Anger bubbled up in my chest. "These supposedly impartial crones." I wanted to rage at the very thought of those so-called Gods who'd visited us, with their charming smiles and electric energy. The Goddess had been completely taken, of course; they were beautiful and charismatic. But something about them had sat wrong with me.

I could tell Wren wanted to hold me, her fingers clenching at her sides until she clasped them in front of her. I wouldn't admit it, but I wanted her to hold me too. When was the last time anyone had comforted me? But I wouldn't risk tying myself to her, or worse, *not* being tied to her. That possibility somehow seemed worse than tying our fates together—what if I hadn't been deemed worthy of protecting her?

Shaking my head, I went back to my story. My history. "The new Gods left, and we went back to life for another century. It was business as usual, except for a few visits from the mainland, and the humans sending sacrifices to the Minotaurs." I scoffed, because that really had been the most insane thing. Minotaurs didn't even eat meat in the bull form.

"But one day, an Oracle arrived at the Goddess's Temple, seeking an audience. It was quite unusual for an Oracle to travel from Delphi. We didn't have experience with them; there'd never been one on the island. They didn't figure in our worship. This one didn't waste time on niceties either. As soon as she sat, her eyes went white, and she said, 'The tail is bitten. Storm clouds rise. Arms and hearts will be sacrificed.'

"That was it. She woke up, gave us a sheepish expression because she couldn't remember her vision, just knew she needed to deliver one to us. She left after that, and we were so confused about what this child—she would only have been about fourteen—was trying to tell us." It had sounded like gibberish.

"We decided to ignore it, because what did it even mean? It's the greatest regret of my life that I didn't listen. Didn't try to decode her prophecy." Hindsight was a vicious bitch. "She meant we were at the end of an age. She meant a war was coming. That we'd need to fight, and to do so, we'd need an army. But we didn't listen and had none of that. So when the war came, we were defenseless."

I pointed to the tapestry. It showed the great battle, hundreds of Minotaurs charging, the Gryphon in the sky, the Goddess's snakes pouring across the ground. *Everything* fought. Human men against Gods. "We fought, of course. And we lost. However, the Minotaur king at the time, Catreus, and his advisor put forward a rather drastic solution. He would sacrifice some of his people to create a ward around the island to keep out this invading Pantheon, and the Goddess would use her magic to create it.

"She argued against it. Milo, who had been given the title of the Great Bull, raising him to his own Demigod-hood, also protested against it. But as more and more of us died, she relented. They performed the magic needed to create the ward. But instead of sacrificing some of the Minotaurs, it sacrificed them *all*, except Milo."

Wren gasped, tears pouring down her face, like she could feel his heartache. But I doubted anyone could have understood the depth of his pain that day. He still felt echoes of it, thousands of years later.

"The magic worked. A barrier was formed. They couldn't cross onto the island, but by extension, we could never leave. Our fortress became our prison." I let out a shuddering breath. "The Goddess couldn't live with the sadness of what she'd done. For so long, there were only a few families of shell-shocked humans left on the island. Her snake companions had died in the war. So many had died in the war. No one worshiped her anymore. She faded from us within centuries of the ward going up. Erus learned what he needed to maintain and enhance it before that, though, and we've managed to keep it strong all these years since."

"Demke..." Wren said in a soft voice, still crying sadly. "I'm so sorry."

She was staring at the tapestry on the wall. Slain bodies of animals that fought for their Goddess, of Minotaurs and men. The tapestry had been woven by one of the widows, and it was aptly named *The Massacre*. It had been left on our doorstep, not as a tribute, but as an accusation. The already fading Goddess had made me hang it, and I'd never removed it. It was a penance that I looked at every day, so I knew my failures.

Clearing my throat, I turned back to her. "So I want you to know why we are so willing to fight for you, for the babies. You are our revenge. You are our penance. You are our chance to rewrite history. We will fight, and we will win. A new age will come, and I know you will raise these infants—if they *are* the Fates—with empathy and compassion. They will not be the power-hungry Moirai, weaving the threads in a way that fits them."

I stepped forward. I couldn't resist this anymore. I needed this; I could feel the Great Weaver pushing me to do it. Grasping her hands, I pulled her tightly to me. "You will birth a better age, because you are kind and compassionate. The fruit you bear won't be rotten."

She inhaled sharply, her eyes watching something I couldn't see, but I hoped it was the threads wrapping around us.

I fell to my knees in front of her. "I will protect them until my very last breath, for those ghosts of my past. For my brethren. For you."

She stared down at me, her eyes impossibly wide. "Demke..." she breathed once more.

I didn't need to ask if the threads of fate had bonded me to her, because I could feel it in my chest. The aching tug that pulled toward her, even though I was gripping her hands in mine. Like it wanted us to be as close as can be.

"Do you accept my arms to help you weather this

storm? Do you accept my heart to help you be triumphant in this battle?"

She was nodding, but she looked shell-shocked. I didn't blame her. I hadn't known I was going to do this when I led her in here, but it felt so right.

"You need the words out in the universe, Wren."

I could feel the others gathering behind me in the hall, because it felt significant. Some moments felt electric, like they were important points in the tapestry, a place where the pattern could continue, or it could shift into something new. This was one of those moments. I could *feel* it.

She lifted a hand to cup my face. "I accept your help, Demke. I need it."

Tension that had been straining in my shoulders relaxed, and I sighed as rightness washed over me. I'd been holding myself separate ever since she'd arrived, not realizing how much effort it was taking me to defy fate. But this was the moment. I felt it in my chest.

She was still staring down at me. "Can I, uh, hug you now? Because I think I need one."

Laughter bubbled past my lips, and the sound shocked me. How long had it been since I laughed? I stood and wrapped her in my arms, like I could protect them purely in the shelter of my body.

I looked back at the others, and Teron inclined his head. His approval was as clear as day. Teron had been my touchpoint for so long, that if he thought it was right, that was the last reassurance I needed. The others all looked various shades of happy and content, like it was inevitable, except the God of War.

He looked worried. I understood it. I was worried too.

I inclined my head at him, out of respect. Out of brotherhood. He had to know that I would protect them with my life now. I would stand shoulder to shoulder with him against anything that might hurt them.

He dipped his chin at me, but then turned and left. I would talk to him tomorrow, once we'd all had a chance to sleep.

For the last time, I silently prayed to my Goddess, who had been faded and gone for so long now, I could barely remember her face.

Goddess, give me the strength to protect them in a way that I couldn't protect you.

And just like the last thousand times I'd prayed to her, there was nothing but an aching silence.

CHAPTER 36
TERON

I wasn't sure if it was the potential bond between Wren and I, or the circumstances of the last couple of days, but I found myself doing a version of nesting. Well, not nesting, but preparing. The attack had proved that we needed to prepare for any eventuality, and more than that, it had proved that it wouldn't be safe for her to travel to the human hospital in Heraklion to deliver her babies.

I'd already been discussing Wren's health with Dr. Eladio, talking about needs and necessities for a home birth. We had looked at the research, the guidelines and best practices, and had come up with a plan, in case she needed to deliver locally.

After the attack, her giving birth here in the compound was a foregone conclusion. I would have to convince Wren, of course, and probably Néit. I would also read every ounce of literature I could get my hands on.

Hope for the best, but prepare for the worst.

I looked around the room I was currently converting to an operating room. I was slowly stocking it with everything that was needed, and was working toward making everything as sterile as I could physically make it, because humans were alarmingly fragile and prone to death.

The Gryphon made an irritated squawk at the idea that his mate was anything less than perfection. His mate. My mate. *Fuck.* He huffed in my mind as if I was being a baby, and I rolled my eyes. She was human. What if something happened to her? What if nothing happened to her and she just died in seventy years, like a normal human?

I hated the uncertainty of it all, and I added it to the ever-growing list of things I needed to research. Going back to making sure all the instruments I'd borrowed from Eladio were sterilized within an inch of their life, I continued down my mental checklist.

A knock at the door had me turning, and the subject of my pining thoughts appeared. The Gryphon ruffled his feathers in my mind, which made me smile. *Vain bastard.*

I wasn't surprised that Milo was behind her. She was rarely alone these days, and I wondered if that grated on her. Maybe I'd casually ask if she needed some space from their constant hovering.

The Gryphon showed me an image of him snapping at them, keeping everyone away so she could rest. I didn't have the heart to tell him that "alone" meant without him too.

"Wren, how are you feeling?"

"Like I've spent a week eating at an all-you-can-eat taco restaurant and there's no longer room for my organs." Milo laughed behind her, his fingers tracing any bare skin they could find, like he was addicted to the feel of it.

"It's a fairly good analogy. Come out into the other room so you can sit." *And not contaminate the clean room.* I didn't say that, though, not wanting to freak her out just yet. That would be coming in a moment.

I led her into a connecting sitting room, the one where I'd been checking her vitals and doing ultrasounds for the last few weeks. She slumped down on the couch, her hands propping up her growing stomach.

Clearing my throat, I sat down opposite her. My heart was thumping in my chest; it was time to lay it all out on the line. I didn't know why I felt so vulnerable. Looking over, Milo gave me a reassuring nod.

"I'm glad you stopped by, because there are a couple of things I was hoping to talk to you about."

I'm your mate. Maybe we'd start with the birth plan first. How was *I want to cut you open in a rudimentary operating room* the easier topic of conversation?

"Firstly, I know you said you wanted to go to the hospital in Heraklion for the birth of the babies, but after the breach of the island's wards the other night, I worry about the safety of you, the babies, and the other people at the hospital. I'm hoping you might consider birthing here, in the compound, where we can keep you all safe. I promise, I am up-to-date on all the skills and practices needed to birth triplets, as well as planning for all eventualities."

I was going to get the guys to let me practice giving epidurals. Not that I wasn't confident, but I didn't want the first time I'd done it in twenty years to be on the woman in front of me.

She looked wary, which was understandable. In emergencies, humans were programmed to seek out the closest hospital. Closing her eyes, she rubbed a hand over her belly and sighed. "I trust you. If it comes to that, I can deliver here."

I stifled my relieved breath. The Gryphon hated the thought of her being out of our territory, out of our protection, but a damn Gryphon couldn't wander the halls of a hospital either. I nodded. I hoped it wasn't necessary, that this all went away for her.

But I wouldn't hold my breath. If there was anything Mythics did well, it was hold onto grudges.

Nodding, I gave her a reassuring smile. "Good. Okay." Sucking in a deep breath, I just let the next words spew from my mouth with no finesse. "My Gryphon believes you're his mate."

She blinked at me, and Milo snorted a laugh. "Mate?"

I swallowed hard. "The person he's meant to be with forever. His person. His fated partner in life."

This was so fucking weird. She was looking at me

like I'd lost my mind, and I could feel my ears turning red. I wasn't this fumbling person; I was cool and level-headed at all times. But right now, I wanted to run for the hills, dig a hole to the Underworld, and never emerge.

She paused. "Oh. Uh, I see. Does he know I'm not a Gryphon?"

The Gryphon was pressing against my skin. He wanted to show her how devoted he could be as a mate, and chase that look of uncertainty from her expression. I warned him that it would probably have the opposite effect.

"He's aware you're not a Gryphon. It is a soul connection, and not a, uh, physical connection."

Now Milo was outright laughing, his hands still running up and down her back. "He means the Gryphon isn't going to want to go at it, bird-lion style."

Her cheeks were now so pink, I was tempted to check her blood pressure. "All right. Huh. And you? What does this mean for you? Are you kind of... stuck with me just because your Gryphon likes me?" she asked with a frown.

The Gryphon was getting irate that I wasn't conveying the true depths of his feelings and thought I was fucking this up. *Temperamental bastard.* "I wouldn't say 'stuck with you' is the right phrasing." I wanted her so bad that it was a damn ache in my balls, all the time. I wanted to lay her down and study every inch of her with my eyes, taste every freckle with my tongue, hear every little noise she made until she sang me a symphony every night. "On this, my Gryphon and I agree wholeheartedly. We're yours, if you want us."

She blinked at me, her eyes tracing my face as if she could divine the real truth. With Demke now completely on board, I was the last one holding out. I didn't know if it was because the thread that was meant to tie us together was the Gryphon, not the man, or if we both had to be on board before we could bond. Whatever it was, it wasn't a lack of desire. I wanted to bond with her, to protect her and the babies with every ounce of my immortal abilities.

She gave me a lopsided smile. "Okay then. I guess I better meet him. My… mate." There was only a slight hesitation in her voice, and I couldn't have respected her more in that moment.

I nodded and stood, my fingers on the buttons of my shirt. "I should warn you, though, he'll probably be quite… affectionate. Much like Tryp and Erus, he'll attempt to mark you as his. A lot. Just know that he'll never, ever hurt you. And Milo is here, in case you feel too uncomfortable."

The Gryphon huffed again at the insinuation that Milo could stop him at all, but didn't protest him being in the room. The Gryphon might be a beast, but he was so fucking smart. Just because he was animalistic in his urges, it didn't mean that half my knowledge didn't come from him.

"Can he speak? Like Milo can in bull form?"

I shook my head, and the Gryphon keened at the idea of inadequacy. "No. But if you bond as mates eventually, you'll be able to speak mind to mind." *Which is even better than what the others have*, I told him, soothing his bruised ego.

She nodded, getting to her feet. "Let's do this." So brave. Even with the quake in her voice, she held her head high. I wanted to kiss her, but I could wait. If she rejected the Gryphon, I didn't want to know the taste of what I was missing and could never have.

Impatience that didn't belong to me rolled across my skin, and I shook my head. Pulling off my clothes—all my clothes—I was amused by the fact that Wren didn't look away. Her eyes ate up my exposed body, heat and hunger warring for supremacy in her gaze.

I needed to hurry this along, before my dick got harder and I decided this little meet and greet could wait until I'd been balls deep inside her.

Ready? I asked the Gryphon.

I've been ready for millennia, he replied.

And if she dies in seventy years? I asked, because I had to. I had to know.

Then it would be better than one more minute without her.

I swallowed hard. I had my answer. In a shower of magic, I was pushed down, and the Gryphon emerged.

CHAPTER 37
WREN

My brain short-circuited as it tried to comprehend the creature now before me. While I'd seen flashes of Teron's other form, it had just been that. Just the shadow of an eagle's head overlaying Teron's own face.

However, there was no sign of Teron in the magnificent beast before me. Well, maybe the molten gold eye color that they shared.

My heart pounded in my chest, and I tried my best to even it out. I knew the Gryphon could hear my galloping heartbeats. Knew he would be able to scent my distress. They were abilities that were loaned to the human version of Teron.

How did you greet a huge eagle-lion that was supposedly your mate? "Uh, hello?"

He made a strange thumping noise, like the sound was coming from behind his ribcage rather than his mouth. It sounded terrifying.

I mustn't have kept my feelings from my face well enough, because his head dropped. He made a soft chirp noise, lowering itself to his belly, cooing at me. He didn't need to talk to say *I'm no threat to you. I'm just a cute chicken-cat, not something that would rend a rhino with little effort.*

Sucking in a fortifying breath, I stepped forward, holding out my hand. I cast a quick look at Milo, but his face was encouraging. He didn't seem worried at all, and that bolstered my confidence a little more. I aimed for the soft feathers of the Gryphon's neck, voluminous and wild, a mane of feathers of pure gold. He was so freaking beautiful.

"You are so handsome," I murmured at him, and he chirped, pushing the top of his head toward my open palm until I could run my fingers down the long, strong column of his neck.

The zap of the bond snapping into place no longer surprised me. A sense of right settled in my chest. This was how it was meant to be.

Standing, he towered over me, but kneeling down like this, he was beak to eyes with me. That wasn't daunting at all.

"Teron says I'm your mate?" Another odd trill that was definitely an agreement. "Are you sure? There's no one out there—another Mythic or something—who would be a better match for you?"

Wings I hadn't noticed unfurled from his back, ruffling with what felt like disgruntlement. He nudged my cheek with his face, and I suddenly had an overwhelming feeling of happiness. Contentment. Purpose. I was who he wanted.

I laughed, a sound of joy that I hadn't really felt in a long time, and the Gryphon responded by curling around my legs, careful to never to jostle me so I became unsteady. The brush of fur seemed so at odds with the slight scratch of his flight feathers. His beak slid across my cheek, and he clicked it through my hair like he was grooming me. He moved down over my shoulder and rested his giant eagle head against my stomach, making a soft thrumming noise, and the babies kicked as if responding to his words.

It was magic. I stared down in awe.

And just like that, any fear I had disappeared. This ancient being was mine. A part of my soul. I could *feel* it, even if I logically didn't understand it.

I yawned, and the Gryphon pulled back to look at me quizzically, making me flush. "No, I'm sorry, I'm not bored or anything. I didn't mean to insult you. I'm just tired. Sleeping is hard with all this." I pointed to my stomach, hoping he understood me.

The Gryphon huffed, nudging me softly on the arm and pushing me toward the door. He followed along behind me, gently ushering me from the room. I soon realized he was sending me back to my suite. I looked over my shoulder at Milo, who was casually wandering behind us, like being herded by a giant mythological creature wasn't weird at all.

We ran into Demke in the hall, though, and while

the Gryphon didn't bristle, he did wind around the front of me.

Demke halted in his tracks and stared. "Oh. I see. Hello, old friend. I see you've finally met your mate?"

I glared incredulously at Demke. "You knew?"

The God before me just shrugged. "When Teron knew. We discussed it, but it wasn't my information to give. Teron had to be ready to give up control to the Gryphon, and the Gryphon needed to be ready to meet his mate."

I swear, Griff rolled his eyes. Yeah, Griff. That was a good name—a little cliché, but I couldn't walk around calling him the Gryphon every day. It'd be odd.

"Can I call you Griff?" I asked him, watching his intelligent eyes for something like disdain.

He inclined his head and cooed, making Demke stare even harder. Milo was outright laughing now, and Griff glared at him until he shut his mouth with an audible click.

I reached out and gripped Demke's hand. It was nice to be able to touch him now, to be able to feel his warmth and the golden glow of safety that spread through my bones whenever I was near him. "I think he's sending me to bed for a nap. I'll see you tonight?"

Demke nodded, still speechless.

I paused. "Griff will let Teron back out, right?"

Another huff from Griff. But Demke looked amused more than anything. "Yes, I think so. But I think we'll all have to get used to seeing the Gryphon around more often, until you share a mate bond. I don't know how Teron will feel about that."

I wanted to question him more, but Griff had run out of patience. He pushed me back down the hall gently, keeping pace with my much shorter stride. Honestly, he was only taking one step for my six. He looked like he was doing the wedding march or something.

The only real hurdle we hit was the fact that Nate was already in my bedroom when we arrived. In the instant between Nate taking in the scene and standing, he had his ax in his hand and had grown three feet.

Griff gave a roar-scream and weaved in front of me, standing between me and Nate. I reached up and grabbed a handful of his feathers. "Wait! Nate! Griff! It's okay." Milo appeared between them too, which wasn't as reassuring as you'd think. "Nate, this is Teron. Well, Teron's Gryphon. I call him Griff." I stepped in front of Griff once more, meeting his golden eyes. "This is my lover and best friend, Nate. He's part of our pack, our family." I sent a frantic look at Milo. "Do Gryphons have packs?"

My Minotaur nodded. "They call them flights, but yeah, they lived in packs."

I obviously took leave of my senses, because I gripped Griff's beak and dragged him down to eye level. "Nate is part of our flight, Griff. You, me, the babies"—I rubbed my stomach, and his eyes flicked down to the movement—"Nate, Milo, Tryp and Erus. Demke. Teron," I said softly. "We are all a flight. You're my mate, but they are my bonds. That means they're yours too."

Rubbing his face feathers across my cheeks once more, he stood tall, eyeing Nate with a regal stance that proved to me exactly why they'd been considered the insignia of royalty for so many years. He made a terrifying noise once again, then flicked his wings out. They were so big, they pressed from wall to wall, even in my giant suite. It was a show of dominance, that much was obvious, and I looked pleadingly at Nate.

Grumbling, he put the ax down, shrinking back to what I considered fuckable Nate-size. I mean, his God form was fuckable too—God knows I wouldn't back down from the challenge—but it would be a lot.

Never say never, though.

He bowed his head at the Gryphon. "We've met. I watched him tear a demon to pieces with that beak you just held like it was the remote control for a monster."

Griff folded his wings back in, giving me a smug expression. If anyone had asked me before today to describe what smug looked like on a bird face, I would have said they were nuts. But he definitely looked haughty as Nate mentioned his kill.

Then he nudged me toward the bed, and I laughed, climbing into it. He grabbed the blanket in his beak, dragging it up over my body and tucking it around me. Then he left and came back with more blankets and pillows clutched in his beak. He placed them down around me, then left, getting more.

"What's he doing?" I asked, with another yawn.

Milo shrugged, and surprisingly, it was Nate who answered. "He's making you a nest."

He was cut off by Griff returning, pushing pillows up around my body, nudging them under the heavy mound of my stomach. That was really freaking sweet.

I closed my eyes, actually exhausted, and sighed happily. Was it weird that I could sleep while a giant beast made me a pretty nest? Who cared? My life was weirder than fiction now.

SOMETHING TICKLING my nose woke me later, tempting me from sleep. Blinking groggily in the darkness, I realized I was lying beside a naked Teron. And I was surrounded by feathers. Dozens of them. The walls of my "nest" were at least half a foot high and went right around the edge of my bed, except right at the foot. And in between all the blankets and pillows were golden feathers.

Did he even have any feathers left?

"He's pretty damn proud of his work," Teron said groggily, stretching. Naked.

Did I mention he was stretching naked?

I looked up at the ceiling, my cheeks so red that I was happy the room was shadowy with the falling light of dusk. "He should be. This is a beautiful nest."

Teron nodded. "It's one of the courtship rituals for the Gryphons. They make their proposed mate a nest, but it's up to you if you accept it or not."

How could I not accept this? He'd gone to so much

effort to create this for me, for my comfort. To keep me safe and warm.

"I accept it, of course." I looked down at the man beside me, keeping my eyes on his. "Teron, he's amazing," I breathed. And he was. He was the most beautiful thing I'd ever seen in my life.

Teron laughed, his eyes closing. "He said the exact same thing about you." He opened one eye to watch me. "You have questions?"

I scoffed. "*So many* damn questions."

He dragged me closer, and the heat of his skin felt like it was searing my own. However, the only parts of us touching were our arms. There were things I needed to know. Things we needed to talk about before we could take this any further.

"Do you still want this? Want me too?"

He didn't answer with words. Instead, he leaned forward and kissed me with so much passion, I felt like I was going to burn.

I was going to take that as a yes.

CHAPTER 38
WREN

With the attack on the compound, I knew that going home would probably be a long shot, so I threw myself into creating a nursery here, in Amourgeles, with the help of the guys. Right now, it was Nate who was building furniture as I sorted through everything again.

I needed to talk to him about all this. I needed him to know that he could go home if he wanted. I hated the idea that he'd been torn from his home, from his friends, just because he was tied to me and my bullshit.

But I was scared that he would want to go. So scared he'd leave me.

"*Mo stóirín*, you're thinking way too hard over there. What's wrong?"

Sighing, I moved toward him, unable to help myself. I wanted to be with him all the time. When he pulled my back against his chest and held up my stomach for me, I sighed, immediately relaxing against him. Nate knew me, knew what I needed without me voicing it.

And I loved him. It was so obvious to me now. And that scared the shit out of me too.

He kissed the spot behind my ear. "What is it, Wren?"

Sucking in a breath, I held it. "Do you want to go home?" It sounded like an accusation, but I hadn't meant it to come out that way. Trying again, I softened my tone. "It's okay if you want to return to your life. We have some unnatural bond chaining you to me, but if you want to return to Boston, to Clio and the house, to your friends, you can. I'd be okay with it. We could figure it out."

Big fucking lie.

He went stiff behind me. "Do you want me to go?" His fingers flexed, like he wanted to move them away, but I linked mine over his, keeping them where they were, against my stomach.

"No! Never. I selfishly want you here with me." Forever, but I didn't tell him that. I didn't need to guilt him into staying. "I just hate that I've trapped you in this nightmare with me."

He spun me gently, tucking his fingers under my chin, tilting my head back so I was forced to look into his eyes. "Wren, fate might have tied us, but I promise you, there is something even stronger tying me to you." His thumb dragged at my bottom lip. "*Mo shíorghra,* I love you." He put my hand on his chest, right over his heart. "I'd forgotten this organ could even beat, but now it does, for you. I am right here, with you, with them"—he used his other hand to cup my stomach—"forever. You are my home. I don't need to go anywhere."

I gaped at him, this gruff God, whose eyes were so earnest right now, like he was willing me to believe his words.

I burst into tears. "I love you too, Nate. But I'm too hormonal for you to be so sweet right now." The fucker laughed at me, hugging me close to his chest. "I don't want to chain you to me, but I'm not sure I could do this without you. I would have tried for you, but I don't want to." I sniffled pathetically.

He kissed the top of my head. "You'll never have to." He pulled back a little and brushed another soft kiss across my lips. "Now, I still have the change table to put together, so we better get back to it." He looked over my head at the bed. "Maybe you should get back in your nest and rest a little more."

It was more tempting than I was willing to admit, but I knew I was only going to get more exhausted, so I needed to do this while I still could. Sighing heavily, I went back to sorting through the boxes of stuff that the guys had shipped from the mainland.

A few hours later, we sat around the dinner table, eating moussaka and bread that Demke had baked from scratch. It was the first time that everyone at this table was bonded to me. It was a surreal feeling.

Milo piled more on my plate, even though there was no room left inside me for food. I was always hungry, but I also felt like I was going to puke if I ate more than a few mouthfuls. Being pregnant was beautiful, but it was also fucking miserable.

"The pack has ballooned out to at least seventy dogs now," Tryp told Demke, his mouth filled with food.

Holy shit. There were seventy strays in town now? "Are you sure they're all strays? Maybe some of them are lost."

Demke frowned. "Cy isn't a real dog. He's a… supernatural dog. He's very old. He was once a favored companion of our Goddess."

I raised an eyebrow. "Cy? The chunky white dog that lives in town?"

He nodded. "Yes, that's the one. Sometimes, he'll call out to surrounding dogs if he thinks something is coming, gathering more and more hounds to him. During the last battle, he had an army of hundreds of dogs from all over the island at his back."

I shook my head. "So he's a magic dog, but doesn't live with you?" I chewed my lip. "I get the impression you don't like him much either."

It was Teron who answered. "He was from the enemy side. He is from the Greek Pantheon."

"Oh. He's not, like… Cerberus or anything, right?"

Demke snorted. "No. He's not a Hellhound."

I thought about the seventy dogs outside our walls, and wondered what they were eating. Were they hungry? Were they eating the native wildlife in order to survive? Or were the locals trying to feed them all?

"Are they okay out there? Should we feed them?"

Demke grumbled beneath his breath, and Tryp was actually laughing at him now. "If that's what you want to do, Wren, I'll make arrangements to get food tomorrow."

I grinned at him. "It is." I reached across the table to grab his hand, and once again, the feeling of rightness washed over me.

THE FOLLOWING DAY, a truck arrived at the compound with an entire pallet of dog food bags. I didn't know the brand, but it looked high-end. I made a note to thank Demke for not skimping on the food, despite being reluctant.

We stood close to the doors so the guys could move me back behind the wards at the merest suggestion of danger. Someone in the village had dug large troughs, so that we could feed as many as we could. Milo was pouring in bags of food now, and I watched dog after dog appear from the landscape around us. Big dogs the size of small horses, and small ones the size of designer handbags, and everything in between. Fluffy dogs and ones that looked like they were half pooch, half broom.

What quickly became clear was there were far more than the seventy Tryp had estimated. There must've been at least twice the amount, including a very pregnant mama dog. I spotted Cy walking her to the trough, snapping at any dog that got too close. He sat beside her until he was convinced she'd eaten her fill, then he wandered over to me.

He placed his blocky head on my lap, and I stroked his ears. "Is that your girlfriend?"

The dog gave me an incredulous expression, which made me laugh.

"No? Well in that case, you're a very good dog. Though, Demke tells me you're not really a dog—you're some kind of immortal Greek companion animal?"

Another put-upon huff.

"No offense, but I haven't had a great track record with your Pantheon. But the guys have some kind of weird, symbiotic relationship with you, which means you must be okay, right?"

Cy yipped and nuzzled his head against my belly. Sighing, I sat back on the chair Milo had brought out for me, and watched the dogs eat and play. I gave up on trying to guess breeds. I was pretty sure none of them were pedigree, though.

I wished I could bring them all inside the walls, keep them safe and warm, but even I wasn't delusional enough to think the compound could hold over a hundred dogs without chaos ensuing.

As if to prove my point, a fight broke out, and Cy's head snapped up. He raced over, got between the two dogs and stood over them, growling softly. It was a warning, but in that moment, I could almost see that he wasn't normal. He wasn't your average street mutt. He was something special.

After settling whatever disagreement was occurring between the scrappy little terrier and a big mastiff with hanging jowls, Cy sat there and watched over his pack. His army, Demke had insisted.

A dog with long, skinny legs and a pointy head came over to sniff at my hand. I held it out, so it could get a better sense of me.

"Hello, sweet"—I did a quick check—"girl. Aren't you just the most beautiful thing ever?"

Apparently, that was all that was needed. The dog was up and in my lap a second later, and I leaned back so she could curl up against my stomach. I scratched behind her ears, and she drifted off to sleep, full and content.

When this was over, I would find them all homes. Where they'd be loved and cared for and never know a night of being cold outdoors again. Even if that home was with me.

CHAPTER 39
NÉIT

My phone ringing woke me. I was wrapped around Wren after managing to basically strong-arm my way into her bed without any added participants. She was still sleeping soundly, and I flailed an arm around, searching for the offending noise-maker.

It was probably Clio, who didn't really respect my sleep when we were in the same time zone, so I doubted she'd pay much attention now.

"Hello?"

"Wake up! They're attacking. They've found someone to break the wards, and they're coming for Wren." The line sounded crackly, but the words came through crisp and clear, like the scream of the banshee she was. "I can't get there, but I'm sending help from closer. Accept the aid, Néit. She'll need it." There was a scuffle from the other end. "I need to go. Shit is getting insane here. People have lost their minds."

The line went dead.

Dread I hadn't felt in a long time welled up inside me. Rolling out of the nest, I stepped out of the room, growing to my full Godly height. My trusty ax appeared in my hand, and I wished more than ever that I'd brought my sword too.

I barged into the living quarters of Milo, who was up with a sword in his hand before his eyes had even opened. "What's wrong? Is Wren okay?"

I shook my head. "My source in the States says they've worked out how to break the wards. I need you to make sure they stand. She said they're going to attack."

Fear flashed across his face. "He said they were going to attack tonight?"

I shook my head, frustrated at myself for not asking more questions. "*She* didn't say."

Milo didn't ask anything further, just rushed along the halls toward Erus's room. I wasn't surprised to see Erus and Tryp together in bed, but they both startled awake as the bedroom door banged against the stone wall.

"Fucking hell, Milo. What's wrong?" Tryp grumbled.

"Check the wards." It was an order, even though I didn't think Milo was further up the hierarchy than Erus or Tryp.

Erus was instantly out of bed and moving toward a glass jar that glowed in the corner of the room. Inside it was a single luminous strand of hair. He chanted over it in a language even I didn't know, then suddenly, the jar went dark.

Tryp sucked in a deep breath, his eyes flying to Milo. "They've broken the wards around the island."

"But the compound's wards still stand?"

Erus nodded. "For now."

Milo made a truly horrendous bellowing noise. "They'll attack tonight." Erus and Tryp were already nodding, grabbing weapons.

"We should wake Demke," I said, and they looked at each other. "What?"

Their expression told me we were more fucked than I thought. Clio didn't have to worry about me rejecting help; she should be worried that it wouldn't be enough.

Teron's Gryphon—or Griff, as Wren called him—paced angrily. He'd found a small army of monsters making their way up the coast, and while he'd taken out the scouts, he knew as well as I did that we were vastly outmatched.

Before ceding control to the Gryphon, Teron had given us a bunch of orders and made calls to Gods who scared the shit out of me.

A sound that sent fear down my spine echoed around the building, making it shake slightly, and making Wren whimper and bury her face in Tryp's neck.

"Griff needs to stay with Wren. If we fall, he needs to take her as far away as he can get. Take her somewhere. North, to the Norse—they have no love lost with the Europeans," Erus suggested. I hated the thought of her anywhere but at my side, but in this, I agreed.

"*No.*" Wren shook her head violently. "I'm not leaving you guys."

Tryp smoothed a hand down her spine. "Baby, if it comes down to us or you and those babies, the choice is easy." He gave Griff a hard stare, and the beast clicked his beak.

She was still shaking her head. "I can't leave you." It was a whimper now, but I knew if it came to it, she would, or Griff would make her.

I knelt in front of her. "*Mo stóirín,* I am a blood-soaked God, and I have no intention of dying tonight. But I can't fight if I know you're putting yourself in danger." I looked at Griff. "If you need to go, fly north to Gamla Uppsala in Sweden. Find the Old Gods. They'll protect you out of spite."

A laugh echoed around the hall, and we were all on our feet, weapons drawn in an instant. A woman I didn't know stepped into the room, and behind her were eleven more women. They shone with a golden hue that hurt even my eyes, so I knew it must be incredibly painful for Wren.

"Well, you're right about that, Néit, Old God of War."

Standing in front of her, I raised my ax. "How'd you get in here?"

She shrugged. "That doesn't matter. We were asked to render aid, and if the hoard we passed was any indication, not a moment too soon. I am Mist, and these are my sisters. We are Valkyrie. Cliona is indeed a great friend of yours; she called in a favor that has sat between us for many centuries."

I looked over at Wren, who was squinting in their direction. "We appreciate your help."

Griff huffed an annoyed noise, which made the Valkyrie all laugh as one. It was an unsettling sound. They looked like angels, but there was something bloodthirsty in their eyes that made a man's blood run cold.

Mist walked toward Wren, but Griff inserted himself into her path. She raised an eyebrow at him. "A Gryphon mate? This one is indeed special."

Tryp was clutching Wren close. "She can see through your glamor. Your luminance will hurt her."

Mist turned her head to the side, an action that was definitely not human. Finally, she shrugged. "We all suffer."

I could see Wren straightening her spine, and she dragged her face from Tryp's neck and climbed to her feet to face the woman—the Valkyrie—opposite her.

The Valkyrie took in her stomach, her mouth falling open. "Clio said she was important, but she didn't say why. I understand now." She looked over her shoulder at the other Valkyrie crowding the hall. They had a silent conversation, before moving further into the room as one.

Then they dropped to their knees as one. "Wren,

mother of the cloth of life, we will protect you with our honor and our swords."

Wren looked at me, then back at the Valkyrie heads bowed before her, panic written across her face. I nodded, and she stared at the top of Mist's head, shell-shocked. "Uh, thank you. I accept."

Mist stood, her face solemn. "Cliona should have told us who you were, and kept her debt. We would have come to defend you." Two of the others appeared beside her. "These are my seconds, Hildr and Hrist. If I fall, they will be the ones who will lead the Valkyries."

Wren was still squinting. "I hope none of you fall."

Mist shrugged. "It is the nature of battle," she said simply, before her lips curled into a smile that was definitely chilling. "And I do love a battle."

I still didn't know how they'd gotten in here, and if they wouldn't turn on us at the worst opportunity, but right now, they were Wren's best chance of survival. I would keep an eye on them, but I had to have faith in Clio and in fate.

Saying something to two of the Valkyries in the back, Mist sat down in a chair opposite mine. "Who is in charge?"

Well, that was a million-dollar question.

The guys all looked at me. "He is. He's the God of War," Milo stated simply.

Mist inclined her head, like that was as good of a reason as any to follow me. That made me even more fearful of fucking this up and losing the true love of my life. "Two of my Valkyrie are going to scout how long we have, but I would imagine less than an hour. Do you have a plan?"

Fuck no. I didn't know the enemy. The terrain. I didn't know anyone's fighting experience, or if I could actually trust half of these people to keep Wren safe. Still, they were right. This *was* my area of expertise.

I rattled off a rough plan, including where Wren would be, who we were working with, what to do with the townspeople. The whole time, Wren's pale face haunted me.

A mournful howl from outside had us all tensing. I looked at Wren, at the fear on her face. I wished I could skip this part for her. I wished it had never come to this moment. But it was pointless to wish for something that could never be.

Standing, I went over and kissed her softly. "It's time to go, Wren. That was Cy. They've sighted them." I stroked her stomach, making a silent vow to the babies that I would protect them and their mother with my very life if needed. I didn't say it out loud, though, because Wren was already crying. "Go with Griff. We'll come for you as soon as possible."

"Nate," she sobbed, and I kissed the tears from her cheeks.

"It will all work out how it is supposed to, *mo stóirín.* Have faith."

The guys each kissed her and whispered in her ear. I walked over to the Gryphon, whose face looked solemn. "Her protection is on you. Do what is necessary to protect her, even from herself, no matter how she protests. Protect your mate. Save her young. Trust in Teron." The Gryphon bowed his head low in response.

A chorus of howls went up around the compound. Hundreds of dogs giving a war cry.

I pushed the big bird-lion in front of me. "Go. If a single hair is harmed on her head, I'm plucking you completely to feather that damn nest," I grunted, and Griff chirped a pissed noise, before he began herding her away and up to the roof cavity, where they could hide but also escape if needed.

When she was gone, I turned to the solemn faces in the room. "Tonight, we protect the future. We fight for a new age. We fight for Wren."

The guys nodded, and the Valkyrie pulled their swords. Mist slapped my arm. "Tonight, we bathe in the blood of the unworthy."

With that, we moved to our positions. This was the first battle, but it wasn't the war.

I couldn't protect Wren from her fate, any more than I could protect my heart from her.

CHAPTER 40
WREN

My stomach churned, anxiety burning through my chest like acid. I felt sick. I was so scared, not for me, but for my babies. For my bonded mates. For the innocent lives in the town.

Griff was wrapped entirely around me, his eyes on the door, his head cocked as he listened to the noise of fighting below. I could hear the screams in the darkness, none of them human-sounding at all. It was a terrifying, dark opus, and like the coward I was, I lifted my hands to my ears, blocking it out.

My heart felt like it was being shredded. Was this sensation in my chest the feel of the guys dying? Were they in pain?

And where was Demke?

A shrill cry had me jumping to my feet, moving toward the window just in time to see a huge batlike creature swooping through the sky. The Valkyries rode winged horses in what looked like hard leather armor, and two of them struck at the huge demon in the sky. It fell to the earth, where a writhing mass overtook it.

No, not a mass. An army of dogs. *Holy shit.* The numbers of them were huge, much larger than even yesterday. I watched them tear apart that bat thing, like ants dismembering a bird.

Griff got between me and the window, herding me back into a corner where he could protect me. "I can't just sit here, Griff. Not when they could need help. Not when they could be dying for me."

He chirped at me, and I felt like he was trying to tell me something. His features looked almost frustrated. I understood the feeling.

"Teron says if you bond with me, we can talk in our minds?"

Griff nodded, his face stroking over mine comfortingly.

"You should do it. *We* should bond. I'd be honored to be your mate."

Making another anxious noise, he stood and paced around once more. He was chirping at himself, and I wondered if he was trying to talk himself into it or out of it. Finally, he came back and sat in front of me, his head dipping down until we were eye to eye. The intelligence there would have been terrifying in any other situation. Right now, though, there was something reassuring about the fact that he knew exactly what I was saying.

I lifted my hand to the side of his face. "I swear, this is the right thing to do. I'm not just saying that because

I'm stressed and worried. I wish it was a different time, but life has other plans. Please, Griff."

He clacked his beak again, then nudged my arm, lifting it up. I held it out to him, and he used a sharp claw to cut my wrist. I hissed in pain, while Griff's tail whipped in a frenzy, a show of anxiousness he didn't usually possess, based on the few times I'd met him. Using his beak, he picked up the dagger that Milo had pressed into my hand before he left. Gently, Griff placed the dagger into my lap.

"I have to cut you too?"

A nod. I winced, trying not to feel sick as I cut him along his strong lion shoulder.

"Do I have to mix our blood together?"

Another quick nod.

Lifting my cut wrist, I rubbed the blood into his wound, trying not to feel sick. This was a blood bond. I was vowing to love this creature, care for him, adore him for the rest of my days, and it felt so right that I knew it was written in the stars.

I felt his magic travel through the wound and up my arm, wrapping around my chest like a vice. It was hard to breathe, and I choked on nothing.

Breathe, little one.

I startled at the deep voice echoing around my head. *Holy shit.* "Griff?"

Yes. Mate. My mate. The wonder in his voice made emotions clog my throat. What I would have given to have this moment in a time of peace, with just me and Griff.

There was a soft laugh. *And me. Always the third wheel.* Teron's voice was in my head too, and I squeaked with happiness.

"I can talk to you both?"

Yes. And if we are in Teron's meat sack form, we can still talk. You have me always now, little one. You all do. I will protect our cubs with my very soul.

I was crying again, but it felt so overwhelming, these waves of love and adoration that poured from the connection between our hearts. How was I ever going to get used to this feeling, this blanket of security?

A scream from outside shook me from the moment. On my feet again, I watched something from a nightmare appear in the distance. It was huge, with wings and a snake body. Fire dripped from its mouth.

"What in the actual flying *fuck* is that?" I breathed, and I could feel Griff's concern in my chest. I wasn't sure how I knew the feeling was Griff's and not Teron's, but I did.

Typhon. What the hell did they promise the Father of Monsters to get him here? Griff asked, but I had a feeling he wasn't talking to me.

I was proven right when it was Teron who answered. *I don't know, but if Typhon's here, Ekhidna won't be far behind.*

I didn't know who either of them were, but they weren't monsters I wanted to mess with. The Valkyrie attacked in threes, but they had little to no effect on the huge monster, who batted them out of the air like they were horse flies, rather than feared warriors.

Pain and death were starting to scent the air. Where were the guys?

I tried to lean further out of the window to see, but Griff pulled me back. *You are making yourself a target. Do not make all this for naught by dying like some kind of fool.*

I flushed, properly chastised, as I moved back to the wall where he placed me. "I hate sitting here. You hate it too—I can tell."

He shook his huge eagle head. *No. While I want to be fighting, you are more important than any glory. You are the only thing that matters, Wren. Mate of my heart.*

How the hell did anyone argue with that? "Smooth-talking fucking Gryphon."

I don't think anyone has complimented me quite so aggressively in a very long time, Griff answered, sounding amused.

Another cry from outside was like knives shredding my chest. Leaving me in the corner, Griff looked out the window, and I could feel his worry. We weren't winning; I knew it in my chest. Outside, people were dying for me.

A loud sound I was beginning to recognise as the ward alarms clanged, and Griff whipped his head toward the door in a move that was definitely preter-natural. *They've breached the compound's walls.*

What did that mean for the guys?

"What do we do?" I whispered, and Griff tilted his head to the side, listening for intruders. His tail whipped furiously, the only tell that he was anxious. He backed me further against the wall, his huge body hiding me from the doorway.

Glass shattered, the sound mixing with my screams. A large hand reached into the room through the window. It was gnarled and crusty, and I couldn't see the body attached to it.

Clearly, we'd found the intruder, or the intruder had found us.

Griff let out a blood-curdling screech and attacked the appendage. Claws and beak shredded the hand, magic swirling around it, until the pained shout of whatever the hell was out there shook the walls.

The hand was back now, angrier, flailing wildly. It had to be a giant—we were three stories up.

GO, WREN! To Milo's room. Block the door! Teron's shout in my head was punctuated by Griff's snarls, and I didn't second-guess him. I just ran. Out through the doors, I ran as fast as I could, holding my stomach and the railing as I took the stairs as safely as I could while not losing momentum.

A steady thump on the door was in time with the frantic pounding of my heart. *THUMP! THUMP! THUMP!*

We were fucked. I was fucked.

Still, I ran past Tryp's room, then Teron's. Demke's door was wide open, and I could see straight through it to his private courtyard. I stopped dead, my feet rooted to the ground.

In the courtyard, completely motionless, was Demke.

No.

I felt around for the bond to him in my chest. They'd said I would've known if one of them was dead, but I couldn't feel anything. Not if they were hurt or injured, nothing. Griff was going to be so mad, but I couldn't leave Demke. What if he was hurt?

What if he was dead?

Turning, I sprinted through the room. "Demke!" Maybe he was just sleeping. I skidded to a stop in the soft moss beside him. "Demke, please wake up!" I shouted, shaking his cold, lifeless shoulders.

He was dead.

"No. No, no… Demke, please…" I brushed his hair from his face, searching him for injuries. He was a fucking God; he couldn't be dead. I searched for a pulse, but there was nothing but icy skin beneath my fingertips. This wasn't right. He *couldn't* be dead.

"Please, don't take him too," I whispered to someone. Anyone. Who did you pray to when your Gods either abandoned you or wanted you dead?

Tears streamed down my cheeks and onto his chest. But this wasn't a Disney movie; my tears wouldn't bring him back to life. I pressed my forehead to his heart, feeling my soul break. Wailing softly, I let numbness enclose around me like the darkness.

"Vessel." The sound of the voice sent shivers down my spine. I knew instinctively this creature meant me harm, but I couldn't lift my head to look.

Instead, I buried my face deeper into Demke's silent chest. "She's not here. I'll take a message."

A grating noise, like two rough fabrics rubbing against each other, echoed through the courtyard. Some part of me recognized it as laughter. I looked up at the monster before me, far too large for me to defend myself against. She was beautiful, or at least, her top half was. Like a Greek statue of some goddess. Her bottom half was a dragon, with large wings and a long serpent tail.

"Ekhidna, I assume?"

The monster inclined her head regally. "I am."

Straightening slightly, I didn't bother to stand. Defeat made my limbs feel heavy. "Why? What did I, or my children, ever do to you?"

She looked down at me with pity. "I too birthed offspring destined to die. I understand your feeling of helplessness."

"Then *WHY?*" I screamed. I screamed it not just to the monster before me, but into the universe too.

She sighed, and the sound was like an ancient yawn, filled with exhaustion and helplessness. "Because, like you, I do what is best for my family. The Fates have promised to free my mate, resurrect the last of my children. We could live and be happy once more in this modern world." She looked wistfully at the sky, like one of her children was trapped there in the stars. "You won't ever understand, because you'll be dead, but when you look down at your young, you know you'll do anything for them."

I threw my hands in the air. "You're working with the very same people who killed them in the first place!

I might not be an expert on Mythic politics, but that seems pretty fucking stupid to me."

Another scraping laugh. "I like you, little human. But I won't let my children be written out of the weave. I won't let them be forgotten in this turn of the Ouroboros. You must die. I will make it quick and painless."

She really believed that she was giving me a compassionate ending, and I guess in comparison to the Lamia, that was true. Despite the exhaustion that weighed down every inch of my body, I wouldn't let Demke die in vain.

Grabbing the dagger that winked at Demke's hip, I jutted it out in front of me. "Then you'll understand that I won't just let my children's story end before they've even taken their first breath."

Ekhidna nodded, something that might have been respect glinting in her eye. "So be it." Then she lunged. I scrambled backwards as her talons reached for me, slashing wildly at her hands, or claws or whatever. When it sliced through her toe, she glared down at me. "A God-blessed blade? So many surprises on this island of the weak."

She lunged again, but then a dog was there, its bark echoing loudly through the hills.

"Cy, no!" I shouted. He was going to die, and it would be my fault. The dog didn't even look at me as he stood between me and the monster. He grew bigger, until he was the same white dog, but the size of an elephant. "Holy *shit*. Big puppy."

Giant Cy attacked the she-monster, who hissed. Cy howled again, the sound so fucking eerie that it sent shivers down my spine. Behind Ekhidna, a dark pit opened, its yawning maw hinting at glowing fire below.

Holy shit... Had Cy just opened a mouth to Hell? Dogs appeared from everywhere, biting and converging on Ekhidna, pushing her back toward the Hellmouth, nipping and biting, shredding what they could, even as she flung them away.

But there were too many. "No," Ekhidna breathed, and I saw the moment she knew what was happening. That she was about to lose.

Some part of me wanted to tell them to stop, to give her mercy, but another part of me knew she was going to kill my babies and me. She wouldn't have shown me mercy, and if she lived, she wouldn't stop.

Instead, I gave her the same sympathetic look as she'd given me moments earlier, as she stumbled back into the pit, her screams whistling for far too long. Maybe it really was a pit that went to Hell.

Cy was still massive, and he turned to look at me. Shrinking back down, his tongue hanging out, he stopped when he was head height.

And then he turned into a man.

A naked, handsome man with a lopsided grin on his face. "Hey, Wren."

AFTERWORD

Surprise!

Sorry! I know. Cliffhangers suck, and usually, I'm right there with you on the 'I HATE CLIFFHANGERS' bandwagon.

But this was too sweet to resist. And Book Two in this duet isn't far away. You can preorder it now

Single Thread Of Hope : Book 2 in the Hanging By A Thread Duet

About the Author

Grace McGinty is eclectic. She has worked as a chocolatier, a librarian, a forensic accountant, and finally, a writer. Like her professional career, the genres she writes are chaotic and out of control. From contemporary new adult to smutty reverse harem novels of every sub-genre, if you like it, she's probably written it.

Except dark romance. She's a marshmallow, and somehow the mean guys always end up cinnamon rolls.

Grace lives in rural Australia with her crazy family, an entire menagerie of pets, and will one day be crushed by the giant piles of books that litter every room.

Head over to www.gracemcginty.com and join the mailing list for sneak previews into what she is working on and to stay up-to-date with new releases and giveaways!

New to Grace McGinty? Like your love interests a little monstrous? Check out Manix over the page.

MANIX

GATLIN

This parking lot smelled overwhelmingly of vomit and dried bodily fluids. How the outdoors, with all this fresh mountain air, could have such overwhelming scents was truly a miracle of nature. The crumbling building, lit only with flashing neon signs, sat in the center of a lot filled with pickup trucks. To the left of my group, a couple were fucking down a side alley and the male sounded like a boar with a hot poker up its ass.

I realized why it smelled so much like puke when I stepped into a small puddle of it, and it splashed up onto the laces of my boots. Humans were fucking disgusting sometimes. I lifted my hand to motion us forward and we walked into the club, which was devoid of security at the front door.

The establishment vibrated with too much bass, like a tribal drumbeat, and it had whipped the crowd into a frenzy. The smell of sweat and lust permeated every corner, and we tightened our formation around Raiden.

The distressed scent of an unfamiliar Omega had me growling low under my breath, and the humans who lingered too close quickly moved away. Not because they could hear the growl, but because they could feel the coiled violence that rolled off my Pack.

Finlo stepped closer to me, leaning in to be heard over the ear-shattering noise of the music. "Are we sure this is the place? Perhaps Seven's nose is broken?" the other Alpha asked.

Seven scowled, baring his teeth at Finlo. Seven was a Beta, but he was a strong Beta. Too strong. It was a generally held belief that a strong Beta would resist orders and cause problems. And it was true, Seven did cause issues at times, especially when given orders. But our Pack weren't hardcore traditionalists when it came to hierarchies. I treated Seven the way I'd treat any other Alpha—hell, any other Manix—with respect and understanding. In return, Seven was grateful to even have a Pack, even if it was one filled with misfits. He was loyal and loved, and that was worth something too.

"My nose didn't lie. There is an Omega here, one that is close to heat."

Ellar hovered over Raiden, practically glued to his side. "I trust Seven's tracking. His nose is his best trait. Goddess knows, it isn't his winning personality," he joked, making Raiden chuckle. Unlike Seven, the family's other Beta was like me. A half-blood Manix. He'd had no other choice than to join us, because no one else would muddy their bloodlines with a half-caste.

This was us. A tiny, ill-formed Pack, except for our one crowning jewel—our Omega.

One of the last male Omegas left, he'd chosen us to be his mates. When an Omega comes of age, he is allowed to choose which Pack he joins. No one had been more shocked than us when he'd chosen ours. Until Raiden, we'd been a rag-tag bunch of mutts on the outskirts of Manix society.

I looked over my shoulder at Raiden, whose soft expression met mine. Just a look from him shored up my resolve. Although our natural instincts wanted to protect and coddle Raiden, he was a warrior in his own right. Maybe that's why he picked us. He didn't want to be pampered and adored. He wanted to fight and fuck, which was wildly un-Omega like. Despite the fact that I *knew* he could defend himself against humans, my Alpha instincts insisted that he be protected at all times. He was the heart of our Pack after all.

I scanned the crowd, but the overwhelming conflicting scents muddled everything. "We'll split up. Raiden will come with me. Trust Seven's nose," I warned Finlo.

Finlo was my childhood best friend, and had chosen to build a Pack with me rather than join one of the more prestigious warrior Packs more suited to his bloodlines. I owed him everything.

He nodded and split off, the two Betas following behind him. I tucked Raiden closer to me as we waded further into the club. There were stages dotted around the room, each lit up with a different color. Blue, red, purple. On each stage, a woman danced, spinning around a pole. I'd been born in human society, raised here until I was eleven, and I knew what a strip club was. But Raiden didn't, and his eyes almost bulged out of his head. He shook his head at me as he grinned.

"My sire was right, the only place you could take me is into the gutter," he teased.

Yeah, not everyone had been overjoyed that Raiden had chosen my Pack. I nudged his shoulder with mine, despite the fact that I wanted to reach out and place a kiss on his temple. "Admit it, you like being dirty down here in the gutter with me."

He laughed, reaching down to squeeze my hand as we parted the crowd. "Wouldn't be anywhere else."

We were getting a few weird looks, and that was another reason we needed to split up. Together, we seemed inhuman. Ridiculously tall and broad, we looked like the warrior race we'd once been, before we were killed off and forced to flee to the mountains of Montana, forever separate until we were slowly dying out for other reasons.

Manix. We were the real reason the word manic entered the English language. It was the way early humans described the rut, where we thirsted for blood or sex, and wreaked havoc. But now there were barely two thousand of us left. Of that, there were less than a hundred full-blooded female Manix. Only twenty-five Omegas, but none of those were female.

We were dying out at a rapid rate. Which is why when Seven said he'd scented an Omega female on the wind, we'd come on this wild goose chase. I was happy to chase a wild goose if it gave my Pack a chance at a real future.

I stayed at Raiden's back, my eyes trawling in front of us for threats. "Scent anything?" I asked, despite the fact it galled me. I was half-blood, the result of a Manix male and a human female. Mating with humans was frowned upon, and according to the Manix Legion, little better than lying with a beast. As a result, I was little better than an animal to the upper crust of Manix society.

I pushed down the residual rage I felt toward the Legion and searched the crowd. Raiden tilted his head, his pupils blowing out wide. "That way," he said softly, his feet taking him in the right direction before he'd even lifted his arm. If I'd had any doubt about Seven's nose, it disappeared at that moment. I kept my hand on Raiden's belt as he moved through the crowd with single-minded focus. He might have been the smallest of us, but he was still over six feet in height, tall in comparison to a human.

He stopped in front of a small platform, bathed in blue light so it appeared like it was in the depths of the sea. Raiden's eyes went wide and his knees nearly buckled as he looked up at the girl on the stage. Finally, her scent permeated my duller senses.

And when I scented her? My dick went rock hard.

She danced in heels that had to be six inches high, her movements easy as her body swayed to the music. She kept her eyes closed, like she could block out the world if she just deprived herself of the sight of these salivating humans.

She was small, tiny in comparison to a Manix female. Her body curved sharply though, her figure like an hourglass of old. Given the overwhelming smell of lust that hung like a cloud around us, she had a body that men would bankrupt themselves to have just a touch.

Wearing basically nothing, her scent was like a caress, followed by a slap to the face. I could feel the Omega presence, scent her oncoming heat cycle. I cast a worried look at Raiden, whose whole body was taut with the urge to rut.

Breeding in Manix society had historically occurred in one of two ways. A female could be impregnated by a single Manix male, and would usually give birth to a solitary offspring. Or, a female and male Omega could mate during a heat cycle, and the male Omega would draw the viable eggs into himself. Afterwards, the pack would lie together during the rut and all the eggs had a chance to be fertilized. It was animalistic, feral sex that would leave the entire Pack drained and weak.

This is why the heat in a female would send us all into an insane rut, but especially Raiden, as our Pack Omega.

I noticed my Packmates on the other side of the stage, also looking up at her like she was a gift from the Goddess. She was definitely the one, and I would make her ours. Raiden was all but shaking with need, and I moved him toward the back wall so we could watch her and be obscured by the shadows a little more.

Her hips swayed with exaggeration to the music. She hooked her leg around the shiny metal pole in the center of the stage, swinging in a slow loop, her left foot barely scraping along the floor. Her breasts were barely contained in a tiny little bikini which matched the barely-there thong that both covered her intimate flesh and attracted the gaze of the audience to it.

As I searched the crowd, watching the hungry eyes of the humans, smelling their lust and violence, my Beast rose up in my chest. They were looking at what was mine, or at least, what would be mine. I looked at the red lever beside me, secure behind its safety glass from accidental knocks. The fire alarm.

Looking over at Finlo, I lifted my chin toward the girl. Finlo would know what to do. He nodded back, so I pushed through the safety glass and pressed the fire alarm. Within seconds, there was a loud whooping noise that blared across the music, the interior fire sprinklers opening the metaphorical heavens.

Panic ensued, and there was a mass exit for the door, people pushing and shoving as they nearly trampled others to make their escape from nothing. As people turned and fled, the girl jumped off the stage, but Finlo moved incredibly fast. He gathered her up into his arms and walked out the rear exit, the girl over his shoulder, Seven and Ellar at his back.

Raiden whined as he lost sight of the other Omega, and we moved with the tail end of the panicked exodus.

The rest of our Pack would get her where we needed her to be. I would just take care of Raiden.

An Omega pair... Could we really be that lucky? Raiden whined low under his breath, his hand gripping mine. "She's close, Gat. So damn close. Maybe a week? It's making my skin itch."

Female Omegas had been the first thing to die out. There were no Omega pairs left. Back when they'd found out the Omega females were dying out, we'd tried the Omegas of different species, but while they might be hierarchically the same, they weren't physiologically similar enough for there to be an Omega bonding. That had led to an uprising against us by shifters, because the Manix of the past didn't exactly ask for the Omegas nicely, which drove us further into the Mountains, isolating us even more.

It had been a bleak time in our history. Because we weren't like shifters, or other supernaturals. We were different completely, an entirely different genus. That was why the girl we'd just pulled off the stage was such a miracle, a true gift from the Goddess.

She was going to save our Pack, and then maybe, our species. But first, we had to get her to like us.